A SUMMER HOUSE ON ARRAN

A Scottish summer romance to fall in love with

ELLIE HENDERSON

Scottish Romances Book 3

Choc Lit

A JOFFE BOOKS COMPANY

Choc Lit
A Joffe Books company
www.choc-lit.com

First published in Great Britain in 2024

© Ellie Henderson 2024

Cover art by Jarmila Takač

ISBN: 978-1781897508

PROLOGUE

A trickle of sweat made its way down Olivia Kennedy's forehead, and she wiped it away with the back of her hand. She was struggling with the Italian heat, unseasonably warm for late May, and was beginning to find the crowds a bit overwhelming. It was only day three on her tour of the Amalfi Coast, and there were another four to go. So far she had visited Naples and Pompeii, though thanks to her current brain fog she could have been anywhere. She could barely recall any actual facts about one of the world's most famous archaeological sites. All she remembered was people, lots of people, and cobbled streets, which frustrated her hugely and made her feel like her brain was shrouded in a cloud of dust. It was no wonder, she supposed.

This hadn't exactly been the best place to lick her wounds, or to have some headspace to contemplate what had gone wrong with her life. Yet, if she was really honest with herself, she already knew the answer to that. It was obvious what had gone wrong. She just wasn't ready to admit it. It was easier and safer just to run.

Naples was the first place she could get a flight to when she'd decided to leave New York. She had recently finished touring with *Let's Dance*, the US's top-rated celeb dance competition. But with no work lined up in the immediate future, and nobody she wanted to stick around for, she decided to bolt. She had always wanted to visit Italy. It was *the* destination for romance, not to mention delicious food and wine and stunning scenery. Yet, ironically, here she was, alone. She hadn't really thought it through before impulsively booking the flight. She took a jagged breath in and pulled her sunglasses down over her eyes as the tears started to well. *Again.*

Today's excursion was to the island of Capri, and the coach had dropped the group off at the port. She fidgeted in the heat as their tour guide, Giuliano, patiently explained the procedure for getting on the boat and where to meet when they reached the island. This then led to the inevitable supplementary questions, with a particular focus on where the toilets were, from the people in the group who seemed to treat Giuliano as their teacher. The usual suspects asked the same questions every time. It was actually quite fascinating to watch grown adults become fairly helpless once out of their comfort zone.

Arriving in Naples, Olivia had signed up to the first tour she could get, hence finding herself with this party of British holidaymakers for a week. It wasn't quite how she imagined her Italian escape. An all-female family from Glasgow had taken her under their wing when they realised she was travelling solo.

'You stick with us, hen,' said the woman she now knew to be Granny Margaret. 'We'll keep an eye on you. You don't want to be wandering these streets on your own.'

Olivia had nodded and smiled, really not wanting to talk to anyone. But Margaret and her daughter, Isobel, and Isobel's daughter, Bella, had persevered when they'd all clambered onto the coach, insisting that she sit in the back row with them.

'Is this your first time in Italy?' asked Bella.

Olivia had nodded, her stomach in knots — she hoped Bella wouldn't probe too deeply.

'Ours too. We normally go to Spain, but we thought we'd do something different this year,' said Margaret. 'Isobel's man has left her, good riddance to him, so me and Bella thought we'd do something a bit more special to cheer her up.'

Olivia had noticed Isobel roll her eyes at her mother.

'You don't have to tell everyone, Mum. I mean, do you want to go down the front and announce it to the whole bus? Maybe they'll give you a microphone so the folk on the street can hear too.'

'Och, stop being so touchy. It's not like I'm telling *everyone*.'

'Aye, you are. You can't keep your mouth shut.'

'Aw wheesht,' said Margaret.

Olivia was transfixed by their interactions, even though she couldn't always quite work out what they were saying. Despite feeling jet-lagged, she couldn't help but smile. When the bus had arrived at the port, they all clambered off and she was grateful for their company.

'Anyway,' continued Margaret, 'Italy's *the* place for romance. And you know what they say about Italian men?' She paused for good measure, looking at Isobel meaningfully. 'A wee holiday fling could do you the world of good.' She cackled, then turned to face Olivia. 'What about you, dear? Do you have a man?'

Olivia shook her head. And she really didn't want another one either.

'Better to be young, free and single. Like me,' said Margaret.

'Oh, Granny,' said Bella, with a scornful smile. 'You're a total embarrassment, so you are.'

Olivia laughed at Bella and then turned to admire the view of the bay, dotted with white boats and people swimming in the deep-blue waters. Despite thinking that male appreciation was beyond her right now, she couldn't help but notice a *really* handsome local who looked like an aftershave model or maybe an actor.

'He's totally checking you out, so he is,' whispered Isobel who stood next to her. She nudged Olivia and jerked her head very obviously in the direction of the tall, broad-shouldered man just metres away. He raked his hand through his hair and smiled at the women. Thank goodness for her sunglasses. She could just pretend she wasn't looking at him at all.

'Oh, will you check him out. He's a total Fabio,' said Isobel, fanning herself with a tourist leaflet.

'Where, who?' said Margaret, spinning around in a frantic circle.

'Over there. You can't miss him,' said Isobel.

'Mum!' Bella said sharply to her mum. 'Will you put your tongue back in your mouth and stop panting.'

'All right. Just pointing out the local talent,' she retorted. 'I thought that was why you brought me here.'

'Yeah, but you're like a dog in heat. Stop staring at him so obviously,' she hissed. 'Talk about objectifying the blokes.'

'It's been happening to women for centuries,' said Margaret. 'It's past time the tables were turned.'

Olivia's woes were soon forgotten as she'd started to chuckle. She was actually so grateful to these women for scooping her up and keeping her safe. Especially when she felt so vulnerable. They asked nothing of her. They seemed to sense that she just needed some support, and to hear some of their dodgy jokes.

* * *

It was early evening when they disembarked the boat that brought them back from Capri to Sorrento, where they were based. They made their way towards the steps that would take them up to the town.

'Fancy a wee aperitif before dinner?' asked Isobel. Isobel was petite, had chin-length wavy dark hair and looked much younger than her fifty years.

'Yes, that would be lovely,' said Olivia. She was normally keen to get back to the peace and quiet of her cool hotel room. After a day of sightseeing she needed time to decompress. But tonight, she wasn't quite ready for the day to end, which was a good sign. She was feeling a bit more like herself.

'Isobel, come on. It's this way.' Margaret pointed towards the lift.

'Come on, Granny,' said Bella. 'It will do us good to get a bit of exercise in after that big lunch we had earlier.'

'Bugger that,' said Margaret. 'Are you trying to kill me off? There's no danger I'm climbing all those steps.'

Bella tossed her ponytail in exasperation. 'Och, Granny, what are you like?'

'I'm with you, Margaret,' said Olivia. Normally she would be the first to up her step count, especially as she usually had to be in shape for touring, but she was starting to relax her strict regime. There was nobody around to tell her that she needed to get to bed, no sharp intakes of breath when she was deemed to be eating too much. What a joy it had been to be here and actually enjoy food for a change.

She could still hear *that* voice telling her that she really needed to watch her calorie intake. He had insisted on doing the shopping and cooking so he could monitor what she was eating. Now in Italy, every time she thought about it, she would defiantly reach for another chunk of bread and a slab of creamy mozzarella. Then top up everyone's glass with more wine.

Margaret put a hand on her arm, pulling her from her food dream. 'Righto. That's my girl. We'll race you to the top,' she said to the other two.

By the time Isobel and Bella got to the bar, Olivia and Margaret were on their second Aperol spritz.

'Jeezo,' said Isobel, her face flushed red. 'I'm gasping for a drink.'

Bella seemed a bit perkier. 'Think of how toned our butts will be after that workout.'

Margaret rolled her eyes. 'Alfonso,' she called over to the barman. 'Same again, *per fevore.*'

He rewarded her attempts at Italian with a wink.

'I think he fancies me.'

'Och, Granny, will you stop it. Honestly, you and Mum are a total disgrace. I feel like the only responsible adult.'

'We're both free and single, Bella. Nothing to stop us admiring the goods on the market,' said Margaret.

Olivia loved their camaraderie, the way they easily joked with each other without anyone going off in a serious huff. From what they had shared with her so far, she knew that Margaret was a widow, and Isobel had had some *man trouble*. What was lovely was that the three women belonged together. Which made her wince in sorrow. Where did she belong? She noticed Bella staring at her and then furrowing her brow. So far, the conversation had been fairly superficial, and Olivia had managed to dodge questions that were too personal. She had a feeling that was about to change.

'So, what's next for you then, Olivia?' asked Bella. 'When do you go back to New York?' She tried to imitate Olivia's American drawl as she said it.

Olivia took a sip through her straw, which gave her a few seconds to gather her thoughts. 'I'm not sure yet. I may stay on . . . I've not decided.'

'If only you could find yourself an Italian stallion and enjoy a summer of wild sex,' said Margaret.

Olivia almost spat out her drink.

'Or . . .' said Isobel, 'if you can't get a man here — though I'm sure you'll bag one no bother, a lovely girl like you — then you should come to Scotland and get yerself one there. You know what they say about a true Scotsman, don't you?'

'Och, Mum,' said Bella. 'It's not like they're all wondering around with their kilts on. Let's face it. A lot of them are total prats. You stick with the Italians, Olivia. Don't listen to what she says.'

'But a good Scots bloke is maybe what you need. They're not all bad,' said Isobel.

Margaret folded her arms, fixing her daughter with a withering stare. 'Tell me one good thing about that eejit you just broke up with? He was a drunken lout.'

Isobel sucked her cheeks in. Olivia had witnessed this before; the cheek sucking was a sign that Isobel was starting to get a bit riled. Keen to avoid a row, she decided to change the subject, pronto.

'You know,' she said, hurriedly, 'my aunt and uncle from California visited Scotland last year and they did Glasgow and Edinburgh. But they also raved about an island they visited and fell in love with.'

'Where was that?' asked Margaret. 'Skye? Islay?' She pulled the slice of orange from her glass and sucked on it.

Olivia shook her head. 'No. I remember it was near Glasgow and you took a ferry there.'

'Millport?' suggested Bella.

'Rothesay?' asked Isobel.

'No. That doesn't sound right. It started with an . . .' She stared at the flickering candle on the table, then shook her head. She had no idea what it started with.

'Och, I know where it was,' said Margaret.

'You do?' Olivia asked.

'It was Arran, wasn't it?'

'Yes!' Olivia beamed. 'That's it. Arran. Something about Scotland and small and . . .'

'It's called "Scotland in miniature,"' said Bella.

'Aye, that is a nice place to go. Mind you, it's not the easiest place to get to, is it?' said Isobel.

'Oh.' Olivia's heart sank slightly. 'I thought it was a short ferry ride away.'

'Aye, it is. That's if the ferries are running. There's been an awful stramash with it all.'

Olivia frowned, unsure what that meant.

'Sorry, love,' said Margaret, 'let me translate. That means it's been a bit of a mess. There's not enough boats, they keep breaking down and being cancelled, and they're spending billions on building new ones, which keep getting delayed and delayed. We would have been quicker doing it ourselves.' Margaret shook her head sadly. 'It's been a right scandal. I mean, there's no danger the Italians would put up with that nonsense. They would be taking to the streets in protest. They're far too *passionate* to let things lie,' she concluded dreamily.

'We used to take Bella there when she was wee,' said Isobel. 'It's definitely worth a trip. And ignore her —' she gestured at her mum — 'she's being a total drama queen. It's not that bad. You'll get there fine. You just have to be flexible and patient.'

As Olivia sipped on the last few drops of her drink, an idea started to form.

'The weather will definitely *not* be like this. Prepare for rain,' said Bella. 'It always pishes down at home. You could join me and my friends instead. We're heading to Corfu in July. It'll be boiling there.'

Olivia laughed. 'I think I'm maybe too old for that.'

'Aye, perhaps,' Bella nodded her head thoughtfully.

Olivia didn't take it personally. Bella was twenty-two compared to Olivia's thirty-five, but she was definitely closer in spirit to Bella's mum, Isobel, if not in years. The truth was, Olivia didn't care about the weather in Scotland, whether it was sunny or it rained or it snowed. She just wanted to find refuge, to take shelter and hide from the world. This island seemed like the perfect place to go.

'Just remember, if you do go there, you must promise to come and see us in Glasgow,' said Margaret.

'Of course I will,' said Olivia. She glanced out across the terrace and watched the sun starting to sink behind the horizon. She had a feeling that things were about to take an interesting turn.

CHAPTER ONE

Two Weeks Later

Kitty's knuckles were white as she gripped the steering wheel, willing herself not to cry. She could do this. She *had* to do this. The last thing Cameron needed was to see his mum break down in tears. She forced a smile, glancing nervously at him in the passenger seat as he clicked his seatbelt in. 'Have you definitely got everything?' she asked for the umpteenth time.

'Yip,' he said, picking at a corner of his fingernail.

'You're going to have the most amazing time, love,' she said brightly. 'I promise. I know it must all feel super scary at the moment. But honestly, you'll be so glad that you've done this.'

'Mmm,' he said.

He was nervous. She could tell. The minute Cameron started to become overwhelmed he would become quiet and monosyllabic. Mind you, she couldn't blame him. Flying across the Atlantic on his own and spending the summer working with lots of American kids was no mean feat. The furthest he had travelled on his own was to the TRNSMT festival in Glasgow last year. Even then, he was with his two

9

best friends, and the deal was that they could go as long as they stayed with her brother, John, who lived in the city centre.

When he had first started talking about the possibility of working abroad for the summer she had listened quietly, nodding and encouraging him to look into it, reassuring him that she would support him to spread his wings and go on this adventure.

Now that he was eighteen it was time for him to gain a bit more independence. He had left school, but wasn't quite sure what he wanted to do next. This seemed the perfect solution to give him a bit of breathing space, to have some freedom so he could get a sense of who he wanted to be.

Little did he know that Kitty felt as though her world was being turned upside down again. As a single parent, she'd vowed she would never become a needy mum, relying on her son for everything, yet it took every single scrap of her willpower not to plead with him to stay at home forever and never leave her on her own.

Surely she should be relishing the thought of time alone, of having a tidy fire and fully stocked fridge. Honestly, that boy could inhale blocks of cheese and packets of bacon in seconds. She was on first-name terms with all the staff at the nearby Co-op because she was such a regular shopper. They even joked with her that she should get a job there — she'd seriously toyed with the idea, if just for the staff discount.

As soon as she waved Cameron goodbye at the departure gate, she would be on her own. For the first time in eighteen years she would be alone.

She always knew that this day would come, but she wasn't sure she was ready for empty-nest syndrome. She was only forty-three. What would she do? Cameron had been her main focus for most of her adult life. Since he was a baby, it had just been him and her. And now it would just be her. Alone.

She could finally put herself first . . . The thought was absolutely terrifying.

Cameron sighed, drawing her back to the present, and she gulped back a sob. She needed to get through the next hour or so, then she could go home and weep and let the sheer sadness overwhelm her in private. She took a deep and steadying breath in.

'I know it must feel daunting,' she said gently. 'But this is just the first step. It will all get easier.'

He shrugged and looked out the window. It was just after 4 a.m. and the sun was already rising. The journey to Inverness Airport from their home in Rosemarkie only took about half an hour. Cameron was catching an early flight to Amsterdam and then making a connection to New York City, where he would then head to his summer placement upstate.

Normally Kitty enjoyed the drive across the Kessock Bridge, which stretched over the Beauly Firth, but this morning it all felt very surreal.

'I'll be okay,' he assured her. 'I'm just tired. Not used to getting up this early.'

That was very true.

'Will you be okay, Mum?' he asked in a quiet voice.

She pleaded with herself not to crumple. 'I'll be just fine.' She forced a jolly tone. 'The house will be tidy for a change. I can watch what I want on telly, and I can eat what I want too. Think of all the egg sandwiches I can make without you moaning what a stink they're making. In fact, I'm looking forward to it. It will be like being a teenager all over again.'

He chuckled. 'You'll miss me though?'

Oh God, come on Kitty, she said to herself, *you can lie through this.* 'Not at all . . . well, maybe a wee tiny bit, but I'll be having far too much fun. It's not just you who's going on an adventure.'

'Well, I'm not sure how exciting spending the summer on a wet Scottish island will be . . . But, okay, if you say so.'

She raised an eyebrow. 'I'll have you know it's got palm trees and a very nice climate.'

'Whatever . . . But what will you do?'

'I'll find plenty to do. I'll sleep in till noon like you do. Go for walks . . . do stuff like reading and pottering and maybe work on my Instagram account. You know, important stuff like that.'

'Sounds riveting. Will you be okay on your own though? I mean, won't you get bored?'

'I'll be just fine. I'll see Fergus a few times, I'm sure. But I really don't mind having some time on my own.'

'And with the Instagram stuff, you know what you're doing now with that? It's all about the photographs.'

She laughed. 'Yes, it's all fine. Who knows, by the time you get back I might be a huge influencer or something. A Kardashian.'

He scoffed. 'Oh, please no. Just remember what I said. Don't overdo the live streaming. It's not that cool.'

'But what about the live cookery demonstrations?'

'Less is more, Mum.'

She shook her head as she followed the exit sign for the airport. Although she worked in a nursery, she had started baking when she realised that Cameron had an allergy to dairy. This had led to her discovering her flair for it, and for making vegan cakes in particular. She was told repeatedly that you wouldn't think her cakes didn't have dairy or eggs in them. They tasted so *normal*. She had become *the* person to go to if someone wanted a birthday cake, and had quite the portfolio of celebration cakes as well as cupcakes and muffins and traybakes. However, she really needed to upload the photos to her Instagram account to showcase what she could do.

Kitty could feel herself starting to wish that Cameron was flying from Glasgow Airport instead. That would have given her more time with her boy. Three more hours. Maybe his flight would be cancelled and she would have to drive him to London Heathrow. She knew she was clutching at straws, but now, as she followed the signs for the car park, it seemed as though they had barely left their house and they were already here. The clock was ticking.

'Right, love.' She pulled into a parking space. 'Here we are. I suppose we should go and get you checked in.'

Cameron jumped out the car and flicked open the boot, hoisting his backpack onto his shoulders.

'Now, remember, brush your teeth, drink lots of water and *be careful*,' she said for the millionth time. They began walking towards the terminal.

'Yes. I'll do everything that you wouldn't do and more.' He linked his arm through hers and grinned. He had the same charming smile as his father. 'Do you want to wait here, and I'll check my bag in?'

'Yes, of course.' She let him walk ahead into the departure zone, watching as her suddenly grown-up baby joined the queue. He was wearing jeans and his favourite blue T-shirt, his mop of curly dark hair falling over his eyes. He towered over the other passengers and stooped a bit, almost to make himself smaller, just like his dad used to do. In fact, he was like Ryan in so many ways she quite often found herself imagining how different their lives would have been if he was still around. As a single parent she had done her best for Cameron, but she would always worry about the lack of a father figure in his life. Her brother, John, was great, but wasn't a substitute for Cameron having his real dad.

Her eyes pricked with tears again. She couldn't think about that just now. She made a mental promise to herself that as soon as she waved goodbye, she would go home and crawl into bed and howl. She plastered on a smile as she saw him walking over to her.

'Okay, so the same goes for you, Mum. Behave, and don't do anything I wouldn't.' He pulled her into a hug and squeezed her tight. He gestured towards passport control. 'I'll just head up there now,' he said, eyes glistening.

'Good plan. Otherwise it could get messy. I don't want to embarrass you by turning into a snivelling mess,' she said. 'Now remember to WhatsApp me when you land in Amsterdam, and keep an eye on the screens in case your flight is announced.'

He rolled his eyes. 'Yes, Mum.'

'And if you get stuck then remember to ask someone for help.'

'Mum . . . I'm not four.'

'I know you're not, love. I know you can do this.' She wanted to sweep him into her arms and take him home. If only he was still a little boy.

She hugged him one last time. 'Off you go, sweetheart. Take care and, most importantly, have fun. Enjoy every minute. You deserve to go off and have a great adventure.'

As he walked away, he turned to give a final wave and she forced another grin, raising her hand. Her shoulders started to shudder, and it took every ounce of self-control to walk back to her car without breaking down. As soon as she closed the car door, she dissolved.

CHAPTER TWO

Logan tried not to wince as Tallulah dug her bright pink nails, which were as hard as talons, into his back. Her arms hooked around his neck and, for a brief moment of horror, he panicked that she was about to kiss him. She had clung to him like a limpet these past few days. He was used to tourists in his group tours thinking they had a crush on him now and again, it was that whole tour leader thing, but he hadn't experienced anyone quite like Tallulah. She was Irish, newly divorced and on the lookout for love — as she kept reminding everyone several times a day.

'There you go,' he said, gently unhooking her and guiding her to where the path broadened out ahead. 'Just that way.'

She flashed him a sorrowful smile. 'You're so strong and manly. Thanks for helping me. That crossing was *very* narrow.' Then she turned, wiggled her bum in her very tight walking shorts and flounced down the path.

Logan felt his cheeks redden. He didn't think he'd ever been called strong and manly before, though he had spent many years in the Navy. If his sisters could see him now they would double over laughing. He looked behind him to make sure the rest of the party were safely passing the narrow walkway, and breathed a sigh of relief. He was escorting a small group on a three-day walking tour of Skye and some parts of the trails were tighter than others. Hence Tallulah's . . . *over-reliance* on him. She was an older woman, confident, flirty   not quietly so   and normally in association with him. He sighed.

Thanks to his two older sisters he was more in touch with his feminine side than he wished to be. Growing up, he had learned all about period pains and hormones and mood swings. He had got used to being sent out to buy emergency stashes of chocolate. Then, as his sisters got older, he became very used to hearing 'all men are wankers' being shouted and doors being slammed. Thanks to his ongoing education, Logan also knew one could never be too careful around hot flushes.

He normally loved his job, but he would be glad when this particular tour had ended. He couldn't remember ever feeling so on edge before. Fortunately his time in the Navy had served him well for dealing with Tallulah and her unwanted advances. She had thrown him a few sad smiles, as today was her last day, which had almost made him feel sorry for her. But never before had he needed to keep such a firm boundary in place for a guest. It was utterly exhausting.

Logan reached the clearing ahead, where the four-strong group were waiting for their next instruction. 'You'll be glad to know that this is where we're going to stop for lunch.' His words were met with an enthusiastic cheer — people sank to the ground and started pulling out their lunchboxes. Logan drained his bottle of water and stretched his neck, then sat down and joined the small circle they'd formed.

'This has been incredible,' said Sam, who was visiting with his wife from New Zealand.

'Just beautiful. The scenery is spectacular,' said Sylvie, a French student, who was trying to cram as much as she could into her year overseas.

'What have your highlights been?' he asked, expecting a little silence as they each pondered over the past few days.

'That's easy,' said Tallulah in a lazy drawl. 'Definitely the Fairy Pools and the *wild* swimming.'

Logan groaned inwardly at the way she lingered on the word *wild*. Crikey, that had been another day he wanted to forget in a hurry. The Fairy Pools were a stunning spot at the foot of the Black Cuillin mountains, attracting visitors from all over the world. Especially now that wild swimming was all the rage, although he had just thought of it as swimming outdoors. He was always a bit baffled by the *wild* part. He had prepared the group in advance, telling them that the water would be extremely cold so there was no pressure to go in. However, that day was warm and sunny, perfect for a quick dip. He had led the way, after stripping to his shorts, aware of Tallulah's eyes on him. He'd always hated attention.

Tallulah was the first of the group to strip off to a bikini that looked like it had been stolen from the set of *Love Island*. It certainly wasn't designed for doing any swimming, especially not in Scotland in some random river pools. He clocked Sam throwing his wife a look of incredulity and tried not to chuckle. Then he said to the rest of the group to take their time getting in the water. He swam over to Sylvie, who looked a bit nervous. 'Once you're in, it will be okay. It's cold but you'll soon warm up.' He tried his best to smile at Tallulah, even though she was now swimming a bit too close for comfort. When he felt her leg brush against his, he manoeuvred himself out the way, then encouraged everyone to enjoy their time in the water but not stay in too long.

'How about you, Logan?' asked Sam. 'You must have done thousands of these walks and know Scotland like the back of your hand.'

That was true. Logan absolutely loved his job — being outdoors, showing off the country he adored to tourists. After leaving the Navy five years ago he had taken some time out to hike and explore Scotland in a way he hadn't before. He had taken his backpack and gone at his own pace, which was a refreshing change after living to such tight routines. It took some getting used to, knowing he could stay in a place for as long or as little as he wanted. He had no ties or responsibilities. The whole experience was really liberating.

Then he had started working for a touring company, which offered guided tours to small groups. He loved being able to take people to hidden parts of Scotland and really show them the best of it. Meeting people from all over the world was a perk of the job too, and he had made some great friends who he still kept in touch with. He had set up an Instagram account, the Tartan Wanderer, and, yes, he knew it was really cheesy, but tourists loved it and it was easy to remember. His sisters had made fun of all the comments he got from 'the ladies' if his face appeared in a post, which was very rare. He tried to focus on showing images and reels of Highland cows, hills, glens, snowy mountains, dolphins, castles and white beaches.

Logan had recently celebrated his landmark birthday of forty, and felt no urge to settle down. He liked his freedom and his space far too much. He couldn't understand why anyone would choose a relationship over that.

'Do you ever get bored of going to the same places time after time?' asked Sam.

'Oh, not at all,' he said with a shrug. 'Never. No two days are the same, no two visits are the same. There's always something different, whether it's the weather or the scenery. I always notice things I haven't before. It's the best job in the world. I'm very lucky.'

'You have an amazing office,' remarked Sam's wife, Naomi.

He nodded.

'Where is your favourite place?' asked Sylvie.

He frowned as he tried to answer her question. 'That's really tricky,' he began. 'I mean, there are so many amazing spots . . . I love Glencoe, and obviously Skye is amazing. In fact, I love all the islands . . .'

'Okay then.' Sam was clearly enthralled. 'How about this? What if you had to choose one island? If you could recommend just one, which would it be?'

Logan took another swig of water from his bottle as he thought. Then he smiled as he felt a slight shiver down his spine. 'Arran,' he said dreamily. 'If I had to choose my favourite spot it would be the Isle of Arran. It's just off the west coast. About an hour's ferry ride away from the mainland.

'Oh,' said Tallulah, a tad breathlessly. 'Have you got time to take us there? It sounds spectacular. And so romantic.'

He briskly shook his head. *Oh, good God, that's the last thing I need.* 'I'm afraid not.' He cleared his throat. 'As you know, this is our *final* day, and it would take us a good day to travel there and then several days to explore.'

Her shoulders slumped and she stuck out her bottom lip. 'What a shame. I was thinking about cancelling my trip to Edinburgh and perhaps trying to see more of the islands.'

'Well, our next few tours there are fully booked,' Logan said quickly. 'Until the end of the season,' he added, crossing his fingers that his boss wouldn't find out he'd said that. 'Edinburgh is a must-see. Especially when you've flown all this way.' What was he talking about? Dublin was only an hour away. He knew he was grasping at straws.

Sylvie nodded in agreement. 'It is stunning, Tallulah. You must go. Edinburgh is such a romantic city.'

Tallulah quickly switched her attentions to the young French woman. 'Oh, do tell me more. Can you give me any recommendations?'

'Of course. I'll make you a list of suggestions. You will not be disappointed, I promise.'

At that moment Logan wanted to high-five Sylvie and thank her profusely. Instead he clasped his hands tightly together. 'I hope you've enjoyed what you've seen of Scotland so far and . . . that you'll feel like coming back some day. There's so much to see and do here. We're so lucky.'

He decided that he wouldn't share details of his next trip, just in case Tallulah made a last-minute change to her plans. He was in fact heading to his favourite destination, to lead a tour around Arran, the island he loved and knew well. He would have a couple of days off before the tour started, then some time off afterwards. He planned to spend it on the island, relaxing and catching up with his good friend, James, who had moved back there last year to run a new distillery.

'Well, we will definitely be back, that's for sure,' said Sam to the rest of the group. 'I think I can safely say we have loved every minute. Thanks for looking after us so well.'

Everyone clapped and nodded.

Logan beamed in pride. 'Thank you. And haste ye back.'

'What does that mean?' asked Tallulah from underneath her eyelashes. She was clearly going for one last ditch attempt.

Logan turned to her and gave her a kind smile. Then he addressed the rest of the group. 'That means you are *all* always welcome here.' He didn't want to say it meant, 'Come back soon.' Because that would give her the wrong end of the stick completely. Honestly, he was mentally exhausted from walking on eggshells these past few days. He just hoped that his next group on Arran wouldn't have any Tallulahs in it. His nerves couldn't take it.

CHAPTER THREE

It was the morning after she had waved goodbye to Cameron, and Kitty sat at the breakfast bar in her kitchen, nursing a mug of tea. It was peaceful, apart from the sound of birds chirping gently outside. She had spent yesterday cleaning the house from top to bottom and decluttering, knowing that she wouldn't hear from Cameron while he was in the air. She should keep herself busy. Then, when she had eventually gone to bed, she hadn't been able to get to sleep until she knew that Cameron had landed safely. He sent her several messages telling her all was fine and not to worry. Despite his reassuring words, she had tossed and turned for ages before finally drifting off. When she woke up, she stared at the ceiling, forgetting for a moment that things were different. It was a mere moment of suspended bliss and then she felt the dread in the pit of her stomach when she remembered. Cameron was gone.

Kitty twirled a lock of her red hair as she thought about how strange it all was. She knew it wouldn't be easy when Cameron left, but she wasn't expecting to feel quite so awful. Friends had warned her what to expect. She had dismissed their concerns and just assumed she would have a quick cry and then get on with things in the way that she always had.

How wrong could she have been? It had been the complete opposite — it was like a tsunami of emotions threatening to drown her.

She wondered if his departure had perhaps triggered all the emotions and feelings that she had managed to bury away for years. But she didn't want to go there just now. Instead, she looked around the kitchen. It was more spotless than it had ever been. But she missed the trails of cornflakes and sticky juice residue on the worktop and the numerous mugs piled in the sink. Looking out through the hallway, she sighed when she saw how empty it was without the shoes. She was so used to climbing over several pairs of size-ten trainers belonging to Cameron and his friends.

A bout of cleaning usually settled her mind, and she hoped yesterday's session would help distract her. But it all just reminded her how empty the house was and how empty her life was. Thank goodness she was heading away for a change of scene. She didn't think she would cope if she was home alone all summer. Just then the doorbell rang, and she could see her best friend Ellen's face through the glass. Flinging the door open, she managed a weak smile and was glad of the warm hug Ellen gave her.

'How are you this morning?' Ellen asked, kicking her trainers off in the hallway on her way to the kitchen.

Kitty smiled wryly to herself. The hallway hadn't been without mess for long. 'Tea?'

'I could murder a coffee actually. But I'll make it,' Ellen said, already reaching for the cafetière in the cupboard by the kettle. 'Sit down and tell me how you *really* are. I was worried about you yesterday, Kitty. Your communication was limited.'

'I know. Sorry, Ellen, but I didn't want to see anyone. I just needed some space.' She almost added that she was an emotional wreck and spent the day wailing, so couldn't have managed to string a sentence together. However, she decided not to share the gruesome details — Ellen would only fret even more.

Ellen frowned. 'But he got to the camp okay?' She paused and reached out to stroke Kitty on the arm.

Kitty nodded. 'Yes. He's there now, and he said he'd FaceTime when he can, but it would probably be quite full-on with the induction and getting settled.'

Ellen poured the boiling water from the kettle into the cafetière and gave it a quick stir before plunging down the lid. 'I know you're supposed to wait for it to percolate or something like that, but I'm desperate for some caffeine.' She poured herself a mug and took a gulp.

'I think I should be asking if you're okay,' said Kitty, surprised at how agitated her friend was.

Ellen wrinkled her nose. 'I am now. I was just desperate for a coffee. Here, sorry, let me pour you one.'

Kitty poured her now cold tea into the sink, rinsed her mug and placed it onto the counter. 'Thank you.'

'I almost forgot. I have biscuits too.' Ellen reached into her huge handbag and pulled out a tinfoil package. 'Don't worry, they're dairy free. It's your cookie recipe.'

Kitty laughed, amused that Ellen, who never ever used to bake, had started to embrace her inner cook.

Ellen shrugged. 'What can I say? You were right. It's a nice thing to do. It's all very relaxing. That is, until you eat all the stuff you've baked and realise you've piled on half a stone.'

'Oh, hardly,' said Kitty, genuinely delighted that Ellen had baked her goodies. Ellen was usually never in her flat long enough to make a cup of tea because she worked so much. 'Anyway, I really appreciate this. It was so thoughtful of you.' She unwrapped the cookies. 'Mind you, I think you've overdone the packaging, Ellen.' Kitty shook her head at the several layers of tinfoil and baking paper. 'It's like you've packed illegal drugs for a flight.'

Ellen gave a belly laugh. 'I just wanted to keep them fresh. Tuck in. We can't have you fading away, can we? Especially when you're also taking off for the summer. Feeding you now is the least I can do.'

Kitty felt a small flicker of guilt when she realised that she wouldn't see Ellen for weeks. 'You could come and visit?'

'I would love to. But I'm just not sure I can get any time off. They're so short-staffed just now.'

Ellen worked in a care home, and the past few years had taken a lot out of her. She loved her job and was so good with the residents. She felt terrible that they were struggling for staff, which was why she worked extra shifts. 'Talking of which,' she said, glancing at her watch, 'I better be off as I'm working later.'

Kitty worried that she was burning the candle at both ends. 'I do worry that you do too much.'

Ellen flicked her hand in dismissal. 'It's fine. Everyone works hard, don't they? These days we're all in the same boat. Look at all you've been doing, these past few years especially.'

Kitty worked full-time at the local nursery after having a bit of a career change just before the pandemic. She had trained as a counsellor when Cameron started school and had a thriving business. Then it had all gotten too much, and she started to feel burned out. She decided she wanted regular hours and to be around kids who were less complicated than the adults she spent her days with.

'Well, look, I appreciate you coming over. I know time is tight for you, and here I am with the whole summer off to just house-sit!'

'Hey,' said Ellen, firmly but gently, 'this is your time now. So don't feel guilty. You have every right to have some time off after all that you've been through. You're an amazing mum to Cameron and have put him first all these years. It's time for you to think of what *you* want to do. And that's okay. A break from the nursery will do you the world of good too.' She paused and winked. 'I reckon a good holiday romance would be just the medicine you need right now.'

Kitty scoffed. 'That's definitely not going to happen.'

'You never know,' said Ellen, winking. 'Promise me that you'll just be open-minded and keep me posted.' She gulped the rest of her coffee down. 'Sorry, Kits, I better run. You're away the day after tomorrow?'

'Yip,' said Kitty.

'Okay, well, I'll try and nip round before then. I'll definitely call though. And don't worry, I'll pop in and out of the house to water your plants. If I remember,' she said sheepishly, pulling Kitty into a warm embrace. 'Don't do anything that I wouldn't do.' She laughed.

'That's exactly what Cameron said to me too. What is it with you pair?'

'We talk a lot of sense. Maybe it's time you listened to us both.'

Kitty was still smiling after waving bye to Ellen. She had a sense that things were going to work out okay, and the feeling of dread was replaced with a fluttering of something she thought was excitement. It was time to pack for her trip.

CHAPTER FOUR

Olivia's wide smile rapidly turned into a frown when she stepped out of Prestwick Airport — straight into torrential rain and a cold and howling gale. It couldn't have been more of a contrast to the lemon trees, sunshine, blue skies and sparkling aqua waters that she had enjoyed the past few weeks in Sorrento and the Amalfi Coast. She shivered. Wasn't it supposed to be summer? She knew that the weather could be changeable in Scotland, but this was more like monsoon weather than a summer shower. This must have been what Bella meant when she said it 'pished down' in the west of Scotland.

Sighing, and reflecting what a great way that was to describe the relentless rain, she turned right back round and into the terminal so she could find her jacket. It was, of course, buried at the bottom of her bag. Then, when she felt her stomach rumble, she decided to get herself a coffee and a snack before making the next part of her very long journey.

Olivia ordered herself an oat milk cappuccino and a banana, then found a seat in the corner of the café. She was tired and irritated and wondered if her decision to come to Scotland had been a bit too hasty. Perhaps she should have extended her stay in Italy and jumped on a train from Naples to sunnier climes. She had toyed with the thought of visiting Florence and exploring Tuscany, but ironically had been put off at the thought of the heat. A further chat with her dynamic aunt Trudy had set the wheels in motion. Trudy insisted that Arran would be the perfect place to retreat, and it would give her some headspace to think about what she wanted to do next.

Trudy had been privy to only limited but significant details of what happened between Olivia and her ex, Patrick, in the run-up to Olivia's last-minute decision to go to Italy. Olivia was grateful that she hadn't tried to pry for more information. Instead, she had reassured Olivia that she was there to listen should she want to talk. Trudy had even managed to sort out this last-minute house-sit for her, which was what had ultimately led her to Scotland. Not to mention that it meant she didn't have to dip into her savings — she had no idea when her next job would be. She knew that she should check her emails and messages about upcoming auditions, but the minute she began thinking about anything normal or everyday she got overwhelmed. It was too much and made her want to keep running, which she was effectively doing now. Olivia had gone so far as to pick up a cheap smartphone in Italy so she could stay in touch with her aunt, while keeping her usual mobile switched off.

Based on what Trudy had managed to organise for her in the last couple of weeks, it did seem as though the planets were finally aligning for her. But now, as she looked out at the pelting rain that showed no sign of abating, she was feeling doubtful. Especially as she had been travelling for what felt like days, which could quite easily have amounted to a long-haul flight. After a few weeks in the Italian sun she had managed to get a cheap flight from Naples to Barcelona, then had taken a connecting flight to Prestwick, which was outside Glasgow. She had been told by Isobel and family that it would be 'dead handy' to then get to Arran. A bus journey and a ferry ride were next. If only it would clear up, she would feel so much better about this trip.

After draining her coffee, she pulled her bag behind her and visited the ladies, before she embarked on the next stage of the marathon journey. By the time she made it to the bus stop across from the terminal building, the sky had turned from a pale grey to a light blue and the sun was trying to shine. Isobel hadn't been kidding when she said you could get all seasons in a day.

* * *

Three hours later, still pulling her bags, she yawned as she walked along the wide pavement that curved its way along the seafront at Brodick. The air was tinged with a salty scent, and she could hear seagulls shrieking at each other as they swooped up and down looking for any scraps of food they could steal. The instructions Trudy had forwarded her said the holiday cottage was about a ten-minute walk from the ferry terminal. She was glad it wasn't any further, as the final stretch was up a hill — she was out of breath as she reached the top, a sign she was definitely losing her fitness.

But then she saw the gate, which had a slate sign on it with the words *Lilybank Cottage* etched in white. She stopped panting. A frill of blue hydrangea flowers fell over the gate, which squeaked as she opened it into a grassy front garden with stepping stones leading up to the door of a converted old stone steading. It was an idyllic spot, and she couldn't help but feel as though she had just walked into an enchanted garden. Putting her bags down on the step, she took a moment to look around and take in her surroundings. The only sound she could hear was bees buzzing in and out of the flowers. It was quite hypnotic. She reached for the key safe by the front door and lined up the required code so that it opened. Inside were two sets of keys. She tried them both, realising one set was a spare, and popped the extra set back in the box, making sure the numbers were mixed up again.

When she opened the door and walked into the hallway, then the room ahead, she gasped. It was beautiful. It looked as though it belonged in the pages of a home magazine. It had clearly been refurbished throughout, with an open-plan layout and sunken sitting room with lots of different seating areas to suit every mood. Looking around she could see there were love seats in the corner, a large squishy sofa to stretch out on or the chaise longue by the window, which looked perfect for lying on and admiring the stunning view of the sea. The kitchen was light and airy and had French windows opening out to the decking area. Wow, thought Olivia, this is so homely and welcoming.

Olivia felt like an excited child as she explored the house, opening all the doors to discover one room after another. There were three generously sized bedrooms, and all had en suite bathrooms with walk-in showers and baths. Which one should she choose? Running between them all, she laughed in delight, then dumped her bags in the first one. It wasn't that she was choosy   she would be happy sleeping in any of the rooms. Maybe she would try them all out while she was here. Why not?

Her throat was parched, and she headed into the kitchen to get a glass of water. The window by the sink looked out across the garden, which had decking, chairs and a table that would be perfect for watching the sunrise. It was an incredible spot with views over the sea. No wonder her aunt had encouraged her to come here. Now she could completely understand why her aunt and uncle were so taken with the place. She was so glad she had made the effort to get here. For the first time in about twenty-four hours she allowed herself a small smile. That was when she spotted a note that had been left on the kitchen island. She picked it up and read.

Hello!

If you're reading this note, then you must have arrived in the cottage. I hope you had a good journey over. A very warm welcome to Arran!

I hope you find everything that you need in the house. All the instructions for how stuff works are in the top

drawer underneath the kettle and are all fairly straightfor-
ward, but just let me know if I can be of any help.

I'm Amy and my sister, Kirsty, and I are just up the
road at Meadowbank Cottage. I hope you have a super
stay here on the island and love it as much as we do. I look
forward to meeting you soon.

Amy x

PS, I've left some essentials in the fridge to get you
started, and a few other local bits and pieces of produce,
including some of Kirsty's very nice shortbread.

PPS, You'll have seen the big Co-op (and the little
one!) in the village for your groceries. There are also lots of
lovely coffee shops and bars. If you want to explore further,
then the bus is handy and regular. There's a timetable in the
lounge with all the other leaflets and books that tell you what
else you can do during your stay.

Olivia glanced over at the small cardboard box next to
the note. She peered inside and pulled out some oatcakes,
a jar of berry jam and another of chilli chutney, along with
some ground coffee and a packet of teabags. There was also
a small box tied with a tartan ribbon. As she opened it, she
could smell a sweet, sugary scent and was delighted to find
small biscuit squares inside. She popped one into her mouth.
It was buttery and crumbly and delicious. That must be the
shortbread. Kirsty was certainly a talented baker. Opening
the fridge door she found milk, butter, cheese and eggs.
Olivia was quite overcome. How kind! It was such a thoughtful gesture, and one she really appreciated.

She must thank Amy. Turning the paper over, she
looked for a business card or a note of her number, but Amy
hadn't left any details. That meant Olivia would need to go
and seek her out to express her thanks. Yet she wasn't quite
sure she was ready for that, it felt too soon to talk to anyone
else after Italy. Just like that, her mind started to race and the
fluttering anxiety started again.

Maybe she would go out later and pop a note through the door to let the sisters know she was there and to say thanks for the thoughtful groceries. That way she wouldn't need to speak to anyone, but at least they would know she was there and was grateful for the gifts.

Olivia reached for a glass from the cupboard by the sink and filled it. She took a gulp of the water, which was refreshing, and also surprisingly tasty for water straight out of a tap. It certainly didn't taste like that in New York, where she tended to buy it in bottles. Then she drank the rest of it and refilled her glass again and drained it. Wow, she was thirsty. Usually she kept a large bottle of water with her all the time — it was easy to get dehydrated when dancing — but that was another thing she had let lapse these past couple of weeks.

Stifling another yawn — she was *so* tired — she went to the bedroom to unpack her clothes. She'd better do something practical and at least get herself settled in before she did anything else. Glancing at her watch, she realised it was gone four in the afternoon. It had been a very long day as her flight from Naples had been at five in the morning.

The bedroom was as stylishly decorated as the rest of the house, and she knew she would quickly settle in. All the walls were painted in a pale grey and the bedding was white, but bright yellow throws and cushions gave it a splash of colour. The curtains were heavy and made of grey material adorned with tiny yellow flowers. Looking through to the en suite she couldn't wait to have a bath in the decadent tub. What a treat. She had to pinch herself. It seemed too good to be true. But perhaps life was evidently looking up for her, and who was she to look a gift horse in the mouth? It was going to be wonderful to have this space all to herself. She'd even just checked with her aunt if she was funding it, as she wouldn't have put it past her. But no, she'd assured her that the owners were simply looking for someone to house-sit; they were thinking of possibly selling or keeping it only for family use.

Olivia emptied her bag. Looking at her crumpled heap of clothes on the floor, she began to think she may need to buy a few more essentials. When she'd thrown some things in her bag for the trip to Italy, she hadn't overthought it. She certainly hadn't expected that she'd be landing in a country where you could have torrential rain and cold, gale-force winds one minute, then bright-blue skies and warm sunshine a couple of hours later. The temperature was also quite a bit cooler than it had been in Italy.

Fortunately she had spotted an outdoor shop in Brodick. She would go there at some point and see what she could find. In the meantime she scooped up her laundry, took it into the kitchen and loaded the washing machine, which seemed tiny compared to the huge ones in the basement of her building.

Once the machine was on, she curled up in one of the seats by the window, appreciating the soothing noise of the laundry tumbling around the machine. Had it really only been four weeks since she left home? It felt so much longer, and she couldn't quite believe how different her life was just a month ago. Things couldn't have been more different to where she was now. But at least she felt safe.

She had taken her old mobile out of her bag and placed it on the table next to her. It had been switched off completely since she left New York — she was still resistant to turning it on, as she knew what would happen when she did. Shuddering, she thought of the missed calls and the voicemails and the emails flooding her inbox. The guilt appeared again. Aside from Trudy, nobody else knew where she was. She had messaged her friends before she left and let them know she was fine and taking some time out. Patrick was out of town when she left. She had moved her possessions into storage and then written him a note to say that things were over. Then she ran.

If she was really honest with herself, she couldn't quite believe what had happened and was still in shock. Her behaviour was so out of character, and she wasn't quite sure what had come over her. But she was so glad that it had. Otherwise, who knows what would have happened. She had been trapped for such a long time and had only recently started to realise it.

Reaching for the phone, that small rectangle that was so significant in her life, she toyed with turning it on. Her thumb rubbed back and forth over the button, and she was tempted. Then she placed it back down on the table. She wasn't ready. She needed some time to rest and recuperate and think about what to do next.

All of a sudden, exhaustion washed over her and she lay back on the seat, closing her eyes just to rest them for five minutes. Within seconds she was fast asleep.

CHAPTER FIVE

After bidding farewell to the group, Logan spent his final night on Skye with just a couple of single malt whiskies for company. He always made sure he stayed in separate accommodation from his guests. Logan liked boundaries and didn't like mixing business with pleasure. It had been a valuable principle to have in place, as Tallulah so aptly demonstrated. With people on holiday, drink flowing, it was best to avoid those occasions when a guest fancied landing themselves a 'kilted hunk' during their visit to Scotland. He was always a bit bemused when asked if he ever did the walking tours wearing kilts, but Logan grimaced at the thought. Aside from the thought of midge bites on his man parts, Logan really only wore kilts to weddings, Highland Games and the odd international rugby game, and certainly didn't think of himself as a hunk. Not at all. He found the attention all quite mortifying.

He poured a splash of cold water into his glass and took a sip of the peaty liquid, enjoying the feeling of warmth trickling down the back of his throat. He was very much looking forward to having a couple of days off before the next trip began. Much as he loved his job, which felt like a way of life rather than work, he needed some time to decompress and recharge his social battery. He enjoyed meeting new people and hearing about their lives and all the stories they had to share, but was glad to have a day or two after a trip when he didn't have to say too much to anyone — that included his sisters, who told him repeatedly that he worked too much and should take more time out to socialise. What they really meant was that *they* thought it was time he should settle down.

His twin sisters, Lucie and Bridget, were older by eight years and they had mothered him from the moment he was born. Their mum had passed away when he was just ten years old, so they had continued with their roles as surrogate mothers, which seemed to give them a free card to boss him about and express their (strong) opinions on how he should or should not be living his life. Both lived in Perth (Scotland, not Australia), and they communicated with him constantly on WhatsApp. They were always telling him off for the length of time he took to reply, and complained that his answers were too short and told them nothing about his life.

Their father hadn't coped well after he lost his beloved wife. Although he did his best at raising the kids, he had turned to drink to help him cope, which led to him sinking into a deep depression from which he'd never been able to recover. He eventually died of liver disease when Logan was twenty-two, which was part of the reason he had joined the Navy. Apart from his sisters, he had no ties to keep him in Scotland. He wanted to explore and leave the sadness of home life behind.

So he embraced the adventure in a way he hoped his late parents would be proud of. He travelled the world and tried to make the most of every minute of it. Wanderlust seemed to suit him and his personality, and although he had many girlfriends along the way there hadn't really been anyone he had fallen head over heels in love with. Not any special person that would have made him swap his freedom and love of exploring for a life of domesticity. No thanks. He was happy with his lot. He had his health, his freedom and his friends, and he was grateful for all of it.

Logan knew his sisters disapproved of his nomadic life-style, but he kept reassuring them that he was happy and he didn't want a life in the suburbs with two-point-four children, thank you very much.

'But it's such a waste,' wailed Lucie one day. 'You could have your pick of women *and* you would be a great dad.'

Logan had shuddered. Fortunately Bridget wasn't quite as dominant as her sister, who was older by twenty minutes and liked to make sure they all knew about it. Bridget was always a lot more measured with her opinions. 'The main thing is that you're happy, Logan. You're healthy and kind and successful and enjoying life. That's all we want for you. Isn't that right, Lucie?'

He couldn't not notice the scornful look Lucie had thrown her.

Raising his glass to inspect the amber liquid, he took another sip of his dram and smiled wryly as he thought about his sisters. He was lucky they cared so much, and he knew a visit back to see them was overdue. The problem was that summer was peak season and his schedule was fairly rammed. Frowning, he flicked through his phone calendar, trying to work out where he might have a window. He was pleased his boss had scheduled him quite a few trips on Arran over the summer. He made a mental note to get in touch with him tomorrow to check on the names of the guests for the next trip. Picking up his phone, he quickly tapped out a message to the friend he would be staying with on Arran.

Hey, James! Looking forward to seeing you very soon. I'll be arriving in Brodick at some point on Monday and will give you a shout then.

That was another perk of the job. He'd get a chance to properly catch up with James and see the new distillery, which he'd been running for the past year. Logan was also curious to meet the mysterious woman, Amy, who seemed to have tamed James's heart. Like Logan, James was a bit of an eternal bachelor and liked to suit himself. He gave a tiny shrug. She must be something special — James was smitten, and that was something Logan certainly did not envy. He couldn't think of anything worse.

CHAPTER SIX

The idea to spend the summer in Arran had all been a bit last minute, only arranged just before Cameron had left. Kitty had the summer off work from the nursery but didn't really have any concrete plans. She thought she *might* do some travelling, but wanted to make sure Cameron was away safely before she made her own plans. It was her cousin, Fergus, who had come up trumps with the holiday house. Fergus had returned to live on Arran after years living away, and a friend of a friend needed someone to house-sit over the summer. Their holiday cottage was in the village of Brodick and they were thinking of stopping the lettings and keeping it for their own use whenever they needed it.

'But doesn't he want to rent it out? Surely it's not too late to try?'

'No,' said Fergus. 'Apparently, they just want to know that it's being looked after, and even better if it's just one reliable and responsible person. Sounds like it's all meant to be.'

'It sounds too good to be true.'

'I would just think of it as a gift coming at the right time,' said Fergus. 'The key safe is outside the front door, and he'll email me the code. It's one of those ones that you line up and it opens. The family who keeps an eye on it for him are just up the road at Meadowbank Cottage and are really helpful. So if you need anything when you're there you can get in touch with them. Obviously, me too, but at least you know they're just a few minutes up the road. Look, I'll forward on the email with the details as soon as I get it.'

'Thank you. It will be so good to see you. Though I know you're busy, so don't worry. I'm really looking forward to meeting Amelia.'

Fergus chuckled. 'I think you'll like her.'

'I'm sure I will.' She paused. 'It's not like you to be so smitten.'

'Do you know which ferry you're getting?' he asked, changing the conversation.

'Yes, I'm going to stay with John the night before and then will aim for one at lunchtime.'

'Are you bringing your car over?'

'No,' she said, 'I couldn't get it booked on, so I'll just park at Ardrossan and come across by foot. I'm not planning on bringing that much stuff anyway.'

Fergus laughed. 'Famous last words. Look, if I can meet you off it, I will. Just text me when you're on the way.'

'Please don't worry. I'll be fine. It looks like it's not so far from the ferry terminal. It's just a short walk, it will do me good to stretch my legs.'

Fergus's words had indeed been famous. Kitty had ended up packing much more stuff than she'd planned. It was both a stroke of luck and a blessing that, when she got to the terminal, there was space for her car on the ferry after all. She messaged Fergus from the boat, letting him know she could make her own way to Lilybank Cottage.

Fergus ran the outdoor centre at Lamlash, and they had never been particularly close growing up as he'd been abroad for many years. It was only when he came back to Scotland for the funerals of his parents that they'd reconnected. Then, when they'd both been visiting John in Glasgow, they'd become closer still. They'd bonded over their shared histories of personal loss and broken hearts. They had a lot in common, and she never had to explain herself to him and vice versa. They both understood each other and in a way were like kindred spirits. She was so looking forward to seeing him again.

Kitty got herself a coffee and took it upstairs to sit on the outside deck. There was a warm breeze, and the sun was trying its best to peek out from beneath the grey cover of clouds. She had checked the forecast for the week ahead and it looked a bit mixed. But that didn't bother her in the slightest. She had packed for the weather and had spares — a couple of pairs of walking shoes in case one got muddy, and two rain jackets to allow for one to dry out. There would be no excuse not to be active. Then again, she reasoned, if it did rain all the time and everything got wet, which meant the walking got a bit miserable, then she would have the perfect excuse to stay in and sleep and read the pile of books she had downloaded onto her Kindle in anticipation of having all this free time. It did feel very indulgent, but she felt a glimmer of excitement, countered by a tinge of sadness that Cameron wasn't there too, as she thought about the long summer that stretched ahead.

It had been years since she'd been to Arran, and she wondered how much she would remember and how much had changed. She had vague memories of a visit during a family holiday when she was around five years old. Her parents had decided to take John and her on a tour of the Scottish islands. As she looked ahead to the mainland, she could see Brodick Castle nestled in the trees. She had definitely been there. She could remember it was a wet day. She and John had had their welly boots on and had loved jumping in all the puddles, and sliding across the grass in the grounds, which were brilliant to play in as a child. She remembered feeling hot and damp and hungry as they trailed after their parents inside the castle, listening to a guide tell them about its history and the stories that lay within its walls. There were huge oil paintings on the walls and the rooms were filled with ornate furniture. She had fidgeted, desperate to go for some juice and cake in the café afterwards.

As the ferry neared the island, the wind started to pick up a bit and the clouds started to clear. Kitty caught a glimpse of Goatfell, the island's highest peak. Maybe she would climb that on one of her days.

Yawning, she realised how tired she was. Yesterday's drive down to Glasgow had been long, thanks to heavy traffic on the A9. Then she and John had sat up late chatting. Maybe once she got to the cottage and unpacked, she could have a little nap. Why not? She could please herself, which made her feel quite liberated. Then she would head out and get some provisions and make a list of all the things that she wanted to do.

When the announcement was made asking passengers to return to their cars ahead of their arrival at Brodick Ferry Terminal, she practically skipped down the stairs in excitement. She couldn't wait to start this next chapter and new adventure.

CHAPTER SEVEN

Olivia had woken early, far too early, to the sound of heavy rain. She stretched out, noticing how comfortable the bed was, before she drifted back off into a peaceful slumber. When she woke again, still feeling tired, she opened the curtains to allow daylight in. Then she hopped back into bed, propped herself up on the fluffy pillows and reached for her phone — the holiday rather than real-life one — popping her earbuds in. Usually listening to a meditation on YouTube did the trick, and she would often fall asleep within a few minutes with no idea of what the meditation had been about. This morning, the coach was telling her to breathe in deeply, exhale slowly and focus on that very moment in time. Olivia was trying her best not to fidget as the soothing voice kept talking. She couldn't keep her eyes closed as she had been invited to. They kept flicking open and noticing things that needed to be done. Important things like her nails — the varnish was chipped — and there was a trail of fluff on the floor, which maybe she should hoover up. She shifted a bit, which then made her focus on the achy pain at the base of her back. She squirmed and tried to find a comfortable position, idly thinking about what to have for breakfast.

It was no use, she was now wide awake. She yanked the earphones off and glanced at the clock. It was almost 2 p.m.

No wonder she was wide awake and hungry. On cue her stomach started to rumble. She had been sleeping for hours and hours! This was so unlike her. When did she last sleep in until after lunch? *Never.* She needed to get up and get on with the day. Then a little voice reminded her that she didn't have anywhere to go and that nobody was expecting her. If she wanted to, she could stay in bed for the whole day — there was nobody to tell her off or remind her about training and schedules and practicing.

Stretching her long limbs out to straighten her back, she kicked off the bedcovers and stood up, gently padding her way through to the kitchen. She gave a loud sigh. Coffee. That was what she needed. A good, strong coffee. Then some food. Filling the kettle at the sink, she paused to watch the birds hopping about on the lawn. The sky was a pale blue and dotted with a few wisps of cloud. She should really go out and get some fresh air and exercise. Then she reminded herself there was time. While she waited for the kettle to boil, she reached for the cafetière and tipped in some of the ground coffee that Amy had thoughtfully left.

She had just poured the water in and was stirring the coffee when she heard the slam of a car door. It reminded her that she wasn't in the middle of nowhere, despite how quiet it was, and that other civilisation did exist. How different it was to the usual sounds she would hear from her apartment, like the constant blast of car horns, the wailing of sirens and the pinging of the elevator.

But then she heard the sound of a key scratching in the lock — her heart skipped a beat. For a moment she was frozen to the spot and all she could do was blink rapidly. Who on earth was that? Had *he* found her? What should she do? Then she reminded herself to breathe. *Come on, Olivia,* she said to herself. There was no reason why he would know she was there. The only person who knew was Trudy, and Olivia knew that she would never betray her confidence like that. Not in a million years.

As she heard the door swing open, her mind did an irrational U-turn. She should have known better than to think Patrick wouldn't track her down. Her breathing quickened and she felt physically sick. Her hands turned clammy, and she rubbed them together, urging herself to think fast. She frantically scanned the kitchen for something, *anything*, and grabbed a rolling pin. She very gingerly peered into the hallway. Olivia's heart threatened to explode in her chest. Her eyes widened when she saw someone, with a mass of red curly hair, turning back to drag in a case. As the sounds of the wheels scratched on the floor, she dropped the rolling pin, which fell to the ground with a clatter. Then Olivia screamed.

CHAPTER EIGHT

Kitty frowned as she was faced with a white-faced woman with blonde curls who dropped a rolling pin at her feet with a clatter and then screamed.

'Oh,' said Kitty, shocked. 'I'm sorry, I didn't mean to scare you.' Kitty wondered if she was perhaps the cleaner who was just finishing off her shift. Though why was she wearing shorts and a vest? Sure, it was summer and quite warm, but not all that balmy. Unless that was what island cleaners wore and, anyway, who was Kitty to judge? She often did her housework in her pyjamas on a Saturday morning. That way she could have a shower afterwards and throw her pyjamas in the wash. But that was all in the privacy of her own home. She chastised herself for being judgemental again.

'Can I help you?' said the woman briskly. She was now standing with her hands on her hips, the rolling pin at her feet.

Her bare feet, thought Kitty. What kind of cleaner went about their hoovering and mopping with no shoes on? And what was with the rolling pin? Had she missed some cleaning hack somewhere about how useful rolling pins were for cleaning hard-to-reach places?

'Hello? Did you hear what I said?' said the woman.

Kitty frowned, not liking the demanding tone the woman was taking. She felt her hackles rise. She could also play the confrontational game if that was how it was going to be. *Erm, I think I should be asking you the same question. Can I help you?* But the truth was Kitty hated confrontation. She could feel heat rising across her chest and up to her cheeks. She crossed her arms in front of her and tried to look confident, when all she wanted was to take her bags to her room and get settled in.

'You can't just walk in here,' said the woman, who Kitty realised had an American accent. 'What do you think you're doing? This is private property.'

Kitty felt her resolve falter. 'I . . . I could say the same thing to you.'

Both women were rooted to their own spots — a real stand-off.

Despite her counselling training, Kitty hated awkwardness of any kind and would always go out of her way to appease a situation. 'I've just arrived to stay here,' she said, flustered, 'and . . . I'm taking a bit of a break. And the cottage belongs to a friend of my cousin's . . .'

The woman looked blankly at her. 'But *I'm* staying here,' she said, gesturing around the hall. 'I arrived yesterday.'

Her voice had at least softened slightly.

'Ah, that must be what it is.' Kitty laughed nervously. 'I'm so sorry. I've obviously arrived early. Normally the changeover of holiday lets is in the afternoon. I didn't even think. I was just told the cottage was empty and to arrive here any time.'

Kitty couldn't help noticing how graceful the woman was as she stood opposite her, wearing not very much, with bed-hair that looked as though it had been professionally styled to look casually tousled. Kitty absent-mindedly tucked a strand of her own hair behind an ear, suddenly very self-conscious of her tangled mane.

'I'm not going anywhere,' said Olivia frowning. 'What are you talking about changeovers? I only arrived yesterday. I flew into Prestwick Airport.'

'What do you mean?' Kitty couldn't work out why this woman was being so awkward, especially as she was the one who was supposed to be here.

The woman flicked her hair out the way and sighed loudly. 'It means that I'm going to be here for the next six weeks. I've only just arrived, so I don't have plans to go anywhere else. I have nowhere else to be right now.'

Kitty felt as though her mouth was filled with treacle. Clenching her fists together, she could feel tears of frustration well in her eyes. When it came to being Cameron's mum, well, she was great at asserting herself and not taking any nonsense. She would walk naked through a field of Highland cows or run over a pile of hot stones. But now . . . well, Cameron wasn't here to bolster her resolve, and she could feel her bottom lip start to wobble. 'There's obviously been a mix-up,' she said, realising she was going to have to spell it all out. 'I'm Kitty, and the cottage belongs to friends of my cousin Fergus, who lives in Lamlash. He works at the outdoor centre there and is really nice.' Why on earth was she oversharing like this? It was her usual attack of verbal diarrhoea that appeared when the nerves hit. 'They aren't letting it anymore and said I could have it over the summer as a house-sitter . . .' Kitty's voice trailed away.

'Hmm, that sounds a familiar story,' exclaimed the woman, her gaze roaming Kitty's face. 'I was also promised the cottage. For the very same reasons.'

Kitty sighed. 'I don't believe it.'

'Me neither,' said Olivia.

'What are we going to do?'

'There's clearly been some kind of mix-up.'

You don't say, thought Kitty, folding her arms. She was starting to feel annoyed now, and hot and bothered by what was turning into the adventure from hell. She thought of Cameron and how lucky he was to be across the Atlantic, but oh how she wished she was back at home with him there, safe and sound. Just the two of them, happy in their own little cocoon. Why on earth did she think this was a good idea?

She should have known it was bound to go wrong. There was no such thing as a free holiday.

She stared at the woman, who looked back, her eyes focused and unwavering, waiting to see what Kitty might say next. Kitty could feel her resolve start to crumble. For a moment she tried to bite down hard on her lip. She didn't want to cry. It wouldn't help solve this very big problem that they were both facing. But it was just all too much, and she burst into tears.

CHAPTER NINE

Olivia was horrified when the woman dissolved in front of her. She wasn't just crying, she was sobbing, taking huge shuddering gulps of air. Olivia was going to have to take charge. Grabbing the box of tissues in the hallway, she ushered Kitty into the living area and pointed to a seat. 'Sit down,' she said bossily, though she was trying to be kind. 'Come on, it's not that bad. I'm sure we'll figure something out. Don't cry.' She could have kicked herself. Who was she to tell anyone not to cry? She didn't know the first thing about this woman. Maybe she had every reason to cry.

'Look, whatever it is, I'm sure it's all a misunderstanding and we can sort something out.' She tried to sound convincing, but knew she was unconvincing. She thrust a couple of tissues at Kitty, who took them.

'Th-thank you,' she stammered.

'That's okay. Now have a seat and I'll fetch you a cup of tea.'

'Thanks,' muttered Kitty.

Olivia felt sorry for this woman, who was now looking mortified as she mopped up her tears.

'I'm so sorry about all of this,' Kitty said around her tissue. 'It's just that I was so looking forward to this . . . it's been ages since I've had a holiday or some time alone.'

Olivia nodded kindly and smiled. Then she held out a hand. 'I've not even introduced myself. Kitty, I'm Olivia.'

'And I'm Kitty,' Kitty repeated.

Olivia nodded her head in the direction of the kitchen. 'I'll go and get that cuppa then. What do you take?'

'Just the bag and hot water please,' Kitty said.

'No problem. Two minutes.'

Olivia returned with the tea and placed a mug gently down next to Kitty. The women sat together, quietly sipping, both deep in thought.

'Where are you from?' asked Kitty, taking Olivia by surprise.

'Oh,' she started, caught on the hop. 'I live in New York.'

Kitty's eyes widened. 'Wow. That's where my son has gone for the summer.'

'Right . . . Well, I'm sure that will be a great experience for him. How old is he?'

'Eighteen. First time he's been properly away from home, so I'm a bit on edge.'

'I see . . . what is he doing there?'

'Camp America.'

Olivia flicked her hand dismissively. 'He'll be absolutely fine, you know. That's when I left home and—' She stopped talking when she realised Kitty had fixed her with a steely glare.

'He's still my little boy.'

Uh-oh, thought Olivia, one of those protective types, especially when it came to her beloved son. She had come across mums like Kitty before, and she knew she'd better watch herself and reign it in.

Kitty continued to chat politely to Olivia as they drank their tea and exchanged pleasantries. However, it was clear neither of them wanted to be there with the other. They were nevertheless going through the motions.

Olivia was relieved to be avoiding too many questions about her own background and why she had ended up on Arran. Mind you, she had become quite the expert over the past few weeks at dodging questions and deflecting the conversation away from herself. She wanted to keep it that way. She had managed to share very little with Margaret, Isobel and Bella, yet knew an amazing amount of detail about their lives. It was surprisingly easy to do — people tended to enjoy talking about themselves if they were given the space to talk. It always amazed her how much personal information people would share about their lives, whether it was their health problems, marital woes, job irritations or money problems. Not Kitty though, interestingly. And she was becoming increasingly diffident and monosyllabic with her answers.

Kitty put her mug down on the table, suddenly stood up and announced she was going for a walk. 'I need to clear my head and gather my thoughts,' she said. 'Thanks for the tea. Um, I won't be too long. Will you be here?'

Olivia didn't know what to say. 'Sure. Why?'

'So I can get back in.'

'Of course. Though why not just take the key in the meantime? In case I go out.'

'Can I leave my stuff here? Or would you rather I put it in the car?'

Olivia shook her head. 'It's fine. Just leave it there. Look, I know this isn't ideal, but just put it in one of the bedrooms until we figure out what to do.'

Kitty threw her a grateful smile. 'Thank you. I won't be long.'

Olivia watched Kitty retrace her steps and move her bags into the bedroom at the front of the house. Then she closed the front door behind her.

'I'll get your mug then, shall I?' she said out loud as she picked up Kitty's cold tea and took it through to the kitchen. Boy, this was not what she had signed up for. Something would have to give.

CHAPTER TEN

The truth was Kitty didn't want to be in this predicament at all. She wanted to be alone and have this time out from her usual everyday life. Tears of frustration pooled in her eyes as she walked past her parked car. She hesitated and wondered if she should just get in it and drive somewhere. She gave herself a shake. There was no point in doing that. It was better to just keep moving, so she followed the road down the hill. Reaching for a fresh tissue, she dabbed her face. Hopefully a walk would help her think and formulate a plan. Should she call Fergus and tell him what had happened? Though the last thing she wanted was to cause him hassle and stress, especially when he'd been trying to do her a favour by arranging this house-sit. He would be embarrassed and insist she go and stay in his flat, which may be okay for a couple of nights but wasn't really ideal or the reason she'd come here.

As she walked towards the centre of the village she started to feel a bit calmer, especially when she saw the blue water in the bay stretching out ahead of her. The early afternoon sunshine felt pleasant on her face, and she began thinking about options and what her plan B might be. It wasn't the end of the world. If the house was taken, then that was how it was, and at least the offer of the cottage had made her come out of her comfort zone and actually make the journey over to Arran. She could spend a couple of days with Fergus and hopefully meet his new girlfriend, Amelia. She'd have had a change of scene and then she could go home to Rosemarkie and enjoy the summer there. There was plenty to keep her busy.

As she passed the community centre, she smiled at the elderly gentleman who stood outside the door looking at the board, which had a poster advertising a new art class for beginners.

'I'm just wondering whether this might be fun,' he said as she passed.

'I'm sure it will be,' she said wistfully. She had always wanted to draw, and would definitely have signed up to it if she could. This was supposed to be about new adventures.

'My girls are always telling me to try new things,' he said, scratching his chin. 'Maybe I'll see you there?'

She smiled. 'Perhaps you will. I'm Kitty.'

The man smiled at her. 'Pleasure to meet you, Kitty. I'm Alex. Hope to see you at the class.'

Feeling more relaxed, she walked on and pulled out her phone to call Fergus.

'Hey you,' he said on answering. 'I was just about to call you and find out if you'd found the cottage and settled in okay.'

'Well . . . there has been a bit of an unexpected problem,' she started.

'What's happened?'

'The cottage is already taken.'

'I don't understand,' he said.

'When I arrived there was someone already there.'

'Eh? That makes no sense.'

'It's fine,' she said hurriedly. 'I think there's been a bit of a mix-up or miscommunication. And don't worry, it's not the end of the world. I wondered if I could maybe just stay with you for a couple of nights and then I'll head home.'

'Oh, Kitty. What a nightmare. I'm so sorry. Let me make some calls and find out what's going on. I'm sure we can sort something out.'

'Thanks, Fergus. Look, do you mind if I just pop over now? It's kind of awkward and I'm down in the village to get out the way.'

He groaned. 'I'd love it if you could but I'm not at the flat. There's an issue with the plumbing and all the water has been switched off, so Amelia and I are staying in Coorie Cabin.'

Great, thought Kitty, rolling her eyes in exasperation. She attempted to sound light-hearted. 'Well, it would look like my summer retreat to Arran might be over before it's even got started. Unless you have a spare tent?'

'Don't do anything hasty. Let me make some calls and get back to you. Where are you just now?'

'Out and about walking and exploring. I had to get away from the cottage as it was all getting a bit intense.'

'I'm so sorry,' said Fergus. 'It doesn't sound ideal at all. Did you let yourself in and find someone cooking naked in the kitchen or something like that?'

'Oh, Fergus, trust you to lower the tone. It wasn't quite like that. There was a woman in the kitchen, but it could have turned violent as she had a rolling pin.'

'A rolling pin?' said Fergus, amused. 'Sounds like it could have turned into a potential bloodbath then?'

'Either that or a flour show.'

He chuckled. 'Oh dear, I see your jokes are as dire as ever.'

'Cameron would have laughed at that,' she said indignantly. 'He thinks all my jokes are funny. And anyway, you did laugh.'

'Mmm,' said Fergus. 'I was being polite.'

She sighed. 'It's better to laugh than cry, isn't it?'

'Exactly. Look, I'll call you back as soon as I have some more info.'

Feeling slightly reassured, she thanked him, then started making the walk back up the hill towards Lilybank Cottage.

CHAPTER ELEVEN

Logan lay on his back and gazed around James's spare room. It was the perfect pit stop for him when he was on Arran. He still couldn't believe how lucky it was that James had moved back here for work. Kipping in his mate's spare room — even though it was very functional, with just a double bed and nowhere to put his clothes — was far nicer than staying in a bed in the youth hostel or a hotel room, which was his usual choice of accommodation when he was doing these trips. Mind you, Logan was extremely self-sufficient and didn't need anything more than a bed. He was used to minimalist living; he carried all that he needed in his rucksack.

It had been a while since he and James had seen each other, and he was really looking forward to catching up with him later. They'd arranged to meet for a beer at the pub just after five o'clock. Logan wanted to hear all about his new job and how things were going with his girlfriend. Ever since he had known James, he'd always been full of ambition and didn't seem that interested in relationships. They were very alike there, although Logan would be the first to admit that he didn't have the same driving ambition that James had. Yes, he loved his work, but it didn't feel like work. He was happy with his lot and the fact he could spend most of his days outdoors. The thought of having to stick to long hours in an office filled him with fear.

James seemed like a different man since reconnecting with Amy, which had amused Logan greatly. On the odd occasion they did catch up on the phone, if he wasn't working at the distillery, James was either on his way to see her at Meadowbank Cottage or was in the middle of making dinner for her at his flat. Logan had seen him briefly when he'd arrived and gone to pick up keys to get into the flat. He'd smirked when James sheepishly told him that he was staying with Amy to get out the way, to give Logan a bit of headspace after the intensity of the last tour. Logan knew that was code for, *I'm deeply loved up and don't want to leave Amy's side, and the thought of being apart from her for too long is driving me mad.* But there was no way that James would ever admit that out loud.

Logan knew Amy had recently built a studio at her sister's guesthouse, so James was clearly making sure she was quite settled in to her new abode.

Logan was actually rather intrigued to meet the woman who had tamed his friend. Earlier, when Logan had mentioned this, James had scoffed and tried to laugh off his comments. But the red dots high on his cheeks were a clear giveaway that James was quite smitten. When Logan had teased him and said, 'You're clearly very loved up, mate,' James quickly changed the subject and offered to meet Logan at the pub for a few beers when he'd finished work. He promised to get away early, and Logan had rolled his eyes in response, knowing full well that was unlikely.

Logan yawned and stretched his arms up behind his head. He glanced at his watch and sighed. Where had the time gone today? He'd better make a move, otherwise he'd end up falling asleep. Maybe he should go for a walk before meeting James. He could do with a boost of fresh air. Jumping off the bed, he raked his hands through his hair and pulled on his trainers. Then he gave himself a quick once-over in the hallway mirror and pulled the door closed behind him, jogging lightly down the stairs and into the close, which would take him out to the street.

As he stepped outside, he looked over at the surface of the sea. It resembled glass. It was a warm afternoon and very still, not even a whisper of a breeze. The sky was a rich blue. Logan took his time walking slowly along the road, admiring the scenery.

This was his first tour to Arran this year and it felt good to be back. He always felt at home as soon as he stepped off the ferry. There was something about crossing the water by boat that made this trip feel extra special. As he followed the path that cut across the golf course, he began to think about the next few days and what lay ahead for the next trip. Logan never really switched off from work, he couldn't help himself. He was extremely organised and efficient and liked to make sure he had all eventualities covered.

Tomorrow he would go through his usual checklist of having a look at the forecast for the next few days, checking that he had all the right kit and that everything was clean and nothing was missing. Then he would have a quick recce of the trails to make sure there hadn't been any major changes that might disrupt the routes. At the moment it looked set to be fine, but this was Scotland, and the weather could change rapidly. Logan was due to meet the group on Thursday for the five-day tour, and he was looking forward to exploring with them.

This trip was a bit different to the one on Skye, more informal, which wasn't a bad thing. Guests tended to already be planning a stay on Arran anyway, so it was a case of them meeting Logan each day for a different walk. Although they were encouraged to sign up to all five days of the tour, they could dip in and out of them as they pleased. Fortunately his evenings would be free, which he felt mildly relieved about — he was still recovering from the intensity of Tallulah's attentions.

Checking his watch, he realised that it was just before five. As he neared the bar he idly wondered if James would be there already. But as he walked up the steps and through the entrance, a quick look around told him that he wasn't. He gave a wry smile. That was *so* James. He would most likely still be at work.

The bar hadn't changed a bit since his last visit. The exposed brickwork and the pale, wooden floors offered a nice contrast. The wood-burning stove at the back of the bar was lovely in the winter, when you felt as though you were cosying in from the elements outside. He ordered a couple of pints of IPA and took them outside, finding a quiet spot in the beer garden. Sitting down, he wondered whether he should wait for James to arrive before he started his beer. Watching the condensation run down the glasses, he looked around one last time and decided not. It would be like watching an ice-cream melt. Sipping the cold liquid, he closed his eyes and smiled. Bliss. It was just what he needed, and hit the spot perfectly.

The pub was quiet, although he had to remind himself that it was a Monday night and not the weekend. Often his days and weeks merged together, and it was quite usual for Logan to lose track of what day of the week it was. That was the drawback of working different hours each week and being in so many different places. He would lose a sense of time and place, which didn't land well with the various women he had dated over the years. They took it all very personally, wouldn't accept his apologies, instead assuming the worst — that he was dating lots of other women on his travels.

Logan sat quietly, observing life go on around him. It was always interesting to see how many people actually chatted to each other and how many sat looking at their phones. That also included the ones who were with company as well as those sitting on their own. A woman sat a few tables across from him, tapping her foot agitatedly and rattling her fingers against her phone, which was placed on the table. Frowning, he wondered what her issue was. Then he flicked his gaze across to the couple who sat together but were clearly miles apart, both fixated on their phones. Logan knew he was old-fashioned, and to be honest he didn't really care, but he really loathed mobile phones. This, of course, didn't bode too well for his Instagram account, which had been neglected of late. That was another thing he would need to spend some time on tomorrow.

Over the years, Logan had watched guests come and go and noticed how mobiles had killed the art of conversation dead. Of course there were exceptions to the rule, but he'd noticed how people could no longer be present and just sit in their surroundings. They needed their phone as an emotional crutch. On every tour, someone would always have their phone out to take photos or film some video footage, and he just couldn't get his head around the idea of having to live life through a lens. Why couldn't they just enjoy the view right then as it was and really see it properly? Or make the most of each moment as it unfolded? He had to remind himself to take photos and then would put his phone away. Much to the frustration of his friends, and sisters in particular, he didn't make a point of checking his phone regularly. For Logan it was purely a functional item. He hated seeing people staring down at their phones, scrolling aimlessly for hours.

He watched the woman lift her phone and put it to her ear and then he noticed her brow furrow as she listened. Then she thumped it down on the table, sighed angrily and drained the rest of her glass. Abruptly, she stood up and stomped past. He didn't even attempt to catch her eye. She didn't look the friendly type *at all*. Taking another sip of his pint he wondered if James was actually coming or whether he'd forgotten. Shrugging to himself, he thought about the silver lining of already having his next drink lined up if James didn't manage to make it.

'Hey, hey, hey,' said James, reaching for Logan's hand to shake it and then plonking himself opposite. 'Sorry I'm late,' he said, taking the pint Logan handed to him. 'Thanks, mate. Boy, do I need this.'

Logan raised an eyebrow. 'Has it been that kind of day? It's lucky you arrived when you did, I was just about to tear into your pint too.'

James laughed. 'Cheers.' He clinked his glass against Logan's and took a gulp. 'Not in a bad way, it's just been so busy at work. Everyone seems to want to hold their wedding or party at the distillery. I seem to have spent most of the day answering calls and emails and dealing with suppliers. Life on the edge, eh?'

Logan shook his head. 'Sounds like my worst nightmare.'

'Och, I don't mind.' James shrugged. 'At least the end is in sight, and I can clock off at night and go home to my bed.' He raised an eyebrow. 'I couldn't do your job and have to be with people twenty-four seven.'

'Which is why we are all different,' said Logan. 'We all bring our own talents to the table.'

'Indeed,' said James. 'Anyway, how's tricks? Have you got everything you need in the flat?'

'Yes I do, thanks. A bed and a sink and a kettle are all I require. You know I'm fairly low-maintenance. I have to say it's much tidier than it usually is. It doesn't appear to have been lived in for a while.' He leaned forward. 'So, do tell. How are things with you?'

James cocked his head, feigning confusion.

'Don't give me that. You know exactly what I mean. How is the big romance?'

A huge grin spread across James's face as he cupped his hands around his glass. 'What can I say? It's brilliant. She's wonderful.'

Logan chuckled. 'Who would have thought it?'

'I know, right?' said James. 'It's the last thing I was look-ing for, but then it just kind of happened.'

James and Amy had been sweethearts in their final year of high school. Then she had broken it off, leaving him dev-astated, and they had gone their separate ways. That had been more than seventeen years ago. Then last summer they randomly both met again on the island. Amy was back from Vancouver for her sister's wedding, and James had just started his new role at the distillery. Since then, Amy had left Canada and moved home permanently.

'And it's clearly meant to be. I mean, talk about fate. Who would have thought you'd have reconnected after all these years?'

'I know.' James shook his head. 'It's a funny old world, isn't it?'

'Indeed.'

James finished the rest of his pint and stood up, reaching for Logan's empty glass. 'Same again?' he asked.

'Perfect, thanks buddy.'

While he waited for James to return with the drinks, Logan looked over at the table the angry woman had abandoned and noticed she had left her bag on the chair. He stood up, planning to hand it in at the bar. Just as he reached for it, he felt someone touch his shoulder.

'Thanks, but I'll have that,' said a woman with an American accent, snatching it from him.

'Oh,' said Logan, startled when he realised it was the woman from earlier. 'I was just going to hand it into the bar.'

'Sure you were,' she said, sarcastically.

He felt his hackles rise. Who did she think she was? 'Actually I was. That's what we do here. We look out for each other.' He threw her a look of disdain and walked back to his table. How rude! By the time he sat down she had vanished.

'There you go.' James walked towards him with two fresh pints.

'Cheers.' Logan scowled.

'What's up? Did I miss something?'

Logan shook his head. 'No, I was just trying to be the community hero and was about to hand in a bag that a customer had left behind, but she thought I was nicking it. Clearly, I've lost my touch.'

James clinked his glass against Logan's.

'And that's why I don't get involved with women. They're far more bother than they're worth.' When he realised James was smiling dreamily, Logan shook his head in exasperation. 'Oh man, this is frightening. Amy must be something very special.'

'Oh she is . . . and she has two sisters, though I'm afraid both are taken, which is a bit of a shame.'

'I'm not interested in meeting *anyone* thanks,' protested Logan.

'Famous last words, my friend, famous last words.'

Logan pulled a face. 'No way. I'll be an eternal bachelor. It's far easier that way.'

'Well, watch this space,' said James. 'I'm sure there will come a day when I remind you of this conversation.'

CHAPTER TWELVE

Olivia stomped her way back to Lilybank Cottage, anger fizzing inside her. In a moment of stupidity she thought it would be a good idea to pull her phone out and switch it on in the pub, only to be greeted by a barrage of angry, accusatory voicemails. She had fled hastily and, in the process, forgotten her bag.

She was still in shock as *his* words rattled through her head, though she reminded herself that it was her own fault. She told herself that she didn't need to switch the blooming thing on. Why on earth had she thought it would be a good time to check her messages and emails? All she had wanted to do was sit peacefully in the pub with a cold drink and to take stock of the situation at the cottage.

She sighed noisily, anxiously scratching her arm as she walked up the hill towards the holiday house. Inhaling the delicate scent of lavender that lingered in the air, she stopped and turned to look back at the view. The sparkling blue sea momentarily calmed the angry thoughts racing around her mind. Shaking her head in frustration, she thought about what could have been. It was such a lovely spot, and would have been the perfect place to hide away from the world. Her world that she had left behind. It was so annoying that it hadn't worked out that way. She'd hoped the Arran retreat would give her space to walk and think and read and sleep and just be. Alone. But she *didn't* know how she and Kitty were going to resolve the living 'situation'.

Olivia could hardly argue that because she got to the cottage first and had unpacked her things, she should be the one to stay. That would make her sound like a complete brat, and it was clear that Kitty was feeling a bit frazzled and vulnerable too. She had felt so conflicted as she watched Kitty dissolve into tears earlier. She wanted to be kind and compassionate, yet she was tired of thinking of everyone else. How she longed to be selfish and put herself and her needs first for a change. That horrid, all-too-familiar feeling of walking on eggshells had invited itself back into her life, and as a result she was back to feeling on edge.

She scowled as she thought about that idiot at the pub who had completely humiliated her with his harsh words. How was she to know that he was trying to help? Okay, perhaps she had been a bit quick to jump down his throat. In fact, now she thought about it, she felt mortified when she remembered just how sharp her tone was. But let's face it, her recent experiences of men hadn't exactly left her feeling warm towards members of the opposite sex. What a disaster.

It was all so different to how she felt in Italy with her new friends, Margaret, Isobel and Bella, with sunshine and laughter and the promise of a new beginning. Maybe she should contact them and find out if Bella's offer to go to Corfu was still an option. Though was that really what she wanted to do? She shook herself. That wasn't the answer either. She couldn't just keep running. Perhaps this was a sign that she needed to head back to New York and face the music. As she walked through the gate and up the path towards the cottage, she couldn't help but admire the way the sunlight caught the window. Taking a deep breath, she opened the door.

'Oh, there she is now. We're through here,' called Kitty.

Olivia felt her shoulders tense and fear grip her. Who on earth was here now? Hadn't there been enough surprise visitors already today? Taking a tentative step into the open-plan living room, she glanced over to see another woman, who she didn't recognise, sitting on the sofa.

'Hello,' Olivia said, puzzled.

The woman stood up and pulled her dark blonde hair away from her face, scooping it into a ponytail. She wore workout leggings and a white V-neck shirt. A wide grin spread across her face as she extended a hand. 'Hello, you must be Olivia. I'm Amy and I am so, so sorry about all of this.' She gestured around the room.

'Hi,' said Olivia politely, quickly shaking her hand. It took her a few seconds to work out who Amy was, then she remembered the welcome note in the kitchen from yesterday.

'So . . .' Amy watched her expectantly, as though she couldn't quite decide what to say next.

Kitty started to talk. 'It would seem that there has been a bit of a mix-up with the owners and communication.'

Amy nodded. 'Yes, there has, and I am so sorry. I help my sister up at the B&B and we keep an eye on Lilybank Cottage for the owners. They'd decided not to re-let it, but the couple didn't realise they had then each promised the cottage to someone.' She rolled her eyes. 'Which is why you're both here. I can only apologise.'

'Okay.' Olivia wrapped her arms around herself defensively. 'Look, I've had a think about it and, if you can bear with me, Kitty, I will look into flights and see when I can book myself on one back home. There's no point in your trip being ruined and I, er, I have some stuff I need to deal with back in New York anyway.' She tried to sound as airy as possible, watching as Kitty's smile turned into a frown.

'But that doesn't seem fair at all,' Kitty replied. 'You've never been to Scotland before, and this is a one-off trip for you. You've come so far and it's not right you feel you have to leave. I can. It's easy enough for me to get back to Inverness from here. If I leave in the morning, then I can be back by tomorrow night.'

Olivia bit her bottom lip, not quite knowing what to say. She felt so sorry for Kitty as, despite her kind offer, she looked crestfallen at the thought of her trip being cut prematurely short. She glanced over at Amy, who hovered between the two women.

'Erm, I've just had an idea,' Amy said. 'Can I make a suggestion?'

Kitty shook her head. 'It's okay, Amy. It's just one of those things. I already had a look to see what else was free. My cousin lives round in Lamlash, but his flat is having work done, otherwise I could have gone there. Everything else is booked or a bit beyond my budget.' She paused. 'Well, unless you have a spare tent, and I could head to the campsite.'

Olivia looked at her in horror. 'Don't be silly. That sounds horrendous.'

'I agree,' said Kitty, not missing a beat. 'I would rather be in my own bed. That's why it would be easier for me just to go home.'

Amy cleared her throat. 'Can I make a radical suggestion?'

Kitty raised an eyebrow in expectation.

'Well, how about you both stay?'

'What?' asked Olivia.

'Why don't you both stay here? Together?' She said it quite matter-of-factly and rubbed her hands together, clearly pleased with her suggestion. 'The cottage is big enough. I mean, look at all the rooms, you can take your pick, and I'm sure you'll respect each other's space.' She looked squarely at them both. 'To be quite honest, it sounds like you both could do with this break and you're both here now. It would be a shame not to stay and at least give it a go.'

Olivia turned to Kitty, her mind a whir of possibilities and thoughts. It *might* work. It was the only time that she would probably do this trip, and if not now, then *when*?

'What do you think?' asked Amy.

Olivia eyed Kitty thoughtfully. 'Well . . . I suppose I am up for *trying* it, if you are. I mean, we could see how it goes . . .'

A huge smile spread across Kitty's face. 'Really? I mean, yes, we could just see how it pans out, and if we decide it's not working then we can call it quits.'

Kitty's smile was contagious, and Olivia couldn't help but beam back. Talk about a rollercoaster of emotions. She had been through them all in less than an hour. 'Gosh. Yes. Why not?' she said kindly. 'I mean, I have to warn you that I might not be the tidiest of housemates and I can't cook. But other than that I'll try and keep out of your way.'

'As long as you pick up your clothes from the floor,' said Kitty, 'then it's a deal.'

'Brilliant,' said Amy. 'That's us all sorted then.' She clapped her hands together in excitement. 'Okay, I will leave you to settle in. You know where I am if you need me. And if you ever fancy a yoga session while you're here, do let me know. I've started running classes down in the village hall. Or if you just want to come up and say hello then please do.'

'Thank you,' said Olivia, grateful for the warm fuzzy feeling that was now washing over her, rather than the anger that had threatened to bubble over and erupt earlier. The thought of being part of something and belonging some-where, even for just a few weeks, wasn't actually too scary a thought. Then a little nugget of worry wormed its way into her stomach — she tried to ignore it and focus on the posi-tive. But she felt her lips pursing in worry. There it was again. That flicker of worry and doubt. Why did she have to always think of the things that might go wrong? She noticed Kitty throw her a curious look, and she gave her what she hoped was a reassuring nod.

As if picking up on her worry, Kitty said, 'We can take it a day at a time, Olivia.'

'Yes,' said Olivia. 'And the yoga might be just the thing I need.'

'Well,' said Kitty, 'I've never tried it, but I'm definitely up for giving it a go. Thanks for the offer, Amy.'

Glancing at her watch, Amy yelped. 'I'd better go, or my sister will *kill* me. I said I wouldn't be long. I just hope she heard the oven timer go off, or the shortbread will be incinerated.' With that she turned round and lightly jogged out the door calling 'bye' as she went. The door slammed shut. Olivia and Kitty were left standing in the kitchen, the sounds of evening birdsong chattering through the window.

Olivia turned to Kitty, who was smiling nervously at her. She returned her smile again. This would be fine. It had to be. 'Okay then, I guess that's all settled.'

'And you are sure? You really don't mind sharing?' asked Kitty nervously.

Olivia shrugged and made sure she kept grinning. 'Of course not. I'm sure it will all be just fine. I mean, what could possibly go wrong?'

CHAPTER THIRTEEN

Kitty woke early the next morning. She quickly dressed before slipping out the cottage for a stroll to the village, planning to buy some bread from the bakery. It was peaceful, aside from a few dog walkers who nodded and wished her a 'good morning' as they passed. It had been windy during the night, but this morning the sea was calm again and the air was still and warm.

Cameron had sent her some WhatsApp voicemail messages and photos of the lakeside camp he was staying in. She felt a huge sense of relief that she could now picture where he was, and she was relieved that his tone was chatty and light. It sounded as though he was having a great time and that was all she could hope for. This was such an adventure for her boy, and she had to let him do it. It was time for him to travel and learn and gain new perspectives from the people he met. It didn't make it easy for her, though.

She wiped away a tear as she looked out over the water. This empty-nest malarkey was tough. Thinking about the next chapter in her life was hard, and she knew she didn't have to have the rest of her life all mapped out this minute. But she did have moments of total overwhelm when she wondered what was next for her. What was she supposed to do now?

All she could remember was it being all about him and making sure he had everything he needed. It seemed off to think that she could actually do what she wanted for a change. She could have what she wanted for dinner, and decide when she would have it, if at all. She could lie in bed all day if she wanted, though that wasn't working out that well so far, she thought wryly, given her usual early start. She could watch what she wanted on television and go to bed when she wanted. Though she had always been an early bird, preferring to be in bed by eleven and up early. The problem was that she didn't really know who she was anymore or what she wanted to do.

She thought about Ellen's advice before she left, how she should use this time to try different things. As she neared the door of the bakery, she caught sight of a guy holding the door open for her.

'Good morning,' he said with a warm smile.

Kitty noticed his eyes first, which were intensely dark brown. He had wavy, dark brown hair and looked ruggedly healthy, as though he spent a lot of his time outdoors. He had that strong and self-sufficient look about him. Perhaps he regularly chopped wood, fished, wrestled bears, lit fires or climbed mountains. An alpha male, the type of guy that Ellen would describe as a *provider*.

'Oh. Thank you.' Kitty felt her cheeks flush, which, she told herself, was due to the sunshine rather than the fact he was very good looking, and she'd just made multiple assumptions about his masculine capabilities.

'No worries at all.'

He held the door open until she was all the way through it and then sauntered away, leaving her feeling a tad bereft. She noticed the scent of his spicy aftershave that lingered in the air, and she stared wistfully after him. She wondered if he was a good example of what kind of men were on this island.

'What can I get for you?' said the woman behind the counter.

'Oh hello,' she said, flustered, and then switched her focus to the reason she was there. 'Can I have a loaf of whole-meal sourdough, please?'

'Of course. Would you like that sliced?'

'Yes please,' she said with a nod. As she waited, she glanced at all the cakes and pastries in the glass display case and absent-mindedly wondered if any of them were dairy free.

'There you go, my love,' said the woman, handing her the package of bread. 'Can I get you anything else?'

'Just a coffee to take away please.'

'Milk?'

'No thanks. A black one is fine.'

Kitty glanced at the pile of leaflets on the counter and saw one that was for walks of Arran. Picking it up, she tucked it in her bag, thanked the woman for her coffee and paid. Then she walked across the road and sat on one of the many benches that looked out across the water.

Sighing with contentment, she reached into her bag and pulled out the flyer. It was for a series of walks around Arran over five days. She looked at the dates on the leaflet and saw the next tour would start the day after next. Maybe she should sign up and try and encourage Olivia to do it with her. It would certainly be a good way of getting to know her properly with all that walking and talking.

As she drank her coffee, she contemplated the bizarreness of yesterday, from the moment she walked into the cottage to the truce she and Olivia seemed to have made. Who would have thought she would find herself in a house share with an American woman for the summer? Even more surprising was that she was prepared to give it a go. When her stomach began to rumble, she realised it was time to head back to the cottage.

CHAPTER FOURTEEN

Gently opening the door, Kitty tiptoed back into the house, careful not to wake Olivia up. Until they got used to each other's rhythms she wanted to make sure she was as respectful as possible. Placing the bread on the worktop, she wondered if Olivia would actually eat it. She didn't seem the type to touch carbohydrates, given how slim she was.

She was glad she'd packed some provisions, including a package of oats. Deciding that she would have that and save the bread for later, she tipped some into a saucepan, topping the pot with some water and a sprinkle of salt. It was her go-to method of making porridge — all she needed were the oats and some water. Some of her friends swore by using milk, which made her feel sick. Others added syrup and sugar, but she always preferred salt. Stirring it with the spurtle she found in the utensil pot, she kept a close eye until the oats turned creamy. Then she tipped them into a bowl and sprinkled the top with some flaxseed. As she sat enjoying her breakfast, she made a list of things she could do while she was on Arran. She was definitely up for giving Amy's class a go, and maybe the art class. She would like to do lots of walking, so in a way the tour was perfect. Fergus had also insisted that she go up to the outdoor centre while she was there, to make use of the kayaks. She had drawn the line at sea swimming though, and shivered involuntarily at the thought.

As she finished her porridge she wondered if she should just get on with the day. Then she heard the toilet flush. Olivia was awake and up then, but would she come through, or would she hide in the bedroom until Kitty went out? Getting used to someone else's routine was going to take some time.

'Good morning,' Olivia said brightly as she wandered into the kitchen, rubbing her eyes. 'Wow, when did you get up?' She stifled a yawn.

'I always wake up at seven and it seems it's a habit that's stuck. I mean, how typical is that? For the first time in years I can actually lie in. I don't have to rush to get up for my son or get to work, but here I am, up and about. I'm still on my mum clock.' She laughed. 'Mum clock has me unable to sleep past seven and on constant edge in case anyone needs some food, money, a lift somewhere or some laundry washed and dried at the very last minute.' She hoisted her elbows on the table and sunk her chin into her hands. 'How about you? What's your routine like normally?'

Olivia looked thoughtful for a moment. 'It depends,' she said hesitantly. 'If I'm on tour then it's all go and I'm up sharp, ready for rehearsals and the show . . . but when I'm not working, I do love to sleep. I have the comfiest bed back home and it's my happy place. The space I go to rest and recharge.'

Kitty raised an eyebrow at her and waited expectantly.

'My bedroom is a bit of a refuge,' said Olivia briskly. 'It can be quite common to have to share rooms when away, so I appreciate my space alone even more.'

Kitty was a bit taken aback at her matter-of-fact tone, and didn't know whether to be offended.

'Sorry, I didn't mean that as it sounded. Sometimes I forget I can be a bit blunt,' said Olivia sheepishly. 'It wasn't meant as a dig.'

'That's okay,' said Kitty. 'Can I make you a cup of tea? Mind you,' she said jokingly, 'I won't be making a habit of this. So don't get used to it.'

Olivia pulled out a seat at the table and sat down. 'Thank you. I just take it black, and you can leave the teabag in.'

Kitty chuckled. 'I take it black too, though I need the bag out pronto before it looks like tar. Aren't we funny with our little routines and ways of making things? And I have to admit, when I offer to make tea at work, I don't get a great take-up, so I hope it's okay.'

Olivia laughed.

'So,' said Kitty, 'when you say you go on tour . . . what is it that you do?'

'I'm a dancer.'

'Oh wow,' said Kitty, her interest piqued. 'How interesting. What kind of dancing is it that you do?'

Olivia laughed. 'To be honest, a bit of everything, though mostly commercial stuff now. I started dancing when I was three when my mom enrolled me in ballet. Then I did tap and contemporary and even a bit of ballroom.'

Kitty's eyes widened. 'How interesting. When did you decide to make it your career?'

'I don't know if I decided as such. I just didn't know how to do anything else. I needed to do it. I loved being on stage. I practised all the time, copied the dance routines from MTV and then started getting lucky with auditions.'

Kitty was transfixed as she listened to Olivia talk. It was clearly still her passion, which made it even more surprising and random that she'd ended up on Arran. 'Do you mind if I ask what brought you here?' Kitty said curiously. She watched as Olivia finished her tea in a gulp.

'I needed to have some time out. I just finished a dance tour and before that a stint at Disneyland. I didn't have any teaching commitments over the summer, so it seemed as good a time as ever.'

Kitty tilted her head, still bemused as to what brought her to Scotland when she could have gone anywhere in the world.

Olivia must have read her thoughts as she continued. 'My aunt and uncle were here last summer, and they stayed at Meadowbank Cottage and raved about it. I decided to see what all the fuss was about. I was on a trip to Italy and decided at the last minute to extend my travels. The Meadowbank place was full, but it was the owners there who said this place might be available.' She shrugged. 'It all kind of happened from that. I wasn't planning on coming, it just happened that way.' She pushed a strand of hair back from her face. 'How about you? What brought you here?'

Kitty cleared her throat. 'My son is away for the summer, as you know. It's always been just the two of us, and it's the first time he's been away for such a length of time. Which is why I'm prone to being quite teary.' She smiled ruefully. 'I also had some time off over the summer. I work in a nursery and have six weeks off. I was planning on painting our home and doing some DIY projects, which if I'm honest I wasn't entirely over the moon about. My cousin Fergus works at the outdoor centre here and he knows the owners of this place . . .'

'Well,' Olivia smiled brightly, 'perhaps it's fate that our paths have crossed?'

'Indeed. I just wonder what on earth we're going to get up to,' said Kitty softly, as the reality of the next few weeks finally hit her.

Olivia gave her another bright smile. 'I'm game for adventures if you are.'

Kitty nodded. 'I definitely am.'

CHAPTER FIFTEEN

Logan sat down at the small table in James's kitchen and opened his laptop. He frowned as he read the email he'd just received from Stravaig's head office. The walking tour was due to start the day after tomorrow, and Henry was letting him know that two of the group had pulled out as their flights from Europe had been cancelled. He knew that it would be super frustrating for the guests, but it was a blow for the company. It meant loss of revenue and they had already been hit hard since the pandemic. Every single guest counted, and Logan knew Henry, who ran Stravaig — which was Gaelic for 'wanderer' — would be getting stressed as they had a slow start to the summer season this year. Logan was quite laid-back about doing fewer tours, especially as he only had himself to think about. But he felt sorry for the tour guides who had families to provide for too, and slightly guilty about the small lie to Tallulah about the tour being fully booked. He started to respond.

> *Thanks for letting me know, Henry.*
>   *Don't worry too much. We still have a couple of days to go until the tour starts, so there's still time for a couple of new recruits. I'll see what I can do.*
>   *Cheers,*
>   *Logan*

Taking a sip of coffee, he decided he would go and hand out flyers around Brodick and Lamlash in the hope that he could entice a few tourists to join them last-minute. He had already left some at the bakery, and there was no harm in trying elsewhere. Some of the walking companies offered a package that meant the tour guide would meet them in Glasgow and escort them over to the island. However, Stravaig preferred to try and keep costs down as much as possible and to attract a wider reach of tourists. Unless someone requested a private tour, of course, in which case it would be a completely different and much more expensive package. Numbers for those had been down this year too, which was a worry. But he knew sometimes a few corporate packages were all they needed to pull them out of the red.

When he had woken early that morning, the sky had been a vibrant blue. It made him want to get up and head out for a run. But now when he looked out the window, he could see a few dark clouds scudding along. Hopefully they would keep moving and it would clear up. He had thought about going out in a kayak at some point too, and although a spot of rain didn't deter him from anything, he would have enjoyed being out in the sunshine.

His hand rested gently on his mug of coffee, and he used his other thumb to quickly check in on his Instagram account. It had been a few days since he'd updated it — that might help with marketing.

He was surprised to see there had been *lots* of activity and he had many, many notifications. There were more than one thousands likes of the reel he had posted from Skye. *Strange*, he thought, *that's a bit out of the norm*. Then when he glanced over the comments he could see why. It would seem that Tallulah had been busy. His stomach tightened as he wondered what on earth she may have said or done to gain him so many likes and so many extra followers in just days.

Clicking on Tallulah's page, he wasn't surprised to see her pouting profile picture. He smiled wryly when he read her bio: *A girl who is wild at heart and loves adventures of the outdoor kind.* Scanning through her posts, he recognised some of the photos from the trip to Skye. He opened them, curious to find out what she had written. Then he realised that she had included plenty of pictures featuring him. He read on, feeling his cheeks redden. How mortifying.

> *Experiencing Scotland at its best. And the scenery isn't too bad either. Stravaig Tours are the best and the Tartan Wanderer is even better. Looking for the trip of a lifetime? Go to Skye with Stravaig Tours, where you will leave wanting more ;)*

Logan sighed. His sisters would have an absolute field day with this. He wouldn't hear the end of it. In fact, he was surprised they hadn't already been in touch to tease him, given they were constantly scrolling on their phones.

Laughing, he decided to focus on the positives. Hopefully the higher profile on Instagram may mean more business for Henry and would keep the wolves from the door. He would do anything to help his friend and boss. Perhaps he needed to think about ramping things up himself and doing some pieces to camera. He had watched other tour guides do it and, although they made him cringe a bit, with their weird Scottish transatlantic accents and love of seeing their own reflection in the camera, it would be a good way of showcasing the kind of tours they did. Definitely one to think about. Finishing his coffee, he stood up and stretched. A quick shower was in order and then he would go out and tout for business. If he could replace the two cancelled guests with another two people, then he knew that would make Henry extremely happy.

CHAPTER SIXTEEN

After chatting with Kitty for a while, Olivia excused herself to go for a run. She pulled on her leggings, a sports bra and a vest, then looked around for her trainers. Running wasn't her favourite pastime, but she knew that it would help to clear her head and perk her up a bit.

'I won't be long,' she said to Kitty, who was fastidiously wiping the surfaces in the kitchen.

'No worries, just do what you want to. No need to tell me.' She then turned to say, 'Just remember to take your keys. In case I go out.'

It was going to take a while to get to know her room-mate properly. She had a feeling there was a lot Kitty *wasn't* telling her, but then it was early days. Olivia was certainly being very selective about what she shared of herself too. They had only just met, yet she sensed a sadness in Kitty, as though something had happened. Above and beyond what she was saying about her son being away. Was she divorced or separated? Or perhaps she had chosen to be a single parent deliberately. It was easy to make assumptions about people and create backstories for them, and she reminded herself it wasn't a good thing to do. You never knew what was going on in people's lives, in the same way that nobody really knew what was happening in hers. Only she knew the truth, and it was one she was going to have to deal with.

She began walking. She usually let herself walk for five minutes at the start to warm up her muscles. She decided she'd head up the hill and find out where Amy lived and where Meadowbank Cottage was after hearing so much about it from her aunt. The island properties were so different to what she was used to in New York. They were so cute and charming and the stunning backdrop made it all seem quite idyllic. As she gazed from left to right, taking in the views, she realised that she hadn't needed to walk far. Amy wasn't kidding when she said it was just a few minutes away.

The guesthouse was a substantial blond sandstone villa surrounded by a garden, which was a rainbow of colourful blooms and palm trees. It was strange seeing palm trees and she wondered how on earth they survived in this climate, especially when the Scottish winters could be harsh, according to one of the guidebooks at the cottage. Looking up to the road behind the cottage she could see a wooden arrow-shaped sign with the word *Lamlash* etched onto it. That must have been one of the many walking trails that her aunt had mentioned. As she contemplated whether to run along it and explore, she realised that Amy was in the garden waving at her. *Oh dear*, she thought. She didn't want her to think she was creeping around spying on her. Amy bounced over to the gate.

'Good morning,' she said cheerily. 'Glad you've found us. Is everything okay?'

'Yes, yes,' Olivia said reassuringly. 'Don't worry, we haven't killed each other yet.' She cringed at her attempt at a joke.

'Are you sure you haven't buried her body under the patio?' Amy wisecracked back.

Phew. She smiled with relief. Thank goodness she was playing along. 'No, too much hard work for the first week.'

Amy chuckled. 'So what can I do for you?'

'Oh, don't worry. Nothing at all. I was curious to see where the cottage was, especially after hearing so much about it from my aunt.'

Amy hit the palm of her hand off her forehead. 'Of course. Silly me. It was Trudy and Chuck who stayed last year and, erm, recommended you visit Arran. I keep forgetting the connection.'

'That's right,' said Olivia, detecting a bit of an undertone from the way she said their names. She wondered if they'd been troublesome guests. Mind you, her aunt and uncle did tend to wind people up the wrong way. They were the polar opposite of the laid-back and hippy types that people assumed most Californians were. She could only imagine what they might have said or done when they were here. 'They raved about what a beautiful island it is and how wonderful the guesthouse was,' she breezed in a bid to lay on the compliments.

'Aw, that's so nice to hear. They have been very kind,' said Amy. 'They left us glowing reviews and then recommended us to some of their friends who were looking for a location to film part of a documentary. They stayed earlier in the year, which made for a lot of fun. And now you're here too. Word of mouth is what keeps small businesses like us going.'

'It's a lovely spot,' said Olivia. 'I can understand why they've been telling all their friends. I'm sorry, I didn't mean to intrude.'

Amy shook her head. 'You're not at all. I've been up for hours. I like watching the sky change from pale pink all the way through to bright blue. It's still a bit of a novelty after living away for so long. I lived in Vancouver for many years, and I moved back permanently last year.'

'Ah, I see,' said Olivia, intrigued to hear more about Amy.

The sun was now high in the sky and, if it wasn't for the cooler Scottish air, Olivia could easily have imagined this was a Mediterranean island. Perhaps not quite like Capri but just as beautiful. It was nicely warm actually, and as she looked back to the bay she saw the ferry making its way from the mainland towards Brodick. Her gaze lingered on the sea view.

'Isn't it beautiful? I will never tire of that view,' said Amy. 'Look, you're very welcome to come in and see the guesthouse one day.' She frowned. 'Early afternoons are best, as that's when the guests have left, and we're getting ready for the next ones to arrive. As you can imagine, mornings are a bit chaotic.'

'Of course. I won't take up any more time. I'll let you get on.'

'Oh no, I don't mean that. I just mean I can't show you just now as it's the clear-up after breakfast and things can get a bit intense. But come in and see the garden.' She pulled a face as she tilted her head towards the house. 'It will give me an excuse to stay out of the way as my sister, Kirsty, tends to get a bit bossy and irritable during breakfast. I've learned that it's much easier to stay out the way and leave her and her husband to it.'

'Okay, if you're sure you don't mind, I'd love to have a peek,' said Olivia, curious to see more of the beautiful garden.

As they walked, Amy told Olivia about how much had happened over the course of the past twelve months since her sister Emma's wedding, which had triggered her decision to move back home. 'Until last week, I was leading a bit of a nomadic existence, dividing my time between my dad's cottage in the village, Meadowbank Cottage and my boyfriend's flat.'

Olivia felt a pang of envy as she noticed Amy beaming when she mentioned the word 'boyfriend'. She told Olivia that in between looking after her father, who had dementia, and helping Kirsty and her husband Steve with the guesthouse, and keeping an eye on Lilybank Cottage, she had also managed to start holding regular yoga sessions in the village hall. Meanwhile she had project-managed the conversion of the dilapidated barn in the grounds of the cottage into two small studios — one for her and one for her dad, so he could have his independence but the girls would be nearby if he needed them. She had originally hoped to also have a yoga studio and therapy room in the barn, but had shelved those plans for now.

'Wow, that is impressive. All of that in just one year,' said Olivia.

Amy shrugged. 'I know. Never in a million years did I think my life would work out like that. It's not at all what I'd planned on doing but it's amazing the way things sometimes work out.'

'The garden is lovely,' said Olivia, admiring the colourful flowers and the immaculate grass.

'That's down to my dad, he's very green-fingered, and my nephew when he's back home for the holidays. I can't tell the difference between weeds and plants. I obviously didn't inherit the gene. But enough about me,' she said. 'How about you?'

Olivia felt her cheeks flush as Amy switched her attention to her. 'Oh,' she said, flustered, 'I just wanted a break for a while, and work has been intense and . . . Trudy said I should come here and, well, here I am.' Glancing over, she could see a woman walking towards them.

Amy looked up. 'That's Kirsty, my sister.'

Olivia was relieved at the distraction.

'Good morning.' Kirsty wandered towards them with a mug of coffee. 'If I'd known you were outside, I would have brought you out a cuppa.'

'Don't worry. I'll get one in a minute. Is that the breakfast chaos over then?' asked Amy hopefully.

'Yes, don't worry, the coast is clear. Steve is just finishing with the tidying up.' Kirsty looked at Olivia inquisitively.

'This is Olivia, she's staying at Lilybank,' explained Amy.

'Oh.' Kirsty smiled. 'Hello, Olivia. Great to meet you, sorry that it's all been a bit of a kerfuffle but I'm glad it's all sorted now.'

Olivia didn't know what 'kerfuffle' meant, but assumed she meant 'muddle' so smiled graciously. 'It's all great, thanks, and this place is as beautiful as my aunt said it was.'

Kirsty rewarded her with a warm smile. 'Ah, you're Trudy's niece. Of course. It's so good to welcome you here, and it's all down to them.'

'I've said to Olivia to come back some time and we can show her inside,' said Amy.

'Of course, please do. And I'm glad that everything is fine, and you and Kitty are going to stay. The owners are friends of ours and we keep an eye on things for them when they're away. If you need anything, please just let us know.'

'I think it will be fine. It will be nice to have some company.'

Kirsty frowned at her. 'Just a thought, but wait there until I get some things from inside.' She turned and disappeared back inside the cottage.

'I have no idea what she's gone to get,' said Amy suspiciously.

Kirsty reappeared with a handful of leaflets. 'Lilybank's information drawer could be a little out of date now the owners aren't letting it out. We've just refreshed ours recently, you may find these useful. Just some of the local attractions we would recommend and a couple of maps. If you and Kitty are keen to explore then you might be interested in this walking tour of the island?'

Olivia took the pamphlets from Kirsty and saw the one about the walks was the same one Kitty had shown her earlier. '*Stravaig Tours offer escorted walking tours of some of the island's most beautiful sights.* That's the one Kitty picked up too. I think we might do it.'

'Are they the ones James brought over last night?' asked Amy.

Kirsty nodded. 'Steve has given them to some of our guests, but most of them leave in the next couple of days and have already scheduled what they're doing.'

'Well, if you're interested let us know as we may be able to negotiate a discount for you,' said Amy. 'We know Logan, the tour guide.'

'Thank you. You're both very kind.' Olivia folded the leaflets and tucked them in the pocket of her leggings. 'I'd better get on with that run otherwise it won't happen. It's been lovely chatting.'

'Anytime,' said Amy. 'Just let us know when you want to come back for the inside tour.'

'Will do. Thank you.' Olivia said her goodbyes and walked away from Meadowbank feeling uplifted. She could feel a small glimmer of hope, the possibility of a happy summer starting to form at the back of her mind. It was a feeling she hadn't felt for a very long time, and she liked it. For the first time in ages she felt okay. There was something about this island. It felt almost magical.

CHAPTER SEVENTEEN

Kitty had decided that she would bake. She was in that kind of mood where she had to do something rather than just sit down. She couldn't really clean any more than she already had. The house was immaculate anyway and, even if it was cluttered, which it wasn't, it wasn't her house to start rearranging. The next on her 'how to unwind' list was to bake. As the kitchen was about twice the size of her kitchen back home, it seemed like the perfect opportunity to perfect some of her recipes and update her Instagram account with some pictures. She was thankful she'd brought the car over after all, as it meant she could nip to the big Co-op and stock up on all the things she needed without having to lug heavy bags back up that hill.

Deciding on one of her quick and easy recipes, she stirred up a batch of cinnamon and raisin muffins and popped them in the oven, making sure she'd turned on the timer. More than once she'd become distracted, forgetting about whatever was in the oven, and it was only the smell of burning that let her know her baking efforts had been wasted.

Standing with her back against the kitchen worktop, she scrolled through Instagram and quickly became distracted by the many foodie reels. They made everything look extremely easy to make and delicious. Her early attempts at baking had been rather interesting — nothing like they were now thanks to many, many hours of practice and perfection. Bookmarking some of the recipes she liked the look of, she watched to see how they had been presented. They all seemed to have the same theme, which usually went a bit like this: *You have got to try my delicious/lovely/mouth-watering cake. It has just four ingredients and tastes better than anything you'll buy in the shops.* She knew she would have to put herself out there and do more of those kinds of reels if she wanted to raise her profile, but she wasn't quite ready or confident enough to start talking as she baked.

Kitty had always been an introvert, much preferring to stay behind the scenes and out of the limelight. Her thumb slipped and hit another reel that started to play. Normally Kitty would scroll on, but now she was staring at her phone, transfixed by the rather good-looking bloke staring straight at her and talking in his deep, sexy voice. 'Are you planning a trip to Scotland? Then you must come soon. Come on over.' He paused, looking straight at her, then grinned. 'Visit our remote islands, our mountains, our forests and our beaches. What are you waiting for?' Behind him were panoramic shots of what looked like the Cuillin Ridge on the Isle of Skye, then some shots of the Fairy Pools, which looked vividly blue. He certainly didn't have any problems with his confidence, and he looked kind of familiar. She wondered if she'd seen him on one of those outdoor shows on TV she sometimes flicked past. Looking at his profile, she saw he was called the Tartan Wanderer. Why did that name ring a bell?

Just then the door opened, and Olivia came in, wiping her brow, sweaty from her run. 'Well, that was a bit of an effort,' she said. 'I am definitely out of shape.'

Kitty thought she looked the picture of great health as she strolled into the kitchen, her cheeks glowing from exercise.

'Whatever you're making smells amazing. Is it something with cinnamon?'

'Yes,' Kitty said with a smile. 'Cinnamon and raisin muffins.'

'Will they be ready soon?' Olivia sounded hopeful.

'In a bit.' She grinned. That was the sort of question her son would have asked.

Olivia stepped towards her, pulling a leaflet from her pocket. 'Oh, look, before I forget. Amy gave me this. *And* she said she would get us a discount if we wanted to go. She knows the guy doing the tour.'

Kitty took the leaflet from her and realised it was the same one she'd picked up. She chuckled when she made the connection. 'Oh, well, let's sign up then. I mean, when I show you who the tour guide is, I think you'll agree it's a great idea.' She handed her phone to Olivia and watched her watch the reel again.

'I mean, he seems like a nice guy, doesn't he? Like he knows what he's talking about.' Olivia shot her a look of appreciation, then frowned. 'He looks kind of familiar.'

'That's what I thought too,' said Kitty. 'Like someone off the telly, but I don't know who.'

'Well, there's only one way to find out. Shall we?'

'Let's do it,' said Kitty decisively.

'Deal. When do we go?'

'The day after tomorrow,' said Kitty. 'Plenty of time to prepare.'

'Okay. Well, I'm going to hit the shower, then you can tell me what I need for this walking tour and where we're going.'

'Sure.' Kitty reached down to remove the muffins from the oven. 'These will be ready to eat when you're out the shower. Meantime, I'll call and get us booked on the trip.'

'Brilliant. Thank you. Let's go!'

Kitty started quietly singing a Calvin Harris song and getting the words completely wrong.

Olivia burst into laughter. 'I love that song.'

'Oops, sorry, that's an old habit of mine. Drives Cameron mad. I'm not even aware I'm doing it. I just tend to start singing if someone mentions a song title. I'll try and be more aware. It can be an embarrassing habit, especially if the lyrics are a bit dodgy. Cameron has walked away from me many times when we've been in public.'

'Oh, don't quit on my account,' said Olivia. 'Please keep singing.'

Kitty grinned and gave a small shrug. 'You may live to regret this.' She looked back at her phone. 'Oh, Olivia. What's your surname? Just in case he asks.'

Olivia paused for a fraction of a second, long enough for Kitty to notice. 'Sure. It's Kennedy. My surname is Kennedy. Thanks, Kitty.' She turned and headed to her shower.

When Kitty was sure she could hear the sound of water, she picked up her phone again and typed in *Olivia Kennedy* to Instagram. There were many results, but after a bit of dogged scrolling she saw Olivia's face. The name of her Instagram account was *OliviaKDancing*. She clicked on it and was surprised to see the privacy settings weren't on, which meant Kitty could look through all the pictures Olivia had posted. Her eyes widened as she saw picture after picture of her appearing at Disneyland, on *Let's Dance* and then on stage with some really famous singers. Like *really* famous. Which made it even weirder that she was here. Something must have happened for her to end up on Arran. As she heard the sound of Olivia coming out of the shower, she put her phone away. It really wasn't any of her business, and if Olivia wanted to share details with her, that was her choice. In the same way that Kitty had her story too, and she didn't just share it with anyone.

CHAPTER EIGHTEEN

Logan was back in James's flat after dropping off the leaflets. It hadn't been long since he updated the dreaded Instagram account with the latest pictures of Skye. He scratched his head and sighed. The things he had to do in the name of work. But it would be worth it if it would drum up some more business for Stravaig. He'd been keeping an eye on the sea — the conditions looked good for some kayaking, so he decided he'd head round to the outdoor centre in Lamlash and see if they had a kayak he could take out for a few hours. His phone buzzed, and he grinned when he saw the text message from James.

Amy's found you a couple of recruits for the tour. Can you do a family and friends rate?

He quickly tapped in a reply.

Sure. Only because it's you. What are their names?

James replied immediately.

Olivia and Kitty. Guests at Lilybank Cottage. They should be calling you soon.

Sure enough, a few minutes later Logan's phone rang. 'Hi, is that Logan?' said a woman's voice.

'It is.'

'Hi, Logan. My name's Kitty. I hope you're expecting this call. Amy said I should phone you and mention her name . . .'

He laughed easily. 'Yes,' he said. 'Her boyfriend James just this minute let me know you would be in touch. I hear you want to join the next tour?'

'Please. If there's space for me and another that would be brilliant.'

'Sure. I just need to take some details.'

Logan exchanged pleasantries with the woman, explaining the walks they'd be doing and the kit her and her friend would need.

'Don't worry, I've come prepared,' she said.

It did sound as though she had come to Arran with walking in mind — he was impressed. 'There's an outdoor shop in Brodick, which is brilliant, just in case you need anything else.'

'Yes, thanks. I clocked that when I arrived and thought it might be handy.'

Logan raked his hand through his hair as he found himself wanting to continue the conversation with her. 'Okay . . . well . . . you have my number, Kitty. Just call or drop me a text if you think of anything else you need.' He paused, desperately thinking of something witty to say, but his mind went blank. 'I look forward to meeting you and Olivia on Thursday morning. Remember your snacks and packed lunches.' God, he sounded like a schoolteacher. Why didn't he just add that she better make sure she was on time?

'And our sunscreen, water, layers and waterproof?' she added helpfully.

Logan raised an eyebrow and couldn't stop himself from chuckling. 'Maybe you should just lead the tour, you probably have more clue of what's going on than me,' he said jokily.

'Maybe. I'll see how I feel on the day,' she said smoothly, not missing a beat.

He smiled. This woman sounded like she might add some sparkle to the group and keep him on his toes. At least he hoped so. Then he reprimanded himself for even giving it a second thought. It was so out of character. What was the matter with him?

'Okay, thanks, Logan. We'll see you bright and early on Thursday. And don't worry. We won't be late.'

'Thanks, Kitty . . . Um, see you then.'

Um, see you then. What was that all about? He *never* got stuck for words. It was as though he had reverted to being fourteen again. He shook his head at himself. But there was no denying that he was intrigued to meet the face behind the voice, and all would be revealed on Thursday when they met in person.

He reminded himself that she was perhaps already taken. She said 'they' would see him on Thursday. It suddenly dawned on him — maybe Olivia was Kitty's partner, and she hadn't actually been flirting with him at all but was just being friendly. He groaned, feeling slightly mortified. How typical that he would misread the signs and jump to the wrong conclusions.

Returning his attentions to his laptop, he quickly typed an email to Henry. He'd be pleased that a couple of others had joined the group. He pressed send and then grabbed his bag. It was time to get out on the water for some physical and mental health time, which would hopefully help him switch off and give him a mood boost. He hadn't been out as much as he normally would these last couple of days, and it was clearly affecting his focus.

CHAPTER NINETEEN

It was the night before the walking tour started and Olivia was chatting to her aunt Trudy on the phone, reassuring her that she was okay and that she was falling in love with Arran. 'I now see why you were so enthralled,' she said enthusiastically. 'Thanks for recommending I come and for setting it all up.'

'I'm glad you're there and safely away from everything,' said Trudy. 'It will do you the world of good to have a proper break. Listen, I'd better go, I can hear your uncle Chuck calling. It's been wonderful chatting. Keep in touch and let me know how things are going?'

'Of course. Give Uncle Chuck a hug for me.'

'I will. Goodbye dear and enjoy those walks.'

Olivia ended the call and looked out her bedroom window. In the garden Kitty sat with a glass of rosé and a bowl of olives. She looked up and, on seeing Olivia, gestured for her to join her. A few moments later she sat down at the table next to Kitty, who'd already filled another glass with wine. They'd spent the day making sure they were prepared for their first walk, which would take them to Whiting Bay and a circular route to the waterfalls of Glenashdale Falls and the Giants' Graves.

'I'm excited to see more of the island,' said Olivia, taking a sip.

Kitty nodded. 'I mean, I guess we *could* have taken my car and a guidebook, but sometimes it's just nice to follow the leader and not have to think for a change. I'm so used to always organising things, whether for Cameron and school or when I'm at work . . . I just feel like I'm constantly the one making decisions on everything and having to initiate stuff, you know?'

Olivia eyed her for a moment. 'I guess parenting must be all consuming, huh?'

'Yes, it's a full-time role and more. You never switch off.' Kitty popped an olive in her mouth and chewed thoughtfully. 'Don't get me wrong though. I wouldn't swap it for the world. But it's been hard.'

There was silence for a moment. The women sat, enjoying the warm breeze in the garden, and the heady scent of jasmine wafting from the flowery trails climbing the fence. 'Have you always been on your own?' asked Olivia hesitantly.

'No, not always. I mean, I was married once . . . but I've always been on my own as a parent.'

Olivia waited, in case she wanted to say any more, and noticed Kitty eyeing her for a moment as though deciding whether to add anything else. 'It's okay, Olivia. Everyone new I meet always wants to know where Cameron's dad is and I don't always feel it's necessary to share the details. But seeing as we're living together, and will no doubt get to know each other quite a bit these next few weeks, I'll let you know why I'm a single parent . . . that's if you want to know?'

'Of course,' said Olivia, 'though please don't feel you need to tell me. Only share the details if you're comfortable to do so.'

Kitty sighed and took another sip of wine. 'It's a bit of a story,' she said as she topped up their glasses. 'Okay, bear with me.' Olivia watched as her expression became sombre.

Olivia listened carefully as Kitty told her that, when she was twenty-five years old, she joined a club that she never

ever imagined she would be part of. She became a member of the young widows' club. She and Ryan had been married for less than a year when he died suddenly in a road accident. What made his death even more tragic was that night she had planned to tell him the good news that she was pregnant with Cameron. Instead, she sat anxiously, wondering why he was so late home, and became so concerned and distracted that she failed to notice the smell of the burning chicken in the oven. She couldn't get through to him on his mobile phone, which was switched off, and she left message after frantic message begging him to call her back. A knock at the door several hours later brought her the news that he was dead.

Olivia's eyes were fixed on Kitty, and she touched her hand gently.

'It's okay,' Kitty said. 'I guess I just go onto autopilot when I tell the story.'

Kitty didn't collapse on the floor stricken with grief or even shed a tear to begin with. She was completely numb and in a daze for weeks, as she tried to come to terms with both the death of the love of her life, and the new life flourishing inside her. It was a dark time and often she wondered whether she would manage to navigate herself through it. Her heart had been ripped into millions of pieces, and the visceral grief she felt threatened to destroy her. But amid the black fog that descended upon her she found tiny snippets of rare light and gratitude — that part of Ryan would live on in their unborn child. Yet that responsibility then started to weigh heavily on her as she became increasingly anxious about the pregnancy.

'Oh, you poor thing,' said Olivia. 'I'm so sorry for your loss.'

Kitty gave her a grateful smile. 'Thank you. It was such a long time ago now but when I start to talk about it again it does feel like it was only a few weeks ago that it all happened. It's such a strange thing to try and describe. When Cameron was born it wasn't entirely unexpected that I had awful post-natal depression, which followed on from the depression I had when I was pregnant. I had panic attacks and extreme anxiety that I wouldn't be able to look after Cameron properly. I couldn't shake off the guilt that I hadn't told Ryan that I loved him before he left that morning.'

'Kitty, what an awful thing for you to have gone through.'

'It wasn't the cheeriest time of my life, I have to admit,' she said.

'How did you manage with such a young baby and having to deal with the grief?' Olivia bit back a tear.

'Friends and family,' she said. 'My mum was a lifesaver.' Kitty told her that, although she had been adamant that she wanted to stand on her own two feet, she allowed her mum to temporarily move in with her. Her family and friends rallied around her and, with the help of a counsellor, she eventually started to find more glimmers of light each day and hope that life could go on. Cameron reminded her that she had a reason to live.

'It's such a haze,' she said, her eyes glistening. 'I don't really remember much at all. I was on autopilot trying to get through each day, and I had to keep going for the sake of Cameron.'

Olivia gave small nods of encouragement. 'This must be so hard to go over, but you're doing so well to share it with me. Thank you.'

'When he died, I realised how many other people were affected by grief, and that's what led me to train to be a counsellor. But it's been hard. Especially these past few years. People have lost so much. That's why I decided to take a break and work in the nursery. Being around kids felt better for my mental health. I started to feel burned out in the counselling role.'

'Wow,' said Olivia. 'You are incredibly strong and brave.'

Kitty took a slug of wine. 'Oh no, not me. There are lots of other people out there who go through far worse. I mean, don't get me wrong, there are still days when I get sad. And especially during those milestone years when Cameron took his first steps, his first day at school and now with him flying abroad on his own for the first time. Ryan would have been so proud. But I have so much to be grateful for. I am surrounded by people I love, and am so lucky to have this time to think about what I want to do next.'

Olivia clasped her hands around the wine glass and leaned forward. 'What did you love most about him?'

Kitty beamed. 'That's easy to answer. He was funny and kind and had the most amazing laugh. It was contagious, he would have everyone in stitches.'

'Has there ever been anyone else?' asked Olivia.

Kitty shook her head vigorously. 'No, not really, other than the odd date here and there. But I just wasn't interested. It was too hard when Cameron was little, as he was always my focus. I guess my life was always about him. Until now . . .'

Olivia smiled kindly at her. 'Well, for what it's worth, I think you're amazing.'

Kitty flushed and flicked her hand dismissively. 'Not at all. I just did what anyone else would do.'

'You still did an amazing and selfless job of dedicating your life to your son, Kitty. I hope this next chapter is an exciting adventure for you.'

'Not sure I need any more excitement in my life,' she said. 'I'm quite happy with the olives and the wine.'

'Let's see what adventures the Tartan Wanderer takes us on,' said Olivia, giggling. 'I think it's time we had some fun.'

CHAPTER TWENTY

Kitty was tying her shoelaces when her phone started to buzz. It was Cameron, FaceTiming her.

'Hey, Mum,' he said in a bit of a drawl.

'You're starting to sound like a local,' joked Kitty, delighted to hear from him, but inwardly groaning at his timing. She and Olivia needed to leave in the next couple of minutes if they were to make the start of the tour. 'How are you, sweetie? You're up late or early?' She looked at her watch, realising it must have been about 2 a.m. with him.

'Good, thanks. I was out kayaking with the kids yesterday and then we had a barbecue. Just thought I'd call as I couldn't sleep . . .'

'That's so thoughtful of you, and it's lovely seeing your face. Is it all still going well?'

He paused for only a second — long enough to plant a seed of doubt in Kitty's mind — before continuing. 'Yes, all good. How are you? What have you been doing?'

'It's a long story,' she said with a laugh. 'But, basically, I have a housemate in the cottage on Arran. She's called Olivia and she's American. We're actually about to go out and join a walking tour.'

'Sounds good,' he said.

Kitty was aware of Olivia's presence in the hallway as she gathered her things together and, when she glanced at the clock, she knew they would have to leave in the next sixty seconds if they were to make it to the bus on time. 'Look, honey, can I try and call you again later? It's just that we're booked on this trip, and it leaves in the next few minutes. We really need to get going, otherwise we'll miss the bus.'

'Sure,' he said, sounding a bit deflated. 'That's fine, Mum. Don't worry.'

'I'm so sorry, love. I'll try and get you later?' She felt like the worst mum in the world for cutting their call short.

'Okay, Mum. Speak to you later. Love you.'

'Are you okay, Cam?'

'Yes, honestly, I'm okay. Just missed you so thought I'd phone.'

'Oh,' she said, biting back the emotion she could feel starting to build up. Cameron had *never* admitted to missing her before. *Ever.* 'I miss you too. But I'm so glad you're having a great time. Sounds much more exciting than being here with boring me,' she said, in an attempt at a half-joke.

'True.' He gave her a small smile. 'Okay, you'd better go. You don't want to get into trouble and be branded the bad old lady on the trip.'

'Hey. Less of the bad and the old,' she said, glad he was teasing her again. 'Get to bed.' Blowing him a kiss, she ended the call and then grabbed her rucksack and car keys. 'Come on then,' she called to Olivia. 'We'd better get moving or we won't be popular. We'll need to take the car if we're going to make it.'

As she drove to the car park at the terminal, where they had arranged to meet Logan and the rest of the group, Kitty didn't say a word, not trusting herself to speak in case she started to cry. She knew that the guilt she felt at cutting the call short was irrational, but the last thing she wanted right now was to be in a group with people she had to make polite conversation with.

'I hope I don't get blisters,' said Olivia cheerily.

Kitty appreciated her attempt to distract her. 'I do too. But at least we've packed those special plasters.' She pulled into a parking space and nodded her head in the direction of a minibus. 'Looks like that's us there. Though there's no sign of anyone hanging around. Maybe they're already on it and getting ready to leave. Come on. We'd better hurry. I hate being late.'

'Yes,' sighed Olivia. 'I feel quite nervous now. Why did we think this was a good idea?'

Kitty got out the car and slammed the door shut before opening the boot to retrieve their rucksacks. Olivia gave her a curious look.

'Sorry,' Kitty said. 'It was Cameron. He called just before we left, and I had to cut him short. I'm worried he had something on his mind and now feel like the crappiest mum in the world. I don't feel like doing this anymore.' She jerked her head towards the minibus.

Olivia didn't say anything, instead putting a reassuring hand on Kitty's arm.

Kitty sighed. 'Come on. Best get on with it. It will keep my mind off things. Oh gawd, we're going to be labelled the troublesome pair before we've even started.' She walked purposefully towards the bus, Olivia trailing right behind her. She could see the tour leader — she assumed it was Logan — standing inside the bus, holding court with everyone, and as she looked up at him and felt herself blushing, she realised that she *had* seen him before. He was the handsome guy who held the door open for her at the bakery the other morning.

'Oh jeez,' said Olivia quietly behind her. 'I know him.'

Kitty swung round in confusion to look at Olivia, whose cheeks had flushed red in embarrassment. 'But how?' Then she turned and watched Logan look down at both of them. She saw the look of recognition on his face as it clearly dawned on him that he recognised one of them, too. She knew it certainly wasn't her — he would have barely looked at her at the bakery, other than to hold the door in the polite way that he would have done for anyone.

Great, she thought. Isn't this just typical? What were the chances of her noticing a good-looking guy for the first time in years — actually, make that in more than a decade — and the random housemate she found herself with on Arran had clearly had some kind of fling with him. How could that even be possible? Was Olivia leading some kind of double life? She grimaced as she realised just how little she actually knew about her. This morning was just getting better and better.

CHAPTER TWENTY-ONE

Logan looked down at the door of the bus as he saw the last two members of the group arriving just on time. Straightaway he clocked who he assumed was Kitty. He was sure he recognised her from somewhere. Her lovely smile and red curls were *really* familiar.

'Hi,' she said. 'Sorry we're late.'

Yip. Definitely Kitty. He hadn't been able to get that voice out of his head since their conversation the other night. Then he felt total dismay as he realised that it was her friend standing behind that he *definitely* recognised. She was the mouthy American from the pub who'd accused him of trying to nick her bag. What were the chances of her coming on one of his tours, and being with Kitty?

He forced a smile and stepped forward, extending his hand. 'Good morning. Welcome. I'm Logan, and I'm assuming you're Kitty.' He reached for her hand, which felt soft in his.

'Hello,' she said with a small smile.

Then he turned to Olivia. 'And you're Olivia?'

'Indeed,' she said curtly with a nod. 'Nice to meet you.'

'I was just saying to the rest of the group that the weather looks fair and should last all day, so hopefully we're in for a good few hours of walking. Okay, so we're going to leave any minute . . . unless anyone wants to visit the toilet? If so, go now. It will take us about twenty minutes or so to get to the car park at Whiting Bay, and then we'll start our walk to the falls.'

Logan was relieved when the party agreed they were fine to get going. He was driving the minibus on this tour and it would save him having to make any small talk while they waited. This was going to be awkward enough. He glanced sideways at Kitty, who was getting settled into a window seat near the back of the minibus. He now realised she was the woman he had held the door open for at the bakery the other morning. He had held the door for a while and then watched her walk away and momentarily lost his focus. What were the chances of her being here on this tour?

There were six other people on the tour of varying ages and nationalities — Fred and Tom were South African, Richard and Jill were from Yorkshire and Adam and Liz were Australian. Everyone was quiet during the journey to Whiting Bay as they focused on looking out the window and admiring the stunning scenery. As they followed the road out of Brodick, he asked a few questions about who had visited the island before and listened as they each shouted out a 'yes' or a 'no'. Then, as they approached the top of the hill that would take them through the village of Lamlash, he directed the guests to look at the Holy Isle, a small rocky island in the bay. As well as being a nature reserve it was also home to a community of Buddhist monks.

'It's an incredible view,' he said, taking a hand off the steering wheel to gesture across the bay. 'You can go over and visit for the day or you can go and stay at the Centre for World Peace and Health, which holds courses and retreat programmes. At the south of the island there's a closed Buddhist retreat.'

'Wow,' said Olivia.

'It's quite something, isn't it?' said Kitty.

The rest of the group were quiet as they admired the view, which meant that Logan could easily hear what the women were talking about.

'Did I mention that my cousin lives here?' said Kitty.

'No, you didn't. What a beautiful place to live,' said Olivia.

'I know. It was his idea that I come here for the summer. He got in touch about the house-sit. He runs the outdoor centre there,' she said just as they drove past it. Logan's ears pricked up. Her cousin was Fergus. That was interesting.

'You mentioned the wildlife and what we might see?' piped up an Australian man sitting nearer the front of the bus.

'Absolutely. There's plenty of that here. Loads of different birds, including dunnocks, blackbirds, oyster catchers — with the long orange beak — gannets . . . In fact, in case you didn't know, the Ailsa Craig is one of the largest gannet colonies in the world. There can be up to fifty thousand pairs breeding there. What else? Black guillemot, eider ducks and shelducks. We also have otters, seals, dolphins, porpoises, basking sharks, red deer and red squirrels. There are no grey squirrels on the island, which means the red squirrels aren't under threat.'

'Impressive stuff,' said Olivia. Was there a bit of tension in her voice?

'Mind you,' said Logan lightly, 'I can't promise that we'll see all of them today.' That provoked a ripple of laughter from the group. 'Not long until we're there. Just enjoy the scenery and the rest while you can,' he joked. However, he knew that he would have to try and address the situation with Olivia. He hated any kind of discord within a group, and starting off a new tour with a guest he had exchanged cross words with was not a good start. He would need to try and clear the air as soon as possible.

CHAPTER TWENTY-TWO

'Isn't this absolutely beautiful?' said Olivia as she paused and turned round to look at the view behind. 'It's just so peaceful.'

They were following Logan up the path through woodland. The only sounds were the trickling burn and the sound of boots thunking over the soft ground. The track started to ascend a bit more steeply as it led them higher into the woods.

'I know,' said Kitty. 'It's like we're in the middle of nowhere. It's so very quiet and calm. The trees are incredible.' She pointed behind them.

'Did you know trees talk to each other?' said Olivia thoughtfully as she thought of a book she had recently read.

'What do you mean?' said Kitty.

'It's called the wood-wide web.' Olivia frowned as she tried to recall the exact facts. 'They communicate through their roots and underground fungi. I guess there's a lot more science to it than that. But I remember thinking how beautiful it was.'

Kitty nodded in agreement. 'You wonder what they say to each other and what they have witnessed. They're so solid and constant.'

'I know. I do find it all quite fascinating,' said Olivia. 'It was one of those books that someone gave me, and it took me ages to pick up and read. I was so glad that I did. I found it quite comforting in a way.'

The women had slowed down slightly as they talked and looked ahead. A gap had formed between them and the rest of the group. Olivia could see Logan had turned to stop. He gave them a wave.

'I think that's our cue to get a move on,' said Kitty with a laugh. 'Who would have thought we would be the ones slowing everyone down. Come on, let's up our pace a bit.'

The cool breeze felt lovely as they made their way up the track, the sunshine creating a dappled light on the springy forest floor.

Kitty raised an eyebrow. 'Are you going to tell me how you know him then?' She jerked her head towards Logan, who was now a few hundred metres away.

'I met him the other night in the bar and was really rude.'

'What, like on a date or something?' asked Kitty in surprise.

'No, nothing like that. It was the day you arrived, and I had gone to the pub for some space. Then I left my bag behind. When I went back to get it, he had found it and was standing there. I practically accused him of stealing it. I feel awful,' she wailed.

Kitty nodded. 'That would explain why there was a bit of "tension" when we arrived at the car park. I sensed a bit of an exchange of looks.'

Olivia groaned. 'Was it that obvious?'

'Not at all,' she said dismissively. 'Sometimes I read into things too much. I wondered if you might have had a romantic *liaison* — and I was trying to figure out how you'd found the time.'

'Absolutely not,' blurted Olivia, horrified at the thought. 'No way.'

'Oh, okay, I get the message,' said Kitty, laughing.

'*Shh*, not another word just now,' said Olivia as they neared the group. 'Sorry, sorry, we got so absorbed in the scenery and talking that we didn't realise we had trailed behind.'

Logan took a sip from his water bottle. 'That's okay. I just want to make sure we all stick together.'

Olivia sighed. She was going to have to say something and clear the air, otherwise it would be a long few days. But she was not good at saying sorry. She wished she could just send him a subliminal message like the trees did, then they could move on without actually having a conversation.

'Okay, everyone,' said Logan. 'Let's keep going. I know it's warm today, so do keep sipping your water. I've also got some spray in my bag, so let me know if you need it. Sometimes the cleggs — flies — can be bothersome. We might be okay, but please shout if you find yourself waving your arms about to get rid of them. The last thing we want is anyone toppling over. Shall we go?'

There was a chorus of agreement and Logan started walking. 'Now, remember in the words of Al Green: *let's stay together.*'

There were a few ripples of laughter. Kitty winked at Olivia and started humming, then singing random words to the tune. 'I am out walking. By the waterfall, it's where I want to be. Let's stay together . . .'

Olivia shook her head in mock horror. 'Oh *please*, now I am starting to regret having encouraged you to keep singing. I can see how this would annoy your son.'

Kitty continued humming a jaunty tune.

Olivia managed to crack a smile as she tried her best to humour Kitty, but as she listened to those words her stomach started to twist. She used to love that song but, unbeknown to Kitty, it had just unearthed a painful memory of Patrick.

CHAPTER TWENTY-THREE

Kitty immediately saw the shift in Olivia's eyes and her mood. She wasn't quite sure why Olivia was so peeved, but she knew she needed to try and lighten things.

'Sorry, I know my singing isn't the greatest,' she said jauntily. 'That's it. You never have to listen to it again. I promise.' She didn't know Olivia well enough to pry further, but it wasn't the first time she had sensed such a mood shift. She knew there was more to Olivia being here, and whatever it was she didn't want to make things any worse for her.

Olivia shrugged. 'It's fine. Don't worry about it. Maybe just get some singing lessons. And next time choose a different song to murder.' She laughed ruefully.

Kitty knew to leave things there and not to push. 'I think that's a very good idea.'

They walked in companionable silence for a while and Kitty tried to immerse herself in the present, noticing the nature around her. The ground felt soft and springy below her feet, and as she listened to birdsong she realised she could hear the rumble of water. 'Do you hear that?' she asked Olivia excitedly.

'Yes, we can't be far away now.'

'Hey, guys,' said Logan. 'As you can probably hear, the falls are near. And that actually rhymes. As well as being a tour guide extraordinaire I'm also a bit of a poet, don't you know it?'

Kitty giggled and felt her cheeks colour as he looked back at her and smiled.

'Okay, so when we go over the bridge, there is a viewing platform. Sometimes it can be busy, so just be cautious and patient. We're not in any rush at all. Take as much time as you need to get photographs and just appreciate the view.'

Kitty and Olivia were still at the rear of the group, allowing the more enthusiastic members to take the lead. 'Tell me then, what are the best things about being a dancer?' asked Kitty.

Olivia looked at her in surprise. 'Gosh. I don't think anyone has actually asked me that question before . . .' Her voice trailed away as she closed her eyes and took a moment to think. She started walking beside Kitty again and began to talk. 'Most of all, it's about doing something that I love. I never forget how lucky I am to dance for a living. What else? The feeling of moving to the music, when you get it just right, and how you're lost entirely in the moment. It's unreal. Um, what else can I say? When you're at your ultimate fitness in body and mind, especially when doing a tour, that's an incredible feeling, which always makes me feel strong and powerful. Does that make sense?'

Kitty nodded.

'And the friendships, meeting diverse people in different places and getting to travel and see places that I wouldn't normally get to experience if I was stuck behind a desk in an office.'

'Wow,' said Kitty. 'Your eyes totally light up when you're talking about it. I can tell it's your passion.'

Olivia nodded enthusiastically as her eyes sparkled. 'I've been doing it since I was a little girl. It's just always been part of me. I always remind myself why I dance and it's for the feeling and love of it. I've learned to practice and practice and practice some more, be gracious and humble and know I have something to learn from every other dancer.'

Kitty felt her spine tingle as she listened. 'The way you describe it is incredible. I can tell it's part of you.'

'I've been so lucky. I've travelled the world and experienced different cultures and learned to dance with some of the most amazing people on some of the most amazing dance floors and stages. And I've been able to teach too, which has been so rewarding. That's the other part I love. Being able to inspire others and encourage them to dance, especially when they think they can't.'

Kitty gestured to Olivia to walk across the bridge ahead of her. 'You're first,' she said brightly, relieved that Olivia seemed to be a bit more upbeat.

'Why, thank you,' she said, putting her hands into her pockets and gracefully striding ahead.

She noticed Logan keeping a close eye on everyone, and it reminded her of working at the nursery and having to have eyes in the back of her head. So far, the group seemed quite relaxed and were quietly getting on with things, appreciating their surroundings. From what she could gather there weren't any troublemakers, aside from her and Olivia holding them up at the start. She wondered if Logan had any tales of tricky customers. Then she checked herself as she found herself staring at him and admiring his strong shoulders. Just then he turned round and caught her eyes and weirdly Kitty felt her legs tremble. They actually *trembled*. This was not good.

He grinned. 'All okay?'

Making herself take a steadying breath, she returned the smile. 'Yes, all good.' She was desperately trying to think of something witty or intelligent to say. 'I was just wondering if you ever had any tricky guests. Anyone that caused you any problems?' *Why on earth did I just say that?* She felt like such an idiot.

He paused and rubbed his hand over his chin. 'Apart from you two holding us all up with your constant chatting?' he said wryly.

'Hey, we were just a bit slow to start with,' she said, feeling quite indignant. 'All good now though. Look, Olivia is way at the front. Mind you, she is super fit, so she should be way ahead. She's a dancer.' She gave herself another shake. Why was she just wittering nonsense?

'I'm joking,' he said, a hint of amusement in his eyes. 'Not really, to answer your question . . . Most people who sign up are keen on the outdoors, and they might be on a once-in-a-lifetime trip to Scotland so want to make the most of it. We try and remind people that some of our walks can be quite physical.' He pulled a face. 'I did have someone breaking an ankle once. Though maybe I shouldn't be telling you that.'

She laughed. 'Oh dear, and here was me thinking that we were in safe hands.'

'Fortunately it was towards the end of a tour, and it was just one of those things where someone slipped and went over at a weird angle.'

'Sounds sore.'

'Yes, it wasn't ideal. But we managed to get them seen to fairly quickly. There was no need to call out mountain rescue or anything like that. Fingers crossed and touch wood, that has been the biggest drama so far. I hope it stays that way.'

'Yes, the last thing you want is any stressful situations,' she said brightly.

'And what about you? What brings you to Arran?' he asked.

'Oh, I've a few weeks off work and had the chance to spend the summer here, so thought it would be a bit of an adventure. Hence us signing up for this trip.'

His eyes crinkled as he smiled. 'Well, I hope it lives up to expectations.'

She followed him over the bridge to the rest of the group, who had made their way to the empty viewing platform.

'There you go,' said Logan, raising his voice so everyone could see. 'Bird's-eye view and we even get it all to ourselves. I couldn't have planned it better. Sometimes it can get a bit crowded up here and there can be some *tensions* if people start to hog the best view. These are double falls around forty-five metres high, or one hundred and forty feet if you prefer, and they're also known as the *Eas a' Chrannaig* in Gaelic.'

They all fell silent as they stood in awe, watching the jets of water cascade into a frothy pool below. Kitty found herself mesmerised by the water as it tumbled down over the rocks. There were so many shades of blue and green and brown. As she continued to stare at the scene ahead, she became aware of Logan standing next to her. His arm brushed against hers and she noticed that spicy scent of aftershave that reminded her of the first morning she'd seen him at the bakery. All of a sudden, she felt quite light-headed, as though she was having an out-of-body experience, and she rested her hands on the wooden bar in front of her. Taking a steadying breath, she looked across to Olivia, who was equally transfixed by the waterfall.

'It's quite something isn't it?' murmured Logan.

She nodded, unable to form any words. Kitty had felt this strange sensation once before in her life and it was completely throwing her off balance. Sometimes she wished she wasn't quite so in tune with her intuition. Kitty *knew* there was a connection between her and Logan. It sounded weird, as they didn't even know each other, and she was aware that if she voiced it aloud to anyone else they would think she was mad. Or a bit of a stalker. But what was overwhelming her more than anything else was that it was the same voice within that spoke to her when she last met someone *special*. This was exactly the same trembling and dizzy sensation that she'd had when she first saw Ryan. But there was no way that could happen again. That was a different part of her life and there was no way she was going to put herself through that. Not a chance. Then she felt a glimmer of guilt, realising she'd forgotten the earlier call from Cameron and her sense that he'd been a bit out of sorts. How could she have managed to push that aside? She felt Logan giving her a sideways glance, and she knew she had to say something, otherwise she would come across as being rude. 'I'm just going to go and have a look over there,' she said as politely as she could to Logan. 'Get another perspective of it.'

'Sure,' he said.

Then she slowly weaved her way over to where Olivia stood, determinedly ignoring the fluttering in her stomach.

CHAPTER TWENTY-FOUR

They were on their descent from the falls and making their way down the woodland trail towards the Giants' Graves, when Logan became aware of Olivia next to him. He wasn't going to lie, he was worried that he had offended Kitty, as she had distanced herself since he stood next to her on the viewing platform. He thought they had been getting on well and there had been a definite connection between them when he accidentally brushed his arm against hers. It felt like an electric current. He wondered why she had bolted. Did he smell or have bad breath? Or say something inappropriate? He racked his brain trying to relive their conversation, but all he could remember was some light-hearted banter and laughter. Maybe he had read the situation wrong after all, and she and Olivia were *together*. Then he reminded himself he was working, and needed to focus on the group he was responsible for. The last thing he wanted was to lose concentration right now. This was so unlike him, and he was worried he was losing the plot.

'Are you enjoying it so far?' he said politely to Olivia.

'It's incredible,' she replied. 'Not like anything I've ever done before.'

'First time in Scotland then?'

'Yes.'

Neither of them spoke and Logan watched Kitty, who was now at the head of the group. He couldn't take his eyes of her tumble of red curls.

'Look,' said Olivia, taking a deep breath. 'I think I owe you an apology. I'm so sorry for being rude at the pub the other night. I had a terrible day, and I shouldn't have accused you of trying to steal my bag.'

Logan shrugged. 'That's okay. Apology accepted.'

'I wanted to clear the air. It wasn't fair of me to project my stuff onto you.'

'Please don't worry. We all have bad days. But for the record, I was just trying to help.'

'I know. And I appreciate it.'

Logan turned to her and smiled. 'Thank you. So what brought you to Scotland?'

She chuckled. 'A long story. But in essence, my aunt and uncle visited last year and loved the place, and I had the summer off so randomly ended up coming to Arran. I was in Italy and met some Glaswegians who also raved about it, so I decided to take that as a sign, then took a bit of a leap of faith.'

Logan was impressed. 'That's a brave thing to do.'

She shrugged. 'Not really. I'm just lucky that I have the summer off work and got the chance to come.'

He was intrigued that she hadn't mentioned Kitty and their connection, and he wondered if there was a polite and subtle way of asking if they were together.

'And how do you and Kitty know each other then?'

'Well, we don't. That's the strange thing,' she said.

'What do you mean?' He was surprised.

'We didn't meet until a few days ago.'

'Seriously?' he said, genuinely shocked. 'I just assumed you were here together.'

Olivia raised her shoulders in a shrug. 'We didn't get off to the best start,' she admitted. She filled him in on their clashing summer house plans and their decision to trial a house share at Lilybank Cottage.

'Wow,' he said. 'I would not have guessed that at all. So you're housemates then.'

'Yes,' she said. 'And so far, so good. We seem to be getting along just fine. Well, apart from her dodgy singing,' she joked. 'Kitty's son has gone away to do Camp America and so she thought she would make the most of her summer here as it's just her.'

Logan felt relief wash over him when he heard this. So she *was* single, and she had a son. *Interesting.* And they were staying at Lilybank Cottage. He would have to get more information from James. He chewed his lip thoughtfully as he glanced at Olivia. 'And where is home for you normally?'

'I'm based in New York. Though I can travel a lot with my job . . . I'm a dancer.'

'You're used to living out of a bag then?' He chuckled good-naturedly.

'Yip. So having one base and one bed for six weeks is a treat.'

They were nearing the prehistoric site of the cairns, which were built sometime between 5500–4500 BCE. 'This will be something that you don't see back home,' he said to Olivia, then edged his way ahead to stand at the front of the group. 'Here we are. As you can see, the tombs are mostly ruined, there's a lot of turf covering some of the remains. But this style of cairn is part of the Clyde group; there are many of these Clyde tombs scattered across the island.' He paused to let everyone look around. 'When they were excavated, shreds of pottery, fragments of cremated bone, and flint knives and arrowheads were discovered.'

'When was that?' asked Olivia.

'That was back in 1902.' He looked across at Kitty, who now seemed to be avoiding eye contact. 'Have a look around, take your time.'

He peeled his rucksack from his shoulders and circled them a few times. It was hotter now than it had been when they started their walk, and he was parched. Taking a swig of water, he stood observing the group as they wandered around the site, taking photographs and quietly talking to each other.

He fleetingly thought about the last significant woman in his life. He and Julia had dated for a few months, until she became increasingly keen that they move in together and settle down. She didn't understand his passion for the out-doors and adventure and the need he had to explore. When she started making suggestions that he settle down and work more 'regular' hours he knew that was the end. He never wanted to feel trapped or suffocated in a relationship. He knew he would perhaps never find someone who would understand his nomadic lifestyle. Anyway, he reminded him-self, he had been perfectly happy with that.

Until now, a voice in his head whispered.

His T-shirt was damp and sticking to his back. He would be glad to have a cold shower when he got back to the flat. Glancing at his watch, he was relieved that they were on time. He liked to have a bit of a schedule to follow, as some guests liked to plan their day meticulously, especially if they were here for a short time. However, he would never rush a tour, particularly if conditions were tougher, or they were genuinely immersed in the moment.

When everyone started to gather around him again, he clapped his hands together. 'Okay, let's make our way back to the bus.'

* * *

By the time they arrived back in Brodick, the bus was almost silent, and Logan knew that most of the party would have fallen asleep. There were also a few loud telltale snores, always the sign of a well-walked lot. He was glad that they seemed to have enjoyed their first day of the tour. It was a gentle start to the next four days of walking, and it had gone well. This was one of their easier walking tours, in contrast to the Arran coastal way, which was a path that took them right round the island, staying in different places each night. He would be doing that trip a couple of times later in the summer, and he felt a sense of relief knowing that he would be spending a bit of time on Arran over coming weeks. He had always felt at home here.

Tomorrow they would visit the Machrie Moor Standing Stones and the King's Cave; the day after they would go and explore the northern coast at Lochranza, with an optional stop at the distillery there. Day four would be a walk through forest trails from Brodick to Lamlash, and then the fifth day they would climb the highest peak on the island, Goatfell. He just hoped the weather would stay fair.

He pulled into a parking bay at the ferry terminal and switched off the ignition. 'Wakey, wakey, sleepyheads,' he called gently, and then cleared his throat when he realised that there was no movement. 'That's us back.' He coughed noisily and stood up to face everyone. He was met with a few bleary-eyed looks of surprise as people realised they had arrived in Brodick. They began to slowly gather their belongings together. 'Make sure you remember all your stuff, water bottles too,' he said, pointing to one that had rolled to the front. He picked it up. 'Thanks for today, everyone. I hope you enjoyed it and are raring to go tomorrow?'

There was a collective murmur of 'yay'.

'Glad to hear it,' he said. 'Now, enjoy the rest of the day and I'll see you here at the same time tomorrow. We'll drive to the other side of the island this time, which should take around forty minutes. We'll walk to the standing stones then down to the King's Cave, where we can have lunch on the beach. Just remember the usual stuff. Your water, your lunch, a waterproof jacket just in case . . .'

'Thanks, Logan,' said the Australian man called Adam, who had been sitting at the front of the bus with his wife, Liz. 'Thoroughly enjoyed that. But I'm not going to lie, I'm looking forward to a cold beer now. And maybe a little lie down.'

Logan chuckled. 'Indeed. And so you should. You're on your holidays.'

As everyone clambered down the steps with their backpacks, he braved a glance at Kitty, who was last off the bus behind Olivia. She had scooped her hair into a ponytail and a few tendrils fell around her face. He felt himself wanting to reach out and tuck them behind her ear — he thrust his hands into his pockets so he didn't do anything stupid. He didn't want to end up having a complaint filed against him on day one. 'Did you enjoy the day, girls?' he said brightly.

'It was great,' said Olivia. 'Just loved it. Thank you.'

'Yes. It was lovely. Thank you very much.' Kitty's cheeks were flushed, and he wasn't sure if that was from the sun and fresh air or if she was embarrassed.

'See you tomorrow, Logan,' said Olivia. 'And thanks again.'

He watched the women make their way over to their car, then set about locking up the bus and getting it ready for the next day. When he glanced across, he could see Kitty looking back. She raised her hand in a small wave. It was a tiny gesture, but one that made his heart soar. He lifted his hand and waved back.

CHAPTER TWENTY-FIVE

Over the next couple of days, Olivia enjoyed getting to know Kitty a bit more. Although they both made sure to speak to other members of the group, they always seemed to fall into comfortable conversation with each other as they walked. Olivia felt as though she had known Kitty for years, and was glad to hear that Cameron was once again okay. She knew that had played on Kitty's mind after that call as they were hurrying out the door. However, Kitty had told her that Cameron had since reassured his mum. He said he had felt a bit homesick but was over it, and now having a great time. Olivia couldn't even begin to imagine the rollercoaster of emotions that Kitty must go through as a mum, and not having a partner to share it with must make it even harder, despite Kitty saying she knew it no other way. While Cameron insisted he was fine, Kitty's mood had definitely been a bit strange since they started the tour, and Olivia wondered why.

Today they were doing the trail from Brodick through the forest to Lamlash. Logan had promised them it was quite an easy route, and they would stop in Lamlash before heading back.

Olivia was enjoying the peace that the walks and the island provided. It was a calming contrast to life back at home, when she was constantly rehearsing and surrounded by people and noise. She was starting to realise how much she appreciated quiet and stillness and time to think. This trip was giving her a chance to untangle the mess of all her thoughts and make sense of the last couple of months.

She was happy to walk at the back this morning so she could make a point of noticing the wildlife around her, like the magnificent dragonfly that had just flown past. The day had started grey, but now the sun was shining and she looked up at the sky, which was beginning to turn deep blue as the clouds disappeared. Olivia didn't think she would ever get bored of looking at the rich tapestry of colour on the hills, in the water and in the sky.

Kitty was ahead, also on her own, and maybe she was reading too much into it, but she sensed there was something else on Kitty's mind. She had tried to reach out yesterday when they visited the distillery. After hearing about the special source of fresh water from Loch na Davie, which they used for distilling, everyone was keen to sample a dram. They were invited to try the Robert Burns single malt whisky, and Olivia felt rather embarrassed to admit that she had never tried Scotch, or any whisky for that matter.

'You can have it straight like that,' said Kitty. 'Or add a drop of water.'

'I'll follow your lead,' said Olivia. 'What would you recommend?'

'I like it neat.' Kitty took a sip and closed her eyes, appearing to savour the taste.

Olivia put the glass to her lips and swallowed, feeling a pleasant, warm sensation at the back of her throat. She could taste the hints of vanilla and cinnamon and had to admit she rather liked it.

'What do you think?' Logan had walked over to where they were standing at the bar.

'I really like it,' said Olivia in surprise. 'I wasn't expecting that at all.'

He beamed. 'Glad to hear it. How about you, Kitty? Have you tried this one before?' Logan pulled a stool up next to where she stood.

Olivia watched as Kitty shook her head. 'No. I'm not sure why, but I've never had any Arran whiskies. I used to like the ones from Islay. They're quite peaty,' she said to Olivia. 'But it's been a while since I drank whisky . . . I really like this one too. It's very drinkable.'

'It's one of my favourites,' said Logan. 'Though the downside of the job is that I'm driving, so I'll need to wait until later . . .'

'You should to come to the pub with us one night,' suggested Olivia. She didn't miss the pause before Logan replied.

'Sure,' he said casually. 'Maybe on our final night? After we've conquered Goatfell?' He stood up. 'I'll let you finish your drinks in peace.' He strolled over to have a chat to the distillery manager who had shown them round.

'Is everything okay?' Olivia asked, jerking her head towards Logan.

'What do you mean?'

'Just sensing a bit of *something* between you. I noticed you clammed up when he asked you about whiskies.'

Kitty blushed. 'It's all fine. Just brought back a memory.'

'Do you want to talk about it?' asked Olivia gently.

'Och, no. Not at the moment. Thanks though. How about I get us a bottle for the cottage?' Kitty was already walking towards the till, indicating the conversation was over.

Olivia shrugged. 'Sure. Great idea.'

Now as she swung her arms and followed today's trail, she realised she had no right to pry. Not in her position. There was so much she hadn't shared with Kitty or anyone, and she was happy being quite anonymous here, where nobody knew her or what had happened with Patrick. Only her aunt knew the real truth. She was too embarrassed to tell her friends back home, not that she saw a lot of them, which had been another issue. Her world had shrunk, although she was sure some of them had their suspicions.

She took a gulp of the tangy, salty air as she thought about how different her life had been just a few months ago. It seemed surreal to now be walking through a beautiful forest on a Scottish island that she had arrived at less than a week ago. She didn't miss home or *him* at all, but she did miss dancing. It was a really hard career to make a living from, but she had managed it and knew she was one of the lucky ones. Many of her friends hadn't been so successful, ending up with long-term injuries, and their mental health impacted when they couldn't dance. They felt as though they were letting themselves and others down and felt like failures. Olivia was grateful that it was all she had hoped for and more, although she knew it wouldn't last forever.

She watched the Australian couple, Adam and Liz, who were just ahead of her. They had such a natural and loving rapport together, and she felt a pang of envy for something she had never experienced. Even with Patrick, when times were good, she was always on edge, waiting and wondering what would happen next. Even now, though he was thousands of miles away from her, he still managed to be present in her head. A lurking threat that caught her unaware.

'Hey, you,' she said, catching up with Kitty. 'Isn't this amazing?'

'It is,' she admitted. 'It's so lovely to have this time and space, isn't it?'

'I know. I can't believe that we only have one walk left.'

'But the rest of the summer is stretched out ahead of us. And there's still loads more to do and see. I can take you round to Kildonan if you'd like? I think we'll definitely see otters and seals there.'

'I would love that. And I must visit the castle, you know, being American and all. How about you? What else would you like to do with your time?'

Kitty mulled for a while before answering. 'There's that stuff we talked about before, perhaps that art class and yoga. My Instagram, of course. But I fancy some kayaking and, if you're up for that, I can take you? What do you think?'

'I can't paint or draw at all, so I'll leave you to it,' she said weakly, visibly wincing at the thought. 'Kayaking sounds fun though. And I could just keep walking and walking forever,' said Olivia, gesturing ahead. 'Especially when it all looks like this. It's just so peaceful . . .' Her voice trailed away. 'I mean, I guess I should go over to Glasgow at some stage to see my friends from Italy. But I have to admit that the thought of a city just now doesn't appeal. I'd be reluctant to leave this.'

'Maybe you should ask Logan about other tours he's got coming up?' blurted Kitty.

Olivia frowned. 'Do *you* want to do more walking?'

'No, I've probably had my fill for now. I mean, it will be great to do Goatfell, but after that I may need a rest.' She laughed. 'But perhaps you could do his coastal tour later in the summer?'

'I suppose there's no harm in asking him about it. Hey, Logan,' she called over her shoulder. He was keeping an eye on the stragglers at the back.

'Yes, what can I do you for?' He upped his pace to join them.

'What's the deal with your walking tours. When are you back?'

He grinned. 'Are you missing me already?'

'No,' said Olivia, swatting a fly from her cheek. 'I just want to know what other walks I could do.'

'Well . . . when I finish here, I have a few days off, then I head to the mainland for a week or so for a tour to Loch Lomond and the Trossachs. That takes us along the West Highland Way, through woodland not dissimilar to this, and a chance for a boat trip. And for the energetic, the chance to bag a Munro, Ben Lomond.'

'What's a Munro?' asked Olivia.

'It's a mountain that's over three thousand feet,' said Kitty before Logan had a chance to reply.

'Is that what Goatfell is then? Can I say that I've bagged a Munro once we've climbed it?'

'Afraid not,' said Logan. 'It's not quite high enough.'

'Okay, sorry, I digress. After you've done your Lock Lomond trip, where do you go?'

'*Loch*,' said Kitty and Logan at the same time.

Olivia burst out laughing. 'Sorry, sorry, I'm more than aware that I need to work on my pronunciation.'

Logan smiled kindly at her. 'After the *Loch* Lomond trip, then I have a few days off, then I'm back here. Off the top of my head, that's for another trip like this. The coastal path tour is sometime in August. After the Highland Games.'

'Oh,' said Olivia, her interest piqued. 'Highland Games? Like caber tossing and kilt wearing and things like that?'

'Yes, among other things,' said Logan. 'There's also pipe bands, fancy dress, lots of stalls and dancing. *Lots* of dancing. There's usually a huge ceilidh at the end of the night.'

'That's a big social event with lots of traditional Scottish dances. It's a lot of fun,' said Kitty.

'Sounds like my kind of thing,' said Olivia happily. She felt a ripple of excitement, which was an odd sensation, as it had been a while. 'I'm already looking forward to it.'

CHAPTER TWENTY-SIX

It was the final day of their tour. Kitty was glad that she just had one more day to get through before embracing a quieter life. She had loved having fresh air and exercise and the chance to get to know Olivia and the others, but she was starting to crave some space and time off her feet. They were starting to ache from the thousands of steps she'd been doing every day.

As she brushed her teeth, she looked at herself in the mirror. Her face did have a healthy glow about it, and there was a sparkle in her eyes that hadn't been there for some time. If she was being honest, she had been feeling increasingly panicked by the pull she felt between her and Logan. It didn't matter how much she tried to ignore it, she had loved getting to know him these past few days. Yes, she had been careful to keep a bit of a distance and not be overly friendly or flirtatious when talking to him, and she had refrained from sharing much about herself. But trying to maintain that had become increasingly challenging, and she only hoped she could get through one more day without giving him the wrong idea.

There had been several occasions over the past few days when she longed to lay a friendly hand on his shoulder, to touch his arm or reach for his hand. Then she'd caught herself just in time and reminded herself that would be weird. In normal circumstances, Kitty wouldn't think twice about how she interacted with the opposite sex — it had never been an issue. This time was different though. She felt a strong attraction to Logan and genuinely enjoyed his company. He was an uplifting person to be around, and she felt herself relax when talking to him. Then the little whispering voice would appear, telling her not to relax too much or make a fool of herself. She needed some distance from him, and from that voice in her head.

Rinsing her mouth, she pulled her curls back from her forehead and wrapped her hair into a bun. She smeared some sunscreen on her face, chest and arms and pulled on her outfit for the day. Let's face it, that was the easy bit of all of this walking malarkey. You couldn't really overthink what you wore to go climbing, as it had to be fairly practical. Today she wore grey outdoor trousers and a deep-green T-shirt with a long-sleeved fleece tied around her waist — Logan had warned it could be cooler as they reached the summit. The usual obligatory waterproof and extra tops, in case it was super cold, were stuffed in her backpack.

'Olivia,' she called, 'are you up?'

'Yes,' she yelled back from her room. 'I won't be long.'

It was Kitty's turn to make their packed lunch today, and she found a recipe on Instagram the night before for spicy chickpea wraps. She quickly assembled them, wrapped them in tinfoil and added a parcel of homemade flapjacks to each of their lunches. She got some apples from the fridge and then filled up their water bottles.

'That's me, I'm good to go,' said Olivia, stifling a yawn. 'All this exercise is exhausting. A lie-in tomorrow will be nice.' Olivia eyed Kitty suspiciously. 'You look nice today. Not that you don't usually,' she added hastily, 'but there's something about you that looks *different*.' She raised an eyebrow quizzically and smirked.

'I've brushed my hair, that's what it will be,' said Kitty hurriedly, realising she should have left it tied up as usual rather than leaving it to hang loose. 'Come on, we don't want to be late.' She didn't want to admit to Olivia that she *had* actually spent longer doing her hair this morning, and had even dabbed on some lip gloss.

* * *

They were meeting outside Arran Brewery, where the walk would start, and when Kitty saw Logan she felt the same annoying flutter in her stomach she'd been feeling since she first laid eyes on him.

'It's a shame we aren't starting with a beer,' joked Adam.

'Just think how much you'll enjoy it later,' said Logan. 'Where's Liz today?'

'Ah, she has blisters. Really sore too. She didn't want to hold the group back.'

'Oh, that's such a shame,' said Kitty. 'Isn't she disappointed to miss out?'

Adam thought for a minute and shook his head. 'I don't think she's too gutted. She's booked a facial and a manicure at the spa.'

Olivia burst out laughing. 'I like her style.'

Just then Logan's mobile rang. 'Hello,' he said, frowning as he listened. 'Okay. I understand. Thanks for letting me know.'

'Everything okay?' asked Olivia.

'Well, yes and no. Fred and Tom already let me know last night that they didn't fancy Goatfell. They want to see the castle before they leave so they're doing that instead. We were two down anyway. And that was Jill saying she and Richard can't come either. Her knees are bothering her, and Richard is insisting he stays with her.'

'Oh well,' said Adam, clapping his hands together and shrugging. 'We'll just need to crack on with it then. I guess we're the last ones standing.'

Kitty could feel Logan's eyes on her, and she dropped her gaze to the ground. Keeping her distance was going to be almost impossible when there were only the four of them.

'Okay. Well, Adam,' said Olivia, 'I'll walk with you for now, as I want to know more about Sydney. I'll ask you lots of questions while I'm still able to talk. I was there briefly last year on a tour and it's a place I definitely want to go back to.'

Kitty could have throttled her. She knew *exactly* what her friend was up to.

'Do you want to walk with me, Kitty?' asked Logan.

'Sure,' she said, trying to sound as casual as possible. She would be having words with Olivia later.

'The route is well signposted and visibility looks good today. The forecast certainly doesn't suggest otherwise, but as you know things can change rapidly. It *is* Scotland. Adam and Olivia, you lead the way. We're right behind you.'

They soon fell into a comfortable pace, with Adam and Olivia walking briskly ahead.

'I'm sure this won't take as long as it would if the group was bigger,' said Kitty, now struggling to know what to say.

'True. Normally we would keep stopping to give folks a chance to catch up. It does get a bit more challenging near the top with all the scree. But the four of us are fairly fit, so I don't think we should have any problems.'

They walked in silence for a while as they ascended up through woodland. Kitty occasionally stopped to turn around and marvel at the view behind her.

'There is another lovely walk on the island if you and Olivia fancy it while you're here,' said Logan as they approached another sign for Glen Rosa. 'If you follow that it will take you on a circular route through the edge of the forest. You feel as though you're in the middle of the Highlands. And you get great views of Goatfell. Without the huge climb.'

They continued up the path and Kitty found herself starting to relax. 'How long have you been doing this?'

She listened intently as he told her about his time in the Navy and how his love of the outdoors led him to working outside. 'I can't imagine doing anything else,' he said.

'Do you miss having a permanent base?'

He shook his head. 'Not really. I mean, I guess I kind of do have a base. It's just that I'm never there. I have a small, annexed cottage, more of a studio really, next to my sister's house in Perth. I have two older twin sisters. But she, Lucie, has taken to renting it out on Airbnb, as she says I'm never there. I guess she's right and the income is quite handy. If I do want to go back, I usually have to give her lots of advance warning to make sure it's not occupied, which doesn't really work with my erratic planning. So usually I end up staying with her or my other sister, Bridget.'

'That actually sounds quite liberating,' said Kitty. 'Just suiting yourself and having the freedom and courage not to conform to expectations. That's something I've always admired.'

'I suppose it's a bit different for me as I don't have kids,' he said thoughtfully. 'I don't have anyone depending on me. But I do love spending nights in different places, whether it's a cabin in the woods or a youth hostel on one of the islands or even a tent. There's nothing better than waking up next to a waterfall or sleeping under the stars and then sipping coffee under the shelter of the trees.'

Kitty sighed and allowed herself a small smile. He did have a certain way with words that was *very* attractive.

'Don't get me wrong, I usually relish time alone, especially after doing a tour, but at times it can get a bit lonely.' His eyes rested on her. 'How about you? Have you always lived in Rosemarkie?'

Kitty hesitated.

'Sorry, just ignore me if I'm being nosy. You don't have to answer that.'

'It's okay. Yes, to answer your question, I was born and brought up in Inverness, then I moved to Rosemarkie when I got married.'

Logan choked back a cough.

'I've been there ever since.' Kitty looked at him curiously as he snapped a twig he'd been holding.

'It's a great spot,' said Logan. 'Some of our tours in the Highlands are really popular.'

'And do you normally work up there?'

'Yes,' he said. 'There's a tour that runs most of the year, but I usually lead it in the autumn. We meet in Inverness, walk up the north side of Loch Ness and stay in Fort Augustus, then Loch Oich and Glen Tarff, Glen Moriston and the Dundreggan, then finishing up back in Inverness. That's a five-day tour, and that time of year, as you can imagine, the colours are just stunning.'

'It is a beautiful part of the world,' she said. 'I should really try and get out more and explore. It can be too easy to fall into the same old routine.'

'And how did the summer house here come about?' he asked.

'I think you must know my cousin, Fergus, who runs the outdoor centre in Lamlash?'

'I do know Fergus, yes. He's a great guy. Olivia said that there was a bit of miscommunication, which meant you both ended up in the same house?'

'That's right. Though it seems to have worked out okay — so far, fingers crossed.' She told him about her plans for the rest of the summer, and how nice it was to have a break from work.

'I can only imagine how exhausting that must be. I admire you though. Working with little ones can't be easy.'

She smiled. 'It has its moments, but I wanted to work with kids to get away from adults. I was a counsellor for a while,' she explained, 'and then, well, after the pandemic I was exhausted. I needed a break.'

He looked at her, his brow creased in concern. 'That must have been tough.'

She waved her hand dismissively. 'It's been tough for loads of people and still is. Things could *always* be worse.'

'And your son?'

'Yes,' she said unable to stop herself from smiling. 'Cameron. He's eighteen and has just left school. He's off having the time of his life working at a camp near New York.'

'What a brilliant experience. And really great of you to support him to go off and do that.'

'It was tough saying bye, and I really had to hold it together so I didn't upset him, and I do miss him. But I had to let him go. He's got to go off and live his life. It's just always been me and him . . .' She could feel tears well up and was grateful when she felt Logan place a reassuring hand on her arm.

'Tell me about him,' he said gently.

Kitty was thoughtful as she spoke quietly. 'Well, he's taller than me, funny, kind, smart, handsome and one of the nicest kids I know. Clearly, I'm biased. But I'm so proud of him. It's not been easy.'

'Well, I really admire you, Kitty. I see my sisters with their kids and know how challenging it can be, and they both have partners.' He paused. 'I lost my mum when I was younger, and my dad didn't cope at all. It seems like you've done a great job of raising him on your own.'

They had been walking for some time now and the path was getting steeper as they ascended. Adam and Olivia were about a hundred metres ahead of them. 'Thank you,' she said automatically.

'Do you mind me asking about his dad?'

Normally Kitty would feel her hackles rise when she was asked that question, which she had been many, many times over the years. But she didn't think Logan was being nosy. He was looking at her with kind eyes and she could feel a surge of emotion at the back of her throat. Oh God, the last thing she wanted to do now was start crying. 'He . . .'

Logan looked at her in concern. 'Oh, I'm so sorry, Kitty. The last thing I wanted to do was upset you. Please, let's change the subject.' He reached for her hand and squeezed it.

Kitty wanted to lean into him and open up and let all the words and emotions tumble out of her. So much for trying to keep her distance — he made her want to do the opposite. She had never felt so at ease with any man, other than Ryan, and she wanted to tell him what happened. But she was frightened, so instead she managed to give him a grateful smile and squeezed his hand back.

For just a tiny moment, their gaze connected, and Kitty felt a surge of *something* ripple through her. She could have stared into his deep brown eyes forever and didn't want him to drop her hand. She wanted to tell him what happened. She wanted to tell him *everything*, but a high piercing shriek jolted them both back into the here and now.

CHAPTER TWENTY-SEVEN

Usually it didn't take Logan long to gather his thoughts together, but today was different to anything he had experienced before. His head was in a complete jumble. Although he had been back in the flat for a couple of hours, and showered and had something to eat, he felt completely wired. He couldn't get *that* moment with Kitty out of his head, which was then interrupted by an emergency.

* * *

The shriek came from a woman ahead of Olivia and Adam, who had tumbled over on her ankle. Logan always carried a first-aid kit in his backpack. He knelt down beside her, trying his best to calm her down. Her name was Sara and she looked like she had a nasty sprain — no wonder, given that she wasn't wearing supportive walking shoes. She had a pair of flimsy plimsolls on. If she hadn't hurt herself at this stage of the climb, he was certain she would have done it further up, when it would have been harder to get her to safety.

'Sara, I think you've had a shock,' said Kitty, who had squatted down next to her and was speaking in a soothing voice. She reached into her backpack, pulling out a flask of tea. 'Here,' she said. 'Take a sip of this and have something to eat. It will help.'

Logan watched in admiration as Kitty effortlessly unwrapped a flapjack and handed it to Sara, who did as she was told. Kitty spoke to the woman in a calming voice, rubbing her back gently, and soon her sobs started to subside. No wonder she was good with kids, he thought. She was so patient and reassuring.

'What do you think?' asked Adam. 'What should we do?'

'Well, you're not going to be able to go any further today, Sara,' explained Logan. 'So I'll strap you up, and I suggest you head back down if you can and get it seen to properly in the village.' He opened a bandage, took the woman's foot in his hands and started binding it around her ankle. 'Now,' he said when he'd finished, 'do you think you can stand?'

'I don't know,' she said. 'I'll give it a try.' She stood up gingerly and tested her ankle, wincing in pain. 'Ouch!' she cried.

'Did you come out here on your own?' asked Olivia in concern.

'No,' she said, clearly biting back the tears. 'My boyfriend is here, but he said I was walking too slow, so he went on ahead. He said he'd see me at the top.'

'Nice,' said Logan through gritted teeth.

'Aw love,' said Kitty sympathetically. 'You can't possibly try and head back down on your own. Come on, don't worry, we'll help you.'

The woman threw her a grateful look. 'I'm so sorry for ruining your day,' she said with a hiccup. 'I feel so stupid.'

'Don't you worry about that. It's your *boyfriend* who should be apologising for abandoning you,' said Olivia crossly. 'I can't believe he would just leave you on your own. What a *charmer*.'

More tears pooled in Sara's eyes, and Kitty gave her a pat on the shoulder.

Logan couldn't fail to detect the venom in Olivia's voice and quickly realised there was definitely more to it. He wondered if she either knew Sara's boyfriend or was speaking from personal experience. Maybe that was why she'd ended up in Scotland. He pushed the thought aside and looked to Kitty, who frowned at him as though she sensed the same thing.

'Look, why don't you two go ahead?' said Kitty, looking to Adam and then him, smoothly pointing up to the summit. 'Adam has come all this way and it would be a shame for him to miss out.'

'I don't mind,' said Adam reluctantly.

'It's fine. Olivia and I can do this another time. You're here from Australia, you must make the most of your trip. Aside from that, I don't think your wife will thank you if you reappear early and ruin her spa time.' Her words were met with a peel of laughter.

'True,' he said. 'You know her well.'

'Let Olivia and I focus on helping Sara back down the hill.' Turning her attention to Sara, Kitty said encouragingly, 'Now, if you lean on us both, do you think you can manage?'

Sara bit her lip and took a small step forward. 'Yes,' she said through gritted teeth. 'If we take it slow, with your help I'm sure I'll make it down.'

'And if you're really lucky, I might even treat you to a song or two,' said Kitty.

Olivia groaned. 'Oh great.'

'Okay, guys,' said Kitty brightly. 'You two get going. On you go. Take care and don't fall over, unless you want Olivia and I to come to the rescue. I guess we'll see you at the pub later for a drink.'

Logan held her gaze. 'That's a promise. Take your time getting down. Be careful.'

'You too,' said Kitty.

He was so impressed at how calm and focused she was in a crisis. Her kindness and compassion towards Sara also made him want to reach out and hug her. But his thoughts were interrupted by Olivia.

'And if you see her boyfriend up there, then be sure to shove him over,' she said. 'Hard.'

Logan was relieved Kitty was taking Olivia in the opposite direction to Sara's boyfriend. The thought of trying to diffuse that situation did not appeal. Olivia could be terrifying.

'Come on, Sara,' said Kitty, who was clearly trying to distract her from Olivia's rant. 'Let's get going. See you guys.'

'All right,' said Sara.

Kitty sniggered and started singing the chorus of a Supergrass song. 'Oh dear. Well, you did say, "All right," Sara.'

Logan watched the trio of women start to make their way back down the slope . . . while Kitty belted out the song and Olivia shook her head. What on earth was that about?

* * *

It was now just after eight and Logan stood in the pub with Adam and Liz. It had been a very long day and they had reached the summit, much to Adam's delight.

'Never before has a beer tasted so good,' Logan said as he clinked his glass against Adam's and Liz's.

'I wonder how the girls got on with that woman.' Adam had filled Liz in on the drama from earlier, and how Kitty and Olivia had gone to Sara's rescue.

'Well, Kitty sent me a text message to let me know she was okay, and they made it down. She and Olivia should be here any minute. That's if Olivia isn't trying to track the boyfriend down,' he said wryly.

'Ah, there they are,' said Adam as Kitty and Olivia strolled into the bar.

They clapped as the women neared them. 'You two saved the day,' said Logan. He couldn't take his eyes off Kitty. She wore jeans, a simple yellow top and her hair hung loose around her shoulders. She was beautiful.

'It was nothing, we just chummed her down the path and kept her entertained with some singing. I think you might have helped though with your expert bandaging,' she said.

'I just wish she'd been wearing the proper gear, then it wouldn't have happened. Honestly, the number of times I pass people wearing flip-flops and flimsy summer clothes. It drives me mad,' admitted Logan.

'It wouldn't have happened if her dickhead of a boyfriend hadn't abandoned her,' said Olivia darkly.

'Glass of wine?' asked Logan. 'I think you deserve it.'

'Please,' said Olivia. 'In fact, make it a bottle. Kitty, would you like wine too?'

Kitty nodded, looking a bit concerned by Olivia's mood, which seemed to have declined since that afternoon. 'So how was the climb then, Adam?'

'Tougher than I thought,' he admitted. 'But I'm glad I did it.'

'And how are your blisters, Liz?'

'They were bloody sore. I mean, I could hardly make it to breakfast this morning, never mind hiking up Goatfell. I am sorry, as I was looking forward to it,' she said, before adding, 'but not too sorry as I had a lovely time in the spa.' She spread her hands out and showed her fuchsia-painted nails.

'Very nice,' said Olivia, taking a gulp of wine and quickly draining her glass.

Logan caught Kitty looking at her quizzically.

'What's next for you then?' asked Kitty to Liz and Adam.

'Well, after this, we're off for some dinner at the hotel. In fact, we'd better watch our time, love, so we make our reservation,' Adam said. 'Tomorrow, we leave to get the ferry back to the mainland, then we're off to Inverness.'

'Oh, wonderful,' said Kitty. 'Have you been there before?'

'No,' said Liz. 'Have you any pointers?'

'I do indeed. I live very close. Just about a half-hour drive, in fact — in Rosemarkie, on the Black Isle.'

'Isn't that where you can see dolphins?' asked Liz.

Kitty smiled. 'Yes, it's near Chanonry Point, which is halfway between Rosemarkie and Fortrose. If you're lucky you'll see bottlenose dolphins, but you need to check the tide times to make sure that it's not a wasted journey. The best time to arrive and wait is from low tide.'

'Great, thanks for that tip. We'll definitely need to remember that, Adam. Where else do you recommend?'

'Why don't I make you a wee list?' Kitty quickly jotted down a few suggestions on a piece of paper, and Liz tucked it away in her bag.

'It's been so lovely meeting you all,' said Adam. 'Thank you, Logan, for being such a great guide. I thoroughly enjoyed today and hearing a bit more about your work too.' He glanced at his watch. 'That's us off then.'

'Thanks again, everyone,' Liz said. 'Take care and enjoy the rest of your summer.'

Logan, Kitty and Olivia chorused their goodbyes before Olivia disappeared into the ladies.

'What a day, eh?' And although it was the very last thing Logan wanted to be saying to Kitty, he said, 'I hope I'm not speaking out of turn, but I think it might be a good idea to get Olivia home?' He added softly, 'She's just about finished that bottle of wine and doesn't seem to be in very good spirits.'

'Oh no,' said Kitty. 'I didn't realise she was drinking it so fast, and she had a couple of whiskies too before we came out. She insisted she would just have the one, but I suspect she's had more. Thank God I made her eat some dinner first.'

'I think it may be better if you suggest it rather than me,' said Logan. 'I get the feeling that she has some beef with the opposite sex today.'

'I would agree with you. I had to suggest she dial it down a bit with Sara. She was telling her to ditch the boyfriend and that he was a useless lump, or words to that effect. And she pointed out in no uncertain terms that if he left her stranded on a mountain, at this stage in their relationship, then think what would happen if the going really got tough.'

'Ouch,' winced Logan.

'Yip. I think the poor woman's ankle was the least of her worries by the time we left her.'

Just then, Olivia stumbled out of the ladies and walked towards them. 'I'm tired,' she slurred. 'Do you mind if I go home?'

Kitty's shoulders slumped with relief. 'No, of course not. Come on, let's head back to the cottage.'

'S'okay. You don't have to come. You can stay here with him,' she said, pointing at Logan. 'Have some fun. You deserve to have a wild night out.'

'Come on,' Kitty said gently. 'Let's go back and have a nice cup of tea together. I'm tired too. It's been a long day.'

'Just stay,' Olivia tried to insist. 'I can manage to get back on my own. I'm not a child.'

Logan begged to differ. At this moment in time she looked young and vulnerable. There was no way he was letting either of the women walk home alone, especially when Olivia was so inebriated. 'That's okay. I'll walk you home,' said Logan, looking at Kitty. 'It's been quite the day for everyone. I need my beauty sleep too.' He stifled a yawn.

He gave Kitty an apologetic smile. What he really wanted to do, *once again*, was to reach out and pull her close to him. But the timing really wasn't great. *Again*. He couldn't help but think a trend was starting to emerge here. And it was the final day of the tour. It was fair to say that it hadn't ended in the way that he'd hoped it might.

Olivia began to walk towards the door and Kitty and Logan followed behind, trailing along the road that would then lead them up the steep hill to Lilybank Cottage. It was a warm and light summer's evening, and the water gently lapped the bay as they followed the path along the road.

'When is it you head off to your next tour?' asked Kitty.

'I have a couple of days here and then go to the mainland on Wednesday . . .'

'Right,' she said, keeping her eyes fixed ahead on Olivia.

'Have you seen her like this before?' he said under his breath.

'No, and I'm a bit worried about her. What happened today seemed to trigger something.'

'Yes, I noticed that too,' he said. 'I suppose she'll tell you if and when she's ready.'

Kitty nodded solemnly, and he could tell her mind was elsewhere, as she frowned after Olivia.

He wanted to say something, *anything*, but what? When Olivia started to walk haphazardly across the road, they both flanked her and linked arms on either side.

'Sorry. I'm so sorry about this,' she said.

'That's okay. It will all feel better in the morning,' said Kitty, her tone light.

Before long they had reached Lilybank Cottage, by which time Olivia had started to cry. Loud, gut-wrenching sobs that made her shoulders shudder.

'Will you be okay?' Logan asked Kitty, quietly.

Kitty nodded. 'It's probably better that you go now and I sort her out. But thank you,' she said, touching his arm. 'For everything.'

'Look, why don't I text you tomorrow,' he said hurriedly. 'Maybe . . . you would like to have a coffee or a drink or something. Before I go?'

Kitty smiled shyly and nodded. 'Yes, that sounds nice. I would like that, Logan. Thanks again.' She reached up and briefly kissed him on the cheek.

'Goodnight, Kitty,' he said as she turned away and helped Olivia through the front door. He stood for a moment, enjoying the scent of lavender that lingered in the air, smiling as he felt the warmth of her soft lips that still lingered on his cheek. He was over the moon that she had said yes! What a day, indeed.

CHAPTER TWENTY-EIGHT

When Olivia opened her eyes the next morning, she immediately felt a sense of dread wash over her. She could vaguely remember going to bed with Kitty's help. She knew that she had drunk far too much. The inside of her mouth felt furry, and she reached to take a sip from the glass of water Kitty must have left at the side of her bed. What an angel she was. Her head throbbed so hard that she had to close her eyes again. There was a swirl of nausea in her stomach.

Worst of all was that her anxiety was back with a vengeance. She thought she'd managed to get it under control these past few weeks since leaving home. She'd felt so much better about things, probably because she was in control and didn't feel so scared. But she knew that last night's drinking spree would have sent her body's cortisol levels soaring. Now her body was overly stressed *again*, and she just wanted to bury herself under the covers and hide.

If only she could rewind the clock. If only they hadn't gone to the rescue of that woman who hurt her ankle on the hill. If only she hadn't started to let her anger get the better of her, and started mouthing off about the woman's terrible boyfriend. If only, if only . . . There was no point raking over it. What was done was done, and she would have to face Kitty and Logan at some point, and apologise and explain. They must think she was mad.

She tossed and turned for a while but couldn't get back to sleep. Instead she threw the covers back and slowly swung her legs round, sitting for a moment on the edge of the bed. Then she took a cold shower, which helped wake her up a bit, pulled on some fresh clothes and went to find Kitty, who was enjoying an al fresco breakfast.

'Hey, you, how are you feeling?' asked Kitty, looking up.

'A bit yuck,' admitted Olivia. She pulled a chair out from the table.

'Can I get you a coffee? Or a peppermint tea?' Kitty stood up.

'A peppermint tea would be great, thanks. I'm feeling a bit fragile this morning. Sorry, Kitty, I don't want to interrupt your breakfast.'

'I'm all done, don't worry.'

'I'm so sorry if I did or said anything to offend you or upset you.'

'You didn't,' said Kitty. 'Let me sort your tea out for you and then we can talk. If you want to, of course.'

'Thank you,' said Olivia gratefully. While she waited for Kitty to make her tea, she watched the bees buzzing in and out of the lavender plants that bordered the lawn. They were mesmerising to watch, and she found her breathing slow down as she gazed at them, listening to them busy themselves with their work.

'Here you go.' Kitty placed a mug in front of her. 'And some toast too, just in case you feel up to it.'

'Great,' said Olivia. 'I feel terrible. I am sorry.'

'No need to keep apologising,' said Kitty, dismissing her comments with a wave of her hand. 'We've all been there. But I do worry about you. I know we don't know each other that well, but you were drinking a lot last night and, well, you just seemed so *angry*.'

Olivia was mortified.

'It's okay,' Kitty said. 'I just wondered if there's something on your mind.'

Olivia clutched her head in her hands and groaned. 'There's so much going on and I feel as though my brain's about to explode.'

'Look, why don't you have your tea? I'm here if you want to chat, but please don't feel you need to.'

Olivia spread some butter on a piece of toast, closed her eyes and bit into it, enjoying the salty taste of the warm bread. She didn't feel under any pressure to share anything with Kitty, but the difference was that she wanted to. She felt at ease in her company, and she actually *trusted* her, which was a lot for Olivia to admit.

Taking a sip of tea, she looked at Kitty thoughtfully. 'I'm sure you must have noticed how annoyed I got when I heard that woman's boyfriend had walked away and left her. I just get so *angry* when I hear how men get away with treating their partners. It's so frustrating.' She looked at Kitty sitting opposite, her hands clutched around a mug. Kitty didn't say anything, but instead gave her a reassuring nod.

'I get so angry because I can see myself in these women. The people pleaser. The woman who thinks she can make a difference to her rogue man. The woman who's too embarrassed to admit her partner's a bully, because somehow she thinks that it's her fault.' She paused to reach into her pocket for a tissue, and noisily blew her nose. 'That's me,' she said to Kitty. 'I'm all of these and more. Not so long ago I was that woman from yesterday. Sara. I was the one who was afraid to speak out because I didn't want to criticise my boyfriend. I thought his behaviour was normal and that it was all my fault.' She had another drink from her mug. 'My self-esteem was in shreds, and it was all thanks to my ex.'

'Is that Patrick?' asked Kitty.

'Yes,' she said in surprise. 'How did you know?'

'You mentioned his name a few times last night when I was helping you get into bed.'

Olivia raised her eyebrow. 'Oh dear.'

'Don't worry, you didn't really allude to much. I just got the impression he wasn't your favourite person.'

'That would be right,' admitted Olivia. 'I guess when I see others in the same position I was in, I get angry because I want them to be braver than I was. I want them to wake up and run and get out of there — before it's too late.'

Kitty stood up and walked round to sit beside Olivia. 'What you've told me is really brave. I know it's not easy. I'm so sorry that you've been through all of that.'

Olivia twirled a strand of hair in one hand. 'I'm not sure it ever ends. I mean, I felt so much better after my trip to Italy. I started to get a bit of perspective, you know? And then coming here really did feel like a fresh start. But then I was stupid enough to check my voicemails the other night in the pub. He left several abusive messages on my phone, asking who I thought I was and where the hell was I. I couldn't think straight, so I ran from the pub and realised I'd left my bag behind. Poor Logan, I'm afraid he incurred my wrath that night.'

'You haven't done anything wrong, Olivia. Nothing at all.'

Olivia was unable to speak, but she nodded her head gratefully at Kitty. She sipped her tea, then took a bite of toast and chewed thoughtfully for a minute. 'I thought I was getting there, Kitty,' she whispered. 'But it feels like I'm back *there* and at my most vulnerable. Yesterday scared me. If I had come across that boyfriend of Sara's, I'm worried about what I might have done to him.'

'But you don't need to worry about that. You didn't come across him. You helped a vulnerable young woman and made her feel seen, and you just never know. Maybe she'll find the courage to leave her boyfriend thanks to your pep talk.'

Olivia nodded gratefully. 'I'm just so sorry about all of it, especially last night. I really hope I didn't create too much of a scene.'

'You were fine,' Kitty said. 'Even Logan came to check you got home safely.'

She groaned and sunk lower into her seat. 'I'll get in touch later with him to apologise. And thank you. I don't know if you'll ever realise what you've done for me. I can't even begin to tell you how much I appreciate it, and you and Logan making sure I got home safely.'

Kitty shrugged. 'That's what friends are for.'

Olivia sat for a minute, wondering if she should open up and tell her just how frightened of Patrick she was and how that had triggered yesterday's downward spiral. Sharing this story was not going to be easy, yet somehow she felt that Kitty was the right person to tell it too. 'The truth is that I had to leave Patrick. Because . . . I have no doubt that if I hadn't run when I did, I wouldn't be here.'

'What do you mean when you say that you wouldn't be here?' asked Kitty gently.

Olivia steepled her hands together and stared at Kitty. 'Just that. If I hadn't run when I did, I would be dead. I really think that Patrick would have killed me.'

CHAPTER TWENTY-NINE

Kitty could see the hesitation in Olivia's eyes, and she didn't break her gaze. Instead she just nodded gently and waited.

'When I met him, about five years ago, he was very charming and smooth and I fell for him hook, line and sinker. He was a really successful dancer, handsome, and the sort of person that people would just be drawn to when he walked into a room. Everyone loved him. It was hard not to. We were friends at first and I looked up to him. He was almost like a mentor to me. I suppose, looking back, it was all too good to be true. Hindsight's handy, isn't it?'

Kitty nodded and chewed her bottom lip as she waited for Olivia to continue.

'We had an amazing time together at the start, but then I began to notice things . . .' She hesitated, dropping her eyes to the ground.

'What kind of things did you notice?' asked Kitty.

Olivia lifted her hand to demonstrate. 'He would squeeze me on the arm, hard, especially when we were out in public together and I didn't do as he said. Or if I said something he deemed to be inappropriate. Then he started to monitor what I ate, especially in the lead up to a tour. He had no hesitation about telling me that I was starting to look a bit porky and that my costumes wouldn't fit me. At the time I thought he was being caring, and now of course I realise he was being controlling. It wasn't coming from a loving place.' She sighed.

Kitty knew she had to hide the shock she felt at what Olivia was sharing with her. She tried to remain grounded, keeping her eyes on Olivia's.

'And then there was the money. He kept insisting that we have a joint account together, and I gave in as he went on and on about it constantly. I thought it was because he cared. And he was so charming. I was in love, so I just went along with it. Although I'm so glad that I kept my own bank account too. I didn't tell him that. That's about the only sane thing that I did when I was with him. And I'm so grateful, otherwise I'd never have got away. He has everyone fooled. There was no way I could tell anyone. They would accuse me of being crazy.' She twirled her finger around in the air and rolled her eyes. 'People would tell me all the time how lucky I was to have him as my partner. But behind closed doors he completely changed, and the mask slipped. If a friend called me, he would get jealous. When I was out, he would call my cell phone incessantly. Hundreds and hundreds of times a day. It all got too much, so I started to withdraw from my social circle.' She stopped to wipe away a tear. 'You must think I'm so stupid.'

'I don't at all,' said Kitty. 'It's classic abusive behaviour from a narcissist. And you don't realise it when you're in that space. You think you're going mad.'

Olivia threw her such a look of relief that it was impossible for Kitty not to reach over and draw her into a hug.

'That's it, exactly. I thought I was going crazy. I kept thinking it was all my fault and that I needed to fix it. I was embarrassed to tell anyone, and I felt so alone. I just didn't think my friends would believe me.'

'What changed?' asked Kitty.

She smiled sadly. 'Aunt Trudy was in town, and I was due to see her for lunch the next day. Patrick was also going away the following night for work. He insisted that I should spend the whole day with him, and if I loved him I would put *him* before my aunt. He said he didn't like Trudy and she didn't have my best interests at heart and that I shouldn't go. Of course, I made the mistake of arguing back. I adore my aunt and she has always been my greatest supporter and I will always defend her. She lives in California, and I don't get to see much of her anyway. There was no way I wasn't going to go and meet her when she was in the neighbourhood.'

'What happened?'

'He said if I went out to meet her then it was a sign that I didn't love him. I told him to grow up and that I'd had enough. Then he lost his temper and tried to take my phone off me and my keys . . . then . . .' Her voice trailed away as she choked back a sob of emotion.

'It's okay. Just take your time,' said Kitty. 'You're doing really well.'

'He pushed me down on the bed and he tried to . . . he tried to smother me with a pillow. It was like a red mist had descended and he wasn't actually there. It was as though something else had taken over his body. Does that make sense?'

Kitty nodded. 'And what happened? How did you get away?'

'I really thought that was it. I believed I was going to die. I was screaming and kicking and then the fight went out of me. I thought it was too late and that was my end. That was when he suddenly stopped and got off me. He apologised profusely. Over and over, he kept saying that he was sorry and that he didn't mean to hurt me. But I know he did. I couldn't breathe,' she said, her eyes glazing over. 'At that point I knew I had to get away. I asked him to give me some space, and he packed his things and went to stay with a friend. I said we would talk when he was back from his work trip in a few days' time. But the next day I told my aunt what had happened. Just knowing that he was away gave me space to think and plan. Trudy was great and, as I talked to her, I realised if I didn't go he would kill me. Or I would end up killing myself.'

Kitty felt anger and sadness wash over her. She couldn't quite believe what she was hearing.

'Trudy helped me pack up my stuff that day and move it into storage. I booked the first flight I could and that was it. I left with no idea what I would do next other than to have some time away where I could think clearly.'

'No wonder he was angry,' said Kitty with a shudder. 'What you did was very brave, but also very risky.'

'I know, and I still can't quite believe I found the strength to do it. I keep thinking he'll find me, I'm still petrified at the thought . . . Yet despite that, it was so hard to walk away from him. I felt like such a failure.'

Kitty nodded understandingly. 'There's a real sense of shame around it, isn't there?'

'Yes, I feel so embarrassed about it all. Despite what happened, I feel ashamed.'

'You shouldn't feel like that. This could happen to anyone. But what you're feeling is normal.'

'Is it?'

Kitty nodded.

'But how do you know?'

'Remember I told you I was a counsellor?'

'Of course. I forgot that I'm talking to a pro.'

'I'm not sure about that,' she said kindly. 'But I did support several women affected by domestic abuse in my time as a counsellor. And what you're describing is very common.'

'I guess that makes me feel a bit better, knowing that I'm not alone, but sad that it's so common.'

'I agree,' said Kitty softly.

Olivia swatted a fly away. 'Thanks for listening, Kitty. It's hard to talk about but I do feel better. It feels like a weight has been lifted off my shoulders.'

'Well, for what it's worth, I think you're amazing and so brave to have left and to have travelled halfway across the world.'

'I know. Who would have thought I would have ended up here, with you? I'm so grateful.'

'Me too,' said Kitty.

Olivia groaned. 'I think I'll take a couple of headache tablets and go back to bed for a while. All the walking and talking and alcohol has left me a bit jaded.'

'Of course. You've had an emotional time. You must be exhausted. Go rest, and shout if you need me.'

Olivia reached over to hug her tightly. 'Thank you.' She gathered her dishes together and made to leave the table.

'Leave them, I'll sort it,' said Kitty.

'It's fine. I need to try and salvage my reputation as a housemate. I don't want you thinking that I'm slovenly as well.' She gave a thin laugh.

Kitty smiled and watched as she disappeared back into the house. Kitty's head was a tumble of feelings and emotions as she began processing all that Olivia had told her. She couldn't quite get her head around the awful trauma Olivia had been through. What a nightmare. She wasn't sure what would come next for her friend, but she was glad she'd found her way to Arran. At least she would be safe here until she sorted out the next steps.

CHAPTER THIRTY

Logan picked up his phone and put it down again. Was it too early to text Kitty to suggest meeting up? Should he wait until later in the day? If he texted her now, would she think he was too keen? He was horrified at how nervous and fidgety he had become. It was like he'd regressed to being a teenage boy again. Or maybe he should just call her? But what should he say? 'Hey there,' he said out loud. 'How are you? How about a drink?' He could actually feel a wobble in his voice as he spoke the words, and he cleared his throat, quite horrified. He was a jabbering mess. What was going on with him? He never ever lost his cool. It just didn't happen.

The truth was that he hadn't been able to take his eyes off Kitty since the moment he'd seen her at the bakery. There was something about her that was spellbinding. Not only was she beautiful, but she was intelligent and kind and very funny. He was just relieved that he had managed to keep his professional head in place during the tour. It would have been awful if he had come across as a creepy tour guide who chatted up the customers.

Kitty had got under Logan's skin in a way that nobody else had before. He now had a bit more of an inkling as to how James might feel about Amy. James! Of course. He would know what to do. He would go and grab a coffee at the distillery café and see if James was free for a break. At the very least he needed to get out the flat and move, otherwise his head would explode.

'Everything okay, buddy?' James asked when Logan walked in.

'Yes, just fancied a proper coffee rather than the instant rubbish in your flat,' he joked. 'Have you got time to join me?'

James glanced at the clock on the wall. 'No bother. The next tour won't start for another hour or so.' He glanced over to his colleague at reception. 'I'll just be in the café. Shout if you need me.'

Logan followed James across the lobby and towards the café, where they ordered their drinks and took them to a table by the huge floor-to-ceiling windows.

'Not bad a view, is it?' said James.

'Not bad at all.'

'How's things then? How did the tour go?'

'Aye, it was fine,' Logan said, wrapping his hands around the mug in front of him. 'They were a nice bunch. No tricky customers, although a few called off Goatfell yesterday.'

'Any nice women?' asked James suggestively, as he always did every time Logan finished a tour. There was a silence and Logan didn't respond, which caused James to give a low whistle. 'Okay, mate. Tell me what's going on. You're acting weird.'

'See when you started dating Amy . . .' started Logan.

'Don't try and change the conversation,' said James, laughing.

'I'm not. Honest. I just . . . Oh, this is tougher than I thought. I thought talking to you might help, but now I'm not so sure. You're not being particularly helpful.'

James leaned towards him, both elbows on the table and his hands clasped together. He narrowed his eyes. 'Is there something you want to share, Logan?'

'Um, yes. Well, kind of.' He knew that James was enjoying every minute of watching him squirm. 'There's this woman . . .'

James smirked. 'Oh, how I have waited and waited to hear you say these words.'

Logan felt the blood rush to his cheeks and he gulped some coffee. 'You're really not helping. I'm trying to have a deep and meaningful and you're taking the piss.'

James held up his hands in apology. 'You're right. I'm sorry. Please continue. Tell me about the woman . . .' He winked.

'Okay. Well, I'll admit it, when you started dating Amy again, I thought you'd lost the plot. You just seemed so . . . smitten.'

'I was,' said James dreamily. 'And still am.'

'Right, well, now I think I'm getting a bit of an inkling as to how you felt.'

'Whoa,' said James in shock. 'Can I record this?'

Logan threw him a look.

'What's her name? Start with the basics.'

'Her name is Kitty, and she's staying at Lilybank Cottage.'

James's eyes widened in surprise. 'One of the women that Amy told me about in the shock house share?'

'Yes. She's called Kitty and she's . . . well, she's smart and funny and kind and beautiful and . . . I can't stop thinking about her. There you go, I've laid my soul bare.' Logan shook his head, not quite believing what a mess he was and how on earth he could be uttering these words. 'Please be gentle with me.' He leaned back in his seat.

'This is a *very* unexpected turn of events,' said James, looking so very pleased with himself. 'I mean, I thought you were the eternal bachelor. But this, my friend, sounds like you're *falling in love*.'

'Don't be daft,' said Logan unconvincingly. 'It's early days . . .'

'What's the problem then? Is your love unrequited?'

Logan shook his head in frustration. 'James, will you be serious for just a minute, please?'

'Okay, I'm sorry. I'm all ears.'

'There's definitely something there, and there was almost a moment last night after we left the pub . . . but we had to get her housemate home. That's another story. But I'm leaving the day after next to do the Loch Lomond tour and . . .'

'You're wondering what to do because you're a nomad? And because it's been a while since you asked a woman out?' suggested James.

Logan nodded. 'I told her that I'm back in Arran a couple of times over the summer. But I don't know if that's enough.'

'Enough?' said James questioningly. 'Do you mean for her or for you?'

'I don't know,' admitted Logan. 'Maybe me.'

'Look, one step at a time. How were things left last night?'

'Well, I said I would get in touch so we could meet for a coffee or a drink before I leave.'

'And have you done that yet?'

Logan shrugged. 'I don't know what to say.'

James shook his head in exasperation. 'I can't believe you're sitting here telling me this. You must have it bad, buddy. I'm assuming you have her number?'

Logan nodded.

'Just say something along the lines of, *Are you free later for a drink? Or tomorrow if that's easier for you?* Then the ball is in her court.'

Logan took a deep breath and stood up. 'Okay.' Then he abruptly sat down again. 'Do you mean now?'

'Why not?' said James. 'No time like the present. And let me wage a bet that, if she is keen, she'll have replied by the time you've finished your coffee with me.'

Reluctant to wait any longer, Logan quickly typed out a message.

Hey, Kitty. Hope you're okay and Olivia's head isn't too sore this morning. About that drink. How about later tonight? Or tomorrow if that would work better for you? Logan

'Do I add a kiss? Or an emoji?' he asked James. 'How do you normally sign off texts?'

'Just with my name.'

'Stick with that then. Don't start going all weird already. Save that for later.' James couldn't stop himself from chuckling.

'I know, I know, you'll have a field day with all of this.' Logan pressed send and then put his phone down on the table next to him.

'It's a good thing you've got so many tours planned here this summer,' said James. 'Otherwise, can you imagine what state you'd be in?'

Logan took another sip of coffee, his eyes flitting between James and his phone. 'Did I mention that her cousin is Fergus?'

'Fergus in Lamlash? What a small world. Well, he's a great guy, so based on that we can assume that this Kitty is a good woman. So you better not mess this up.'

Logan nodded, his stomach a knot of tension. He just hoped she was the type to send a rapid response and not leave him hanging. 'Sorry, mate. I'm not being a very good friend. I've not even asked how you're doing? How is work and how is Amy?'

'Great,' he said with a beam. 'We've just booked a holiday to Crete in September. I think we'll both need it by then. She's had a lot on with the building works and her dad and—'

Logan's phone buzzed on the table next to him, making him jump. He held his breath as he picked it up and read the message.

'Is it from her?' asked James.

Logan nodded.

'What did she say?'

He looked up and grinned. 'She said yes. She said a drink tonight would be great.'

'Thank the Lord,' said James, holding his hand up to high-five Logan. 'Now you just need to spend the next eight hours worrying about what to wear.'

CHAPTER THIRTY-ONE

Kitty's finger hovered over the send button.

I'm sorry but something has come up. I need to cancel. Kitty.

But she deleted the message, before typing out another.

Do you mind if we cancel? I can't do this. Kitty x

'Aargh,' she wailed in frustration and deleted that one too. It was far too dramatic. It was the fourth time that afternoon she had written a message to cancel their date, if it even was that, but she couldn't quite bring herself to press send and cancel her plans to see Logan.

The truth was that she was desperate to see him. Despite that, she had spent the last hour staring out the window in a complete tizz about what to do. She kept trying to reason with herself that it was no big deal, that they were only going for a drink. But her stomach was fizzing with nerves, especially when the other voice in her head kept asking if she really wanted to do this. But she felt as though there were invisible threads pulling her and Logan together despite her attempts to resist.

'Everything okay?' Olivia walked into the lounge, rubbing her eyes.

'Mmm, yeah, sure. How are you feeling?'

'Much better after a nap. And for talking it through with you. You're a good listener.'

'Thanks. If only I could listen to my own advice.'

Olivia plonked herself down on the chaise longue by the window, stretching her legs out along it. 'How about you talk to me. What's up?'

Kitty sighed while she considered Olivia's offer. She had thought about calling Ellen back home, but she didn't want to make this into some big drama. Ellen tended to embellish things and, before she knew it, half her village would think she'd hooked up with the first available man she'd bumped into once Cameron had flown the nest. Maybe she was being a bit unkind, but she wanted to keep this all as low-key as possible.

And sometimes it was easier to talk to people who didn't know that much about your past. It did help that she'd told Olivia a bit about what had happened to Ryan, which may help her understand why she was reluctant yet also desperate to go on the date. 'If you don't mind, that may not be a bad idea. I'm driving myself mad with all my pros and cons as to what to do.'

'Okay, shoot,' Olivia said, crunching into an apple she had grabbed from the fruit bowl on the coffee table.

'It's Logan.'

She smiled and raised an eyebrow. 'Uh-huh? What about him?'

'He's asked me out for a drink.'

Olivia slapped her hand on her thigh. 'I *knew* it!'

'Knew what?' said a confused Kitty. 'I don't think you were in much of a state to notice anything last night.'

Olivia squealed. 'Not last night, though park that for a minute, we'll come back to that. I mean, I knew something was going on.'

'Olivia, nothing has been *going on*,' insisted Kitty, her voice going up a pitch.

'I think you're protesting a bit much. I could tell that sparks were flying between you at the falls that day. Then yesterday — well, my friend, you could practically slice the sexual tension between you with a knife. It's just a shame that Sara fell over and hurt her ankle. Otherwise you could have had your first kiss at the top of Goatfell.' She beamed, clearly pleased that she had seen what Kitty had been desperately trying to ignore.

'Hardly,' said Kitty. 'I'm not saying that there wasn't perhaps a wee frisson of *something* that first day. But I really tried to pull back.'

'Why?' asked Olivia, frowning.

'Because I don't want to get involved with anyone.'

Olivia hesitated before swinging her legs round and putting her feet on the floor to face Kitty. 'But why?'

'Because,' said Kitty, 'the way I feel reminds me of when I met my husband, Ryan.'

'Oh wow,' said Olivia. 'You have got it bad for this guy then?'

'Well, I wouldn't say that exactly . . . but I can't face having to deal with any heartache.'

'Hey,' said Olivia gently. 'This is just a drink between friends. You don't have to marry the guy. Just think of it as a new adventure and a new friend. But, for what it's worth, I think if you don't go, Kitty, you'll regret it.'

Kitty knew she was right.

'Does he know about Ryan?' Olivia asked, her face wincing in sympathy.

'No. It's not exactly one to throw into a casual chat, is it?'

'I get that,' said Olivia. 'But it's part of you and your life and your story.'

'I know.'

'What would you say if the roles were reversed, and I was asking you what to do?'

'Oh, you are good at this, Olivia, I'll give you that. I would say just go along and enjoy the moment. And be yourself.'

'What else?' said Olivia encouragingly.

'It's not a lifetime commitment. And I would also say, what have you got to lose?'

'Case closed,' said Olivia. 'Now, what are you going to wear?'

* * *

158

A few hours later, Kitty decided to take the long route to the pub — along Fisherman's Walk, which skirted the beach and the sea. Despite Olivia's suggestion to lend her several floaty dresses, she declined. She would have felt out of place in chiffon, and it was important to her that she was comfortable and felt like herself. That's all she could be. She'd let her hair hang loose over her shoulders and decided on her faded grey jeans and green Converse trainers, a white sleeveless T-shirt and lots of chunky bracelets. Then she had applied a touch of lip gloss and sprayed herself lightly with perfume. She threw a light cardigan and a brolly into her bag, in case the weather changed later.

'You look great,' said Olivia, giving a low whistle. Olivia was wearing her pyjamas and had just taken a pizza from the oven. 'Think you're going to have a more exciting night than me,' she said wryly.

Kitty was just glad that Olivia seemed a bit brighter and more like herself after the emotional outpouring earlier.

'Don't do anything I wouldn't do,' called Olivia. 'In fact, please just forget that I actually said that out loud. I'm not exactly one to be doling out relationship advice.'

Kitty had laughed and hugged her friend. 'Thank you. I'll see you later.'

Now, as she made her way along the boardwalk, she inhaled the coconut scent from the yellow gorse bushes and watched the ducks bobbing about in the water, keeping their distance from a couple of huge swans that were elegantly gliding through the sea. The water was still tonight, and there were a couple of paddleboarders out making the most of the flat conditions.

Although she was nervous, she realised she was also excited about seeing Logan. She just hoped that things wouldn't be too weird when they met. It wasn't the first date she'd had since Ryan, there had been a few disastrous meetings since then, and the memories made her shudder. They had completely put her off dating. Focusing on bringing up Cameron had been her priority. This somehow felt different. It was something that she was looking forward to. She just hoped they would slip into their easy banter when they met, and things wouldn't be awkward because they were on *a kind of date*, if that's what this even was. Think of it as a drink between friends, she reminded herself. As she followed the path onto the sand, she spotted the red funnel of the ferry, which was leaving the port to return to Ardrossan. She shook her head when she thought just how much had happened since she arrived here.

When she started to near the pub, her breath quickened and the fluttering in her stomach intensified. She could hear Olivia asking her what she would tell a friend in this situation. 'I would tell her to breathe and be herself,' she said aloud, glad that nobody was around now that she was talking to herself. Didn't that used to be the first sign of madness? She walked into the beer garden, her eyes darting around. She immediately saw Logan, who had just sat down at a wooden table. He lifted a hand in greeting and smiled warmly at her.

'Hey, Kitty,' he said. 'How are you?' He stood up and reached to give her a hug.

He wore a pair of dark jeans and a grey T-shirt, and his sunglasses were perched on top of his head. She could smell his familiar scent of soap and spice. 'Can I get you a drink?' she offered.

'Let me get this one,' he said. 'What would you like?'

'A gin and tonic please.' It was her safe drink, whereas wine tended to make her overshare, especially when she was nervous.

'No problem. Give me two ticks.'

She dug her toes into the pale stones that were scattered across the beer garden.

'Are you digging to Australia?' said Logan when he reappeared with their drinks.

'Oops,' she said. 'I was miles away there.'

Logan laughed easily. 'Cheers,' he said, holding his beer up to her glass.

'Cheers.' Kitty took a gulp of her drink. It was cold and refreshing and just what she needed.

'How is Olivia today?' said Logan.

'She was a bit rough this morning, and I left her having pizza on the sofa and watching Netflix. I think she'll be fine by tomorrow.' She didn't want to betray Olivia's confidence, but she felt she wanted to give Logan a bit of an explanation as to what had happened. 'She's had a bit of a rough time these past few years.'

Logan put his hands up to stop her. 'You don't need to tell me. It's okay.'

'I don't think she would mind me telling you a bit. But it involved a particularly nasty break up with her ex, and she's staying away from men for the foreseeable.'

He grimaced. 'I got that sense from what happened on the mountain yesterday. I'm really sorry to hear that.'

'Anyway,' said Kitty, keen to steer the conversation away from toxic men and Olivia's relationship, 'tell me about you. Have you enjoyed this trip? Are you excited about the next one?'

He rubbed his hand over his jaw, which had a light smattering of stubble. 'It's been great, and so good to be back on Arran. We've been so lucky with the weather.' He took a drink of beer. 'It can be hard to switch your thoughts to the next tour and location. But I'm really glad I'll be back here soon.'

'And remind me, when is that?' she asked, trying to make her question sound casual.

'I'll be back towards the end of next week.'

She knew he was watching her for a reaction, and she couldn't help but give a small smile as heat flared across her cheeks.

'So, what have you got planned now you have the walks out of the way?' he asked, smiling encouragingly.

'Well, some art, and Amy's yoga class . . .'

'I hear she's very good at it,' said Logan. 'Even James — that's my friend who's going out with her — has become hooked, and that says a lot. He can even touch his toes now, which is no mean feat for a stiff ex-rugby player. That's all down to Amy's careful tuition.'

'Well, there's hope for me yet,' said Kitty. 'I'll let you know how I get on with that. And Olivia and I still want to do Goatfell.'

'And I know just the man to escort you,' said Logan softly.

She dropped her gaze from his, unable to stop herself blushing. 'Sounds good,' she said quickly. 'Okay, can I get you a drink? Same again?' She stood up, feeling completely flustered. Why couldn't she just be herself? So much for her self-talk earlier.

When she returned to their table, she passed a beer to Logan and sat down.

'Is everything okay?' he asked. 'You seem a bit . . . on edge.'

'Yes. Actually no,' she said. So much for gin and tonic being her safe drink. 'It's this whole thing. Being here with you,' she said. 'It's been a while since I had a drink with a bloke who I wasn't related to.'

Logan smiled reassuringly. 'There's no pressure from me at all. Just be yourself. We're two friends having a drink.'

'You're right. That's all this is. Two friends having a drink. Okay, so let's just try and have a laugh. That's what I could do with.'

'Well, you've come to the right place,' said Logan. 'My friends often tell me I'm the funniest person they know.'

Kitty rolled her eyes. 'Of course you are,' she said. 'I think they're pulling your leg.'

When Logan walked her back to Lilybank Cottage later she felt so much more relaxed. They'd ended up having a fun night after all, and she'd managed not to disgrace herself with any singing, especially when there had been so many opportunities. He had mentioned so many song titles tonight, but she hadn't risen to his bait, even when he had unwittingly mentioned he had been all around the world. That Lisa Stansfield song was one of her favourites, and one she liked to belt out at home. She didn't want him running for the hills when he witnessed her questionable musicianship.

'What are you doing tomorrow?' she bravely asked as they reached the door of the cottage.

'I don't have any firm plans yet,' he said, his eyes crinkling in amusement.

'I haven't had a chance to see Fergus yet. Do you fancy coming to Lamlash with me and taking out a couple of kayaks?'

'That sounds a perfect plan,' he said.

'I'll text you in the morning and come and pick you up. And thank you for a lovely evening and making me feel at ease. I really enjoyed it.'

'Anytime,' he said, leaning towards her and kissing her cheek.

'Goodnight, Logan,' she said, watching him as he sauntered back down the path. Part of her wanted to call him back, so she could kiss him properly. Yet the other part of her wanted to make the most of this delicious early stage of getting to know him. But there was a niggle in her stomach, reminding her that she would need to tell him about Ryan. She just didn't quite know how to.

CHAPTER THIRTY-TWO

Olivia was pleased to hear that Kitty's evening with Logan had gone well, and that they were spending the day together before he left for his next tour.

She felt so much better after yesterday's horrid hangover. She decided to have a more productive day and go for a run. After waving off Kitty, Olivia switched her old phone on briefly to remind herself of her email password. Although it pinged incessantly with texts and voicemails, she managed to ignore them. After reminding herself of the information she needed, she quickly switched it off. She knew she would need to log into her emails just to make sure there were no urgent work-related messages. Otherwise, she may well find herself unemployable when she did return home. Although it suddenly dawned on her that she had no idea where that was, now that her possessions were in storage and she had moved out of Patrick's place.

Thinking about next steps was too much right now and she couldn't bring herself to go there. She would ask Kitty if she could borrow her iPad later and log in to check her messages. There was no point in worrying about anything else at the moment. Pulling on her trainers, she lightly jogged on the spot and did a quick few stretches, reaching down to touch her toes. When the doorbell rang, she jerked upright and felt her blood run cold. Who could that be? Creeping to the lounge, she stood to the side and peered out one of the windows at the front. She relaxed when she saw who it was.

'Hi, Amy,' she said, opening the door.

'Sorry, Olivia, is this a bad time? You look like you're on your way out?'

'I'm just going for a run. But it's okay, there's no hurry, come in. What's up?'

Amy stepped inside and followed Olivia through to the lounge.

'Well,' she said, looking around the room. 'I wondered if you might be able to help with something.'

Olivia gestured to her to sit down on one of the chairs. She sat down on the sofa.

'Am I right in thinking that you're a dancer? Or that you teach dance?'

'Yes,' said Olivia hesitantly. 'How do you know that?'

'I'm not quite sure,' she said honestly. 'I think you perhaps mentioned it. Or it might have been Kitty, or it could have been my boyfriend, James. He's friends with Logan. Did you tell him?'

Olivia nodded, still unsure where this was leading.

'Sorry, I'm totally digressing, my memory is brutal. Anyway, you know the Highland Games that are coming up? In August?'

Olivia nodded, intrigued to hear what she was going to say.

'There's always a dance competition for the kids — any kind of dance, by the way, it doesn't have to be Highland dancing. It can be anything — ballet, hip-hop, tap, jazz, anything really,' she added quickly. 'The teacher who normally coaches the kids has been called away to the mainland suddenly. Her father has taken ill.'

Okay, now she had a sense of what Amy was about to ask, and she felt a rush of adrenaline.

'I know it's a big ask. *Huge.* But the kids will be so disappointed if they can't take part. I was just at the post office this morning and heard a couple of parents in the queue talking about it. Apparently one of the wee girls cried herself to sleep last night, she was so sad at the thought they could no longer perform.'

Olivia felt goosebumps form on her arms as she thought about getting back into teaching again and encouraging these kids. 'I would love to help,' she said immediately.

Amy's shoulders slumped in relief. 'Oh, I'm *sooooooo* happy you said that, Olivia. You'll make their day. They'll be delighted.'

'Just tell me what I need to do,' she said. 'Should I talk to their teacher just in case there's anything that she wants me to pick up on?'

'Oh, would you? That would be brilliant. I'll get hold of her number and pass it to you. From what I gather, the kids practice a couple of times a week in the village hall.'

Olivia was immediately thinking about scheduling more rehearsals than that. She wanted to give these kids a fighting chance of *winning*. She thought about the moment of standing on stage in darkness, then the lights going on and the music starting. Then she reminded herself that this wasn't an international tour or a high-stakes competition. It was a chance for the kids to come together and learn, and most of all have fun.

Amy jumped up and clapped her hands together in excitement. 'Honestly, you have no idea how pleased they will be. Especially when they realise who you've danced with.'

Olivia was confused.

'I have a confession to make,' she said sheepishly. 'I checked out your Instagram page. I mean, impressive or what? Janet Jackson? And Pink?'

Olivia's cheeks coloured. 'Oh, it doesn't matter. I don't want to make a big deal about any of that stuff or the kids might be a bit daunted.'

'Sure,' said Amy quickly. 'No big deal at all. Now, I'll go and let them know and be in touch. But you may well have saved the day.' She flung her arms around Olivia and hugged her.

'I'm just glad you thought to ask,' she said when Amy stepped back.

'Okay, I'll let you get on and head off for your run. Thanks again and hopefully I'll see you and Kitty at yoga.'

'Definitely,' said Olivia, waving goodbye. 'We'll try and come along soon.'

As she jogged lightly down the hill, everything felt so much more colourful. She noticed the red sandstone cottages with their dinky doors, the clouds dancing along in the sky and shrouding the top of Goatfell. As she ran along the path by the sea, Olivia felt excited about having a project to focus on over the next few weeks, and was thrilled that she could do something meaningful with her time. She always loved teaching kids, and this would be a brilliant opportunity to help in the community she was growing to love. She started thinking about potential songs she could suggest to the kids, and before long she had covered five kilometres.

When she arrived back at the house, kicking off her trainers in the hallway, she realised her phone was still pinging on the floor. She must have failed to switch it off properly. Pressing her thumb down hard on the off button, she took it into her bedroom and threw it into a drawer.

'Alexa,' she said to the speaker in her room. 'Play Janet Jackson.' She smiled and started to sway her hips in time to 'Control'. That had been one of her favourite routines when she had toured with Janet, and she quickly found her groove, slipping effortlessly back into the moves. Her head was now buzzing with ideas, and she couldn't wait to get started with the kids.

CHAPTER THIRTY-THREE

Logan smiled as he watched Kitty run over to Fergus, throw her arms around him and hug him tightly.

'It's so good to see you, cuz,' he said. 'And I'm sorry that I've not had a chance to catch up properly with you. I feel really bad.' He smiled reassuringly at Logan and waved his hand to welcome him over. 'Hey there. How are you? Good to see you again. I hear you've been keeping Kitty busy?' The corner of his mouth lifted in a mischievous grin.

He looked at Kitty sideways, wondering just what she had told him. Not that there was much to tell. But her face was the picture of innocence.

'Yip, I told Fergus that you'd been cracking the whip with all these walks we've been doing. My feet have been totally shredded.' She grinned at him.

'What do you kiddos want to do today?' he asked. 'Are you still keen to take out the kayaks? Perfect weather for it.'

'Less of the kiddos, Ferg. Remember that I'm older than you, so show some respect.' She laughed and gave him a playful punch on the arm.

He rolled his eyes. 'Sorry.'

'Kayaks would be great if that works for you?' Logan had already checked the weather conditions for the rest of the day, and they were in luck. It was set to be fine and calm. A bubble of anticipation began to form as he thought about the day that stretched ahead of them.

'Okay, no problem. I know that you're savvy enough, Logan, but I have to say that you've come along with the right woman. You're in good hands with Kitty here.' He jerked his thumb towards the shed. 'I've left a couple over there for you and just remember your wetsuits and buoyancy aids. Gail will sort you out with that inside. Just bear in mind the usual safety stuff and be careful. But as I said, Kitty will look after you, mate.'

Logan's gaze swept over Kitty, and he wondered if he had missed something. She looked at him and winked.

'Did I tell you that I'm a qualified instructor?' Her gaze lingered on him.

'No, you did not tell me that.' He grinned back.

'I learned with Cameron when he was younger. He loved sea kayaking in the Moray Firth. I spent so much time helping out that I decided I may as well get the qualification.'

'I'm impressed,' said Logan, genuinely.

Kitty met his eyes. 'No big deal. Right, shall we do this? I'll be ready in ten minutes if you are?'

'Deal,' he said.

When they had their wetsuits and buoyancy aids on, they dragged their kayaks down to the shore. As they walked, he could smell the gentle floral scent of her perfume in the air. 'Ladies first,' he said, gesturing for her to go ahead of him.

'It's fine. You go first. I just want to make sure you know what you're doing,' she said wryly.

'Of course, I keep forgetting that you're in charge.'

They both paddled out towards the Holy Island, Kitty at the front, constantly looking over her shoulder to check he was behind. He wanted to be alongside her, so he paddled a bit faster until he was.

'Isn't it pretty?' said Kitty as she manoeuvred herself around and pointed back at the panoramic view of Lamlash.

'I know,' he said. 'That's what I love about being on the water. The different perspectives it gives and the way you can look back on a place and see it like this. It's amazing.'

'Do you see those terraced cottages there?' said Kitty, pointing at the row of white houses with green doors that were prominent in their view. 'Did you know they're actually of *major* architectural importance? They were designed by Sir John Burnet and built in the late nineteenth century.'

'I did know that actually, but I'm impressed,' said Logan. 'I didn't realise you were so up to speed on the island's history. Did I tell you that on one of the tours when we drove through Lamlash?'

'No,' she said indignantly, then laughed. 'It's something Fergus tells me just about every time I see him.'

'How come?'

'Because he's decided that he wants to buy one of the cottages. So he's been doing his research while he waits for the perfect one to come on the market.'

'Ah, I see.'

'It will actually be good to spend a bit of time with him while I'm here. I haven't seen him properly for ages, and he also has a new girlfriend that he appears quite smitten with.'

Logan considered her words for a moment. 'That sounds like a familiar story. The same thing happened to my friend, James. Until he met Amy, I thought he would be a bachelor forever.'

Kitty turned to him and he allowed his gaze to roam over her face. She opened her mouth as though she was about to say something in response, then appeared to change her mind and clamped it shut again.

'What is it?' he said.

'Nothing.'

'Mmm. You looked like you were going to say something.'

She held up her hands. 'All I was going to say was, first one to the Holy Isle is the winner.' With that, she turned and began paddling furiously.

They paddled quickly, peals of laughter coming from Kitty as she tried her hardest to stay in front. There was no denying that she was good, and he was struggling to keep up. By the time they reached the shore, he was panting for breath, as was Kitty, and she beat him by about a metre. 'I won,' she said, punching the air triumphantly.

'I didn't have you down as the competitive type,' he said, grinning.

'I'm afraid I am. I can't help it. Even when Cameron was small, he would get annoyed with how competitive I could be.'

'What, did you try and tackle him and his friends when they were playing football?'

'Pretty much,' she said, beaming. 'I know I shouldn't be telling you that. You'll think I'm an awful person.'

Logan stepped out of his kayak and pulled it onto the beach, then stretched his arms up. 'That was quite the work-out,' he admitted.

'Did you think you were just going to have a gentle morning on the water?' There was a smile on her lips.

He looked shame-faced. 'I wasn't expecting that. Just goes to show you shouldn't judge a book by its cover.' He reached into his small backpack, which was tucked into the boat. 'I don't know about you, but I'm desperate for a coffee.' He pulled out a flask. 'Can I offer you one?'

'Oh, yes please,' said Kitty, fastening her hair with a clasp. 'I'm parched.'

'There you go,' he said, passing her an enamel mug. 'Hope you don't mind it black. I wasn't sure what you took so thought I'd play it safe.'

'It's perfect,' she said, taking a sip. 'Wow, this is a really good cup of coffee.' Her tone was quite sincere.

'You sound surprised.'

'Well, it just goes back to what you said. We shouldn't judge a book by its cover.'

He laughed and raked his hand through his hair. 'I will admit that I didn't make it. James only has the instant stuff in his flat, so I took it down to the distillery café and asked them to fill it for me.'

They sat in companionable silence for a while. Logan wondered if he should tentatively ask again about her husband and what had happened. But Kitty drained the rest of her coffee then bounced back to her feet, and the moment was gone.

'Right,' she said. 'Are you ready for a rematch back to the other side?'

'You mean you want another race? Oh boy, okay. But you do realise that I was giving you a chance on the way over here. I didn't want to embarrass you by winning. It wouldn't have been very gentlemanly of me.'

He twinkled at her and Kitty narrowed her eyes. 'Sod that nonsense. First one back can buy lunch and, seeing that I'm not feeling very generous, I hope you've brought your wallet.'

Before he could respond, she had jumped in her kayak and was off. 'Hey,' he called after her. 'You didn't give me any warning.'

She looked over her shoulder and grinned. 'Catch me if you can.'

It was an invitation he couldn't refuse.

CHAPTER THIRTY-FOUR

Kitty was exhausted, but there was no way she was going to let him beat her. She was determined to reach Lamlash first, and she could feel her competitive nature powering through her as she paddled furiously. Her arms were burning, but she couldn't help laughing as she heard Logan behind her singing about being a champion. She desperately wanted to turn around and tell him he hadn't won the race yet. But she suspected his singing was a distraction tactic, so she kept her eyes on the land ahead. She focused on the sound of her paddles, swooshing through the water, grateful that there were no waves or strong currents today, which would have made this much harder. It had been a while since she'd been out on the water like this, and she was relieved that she had kept up with her regular Pilates sessions, which seemed to have maintained her core strength and balance. She had no doubt though that she would feel all of this hard work when she woke up tomorrow.

'Not far now,' she whispered to herself. She had about one hundred metres to go, and she realised that Logan had gone quiet. Turning around in a panic, to check he was okay, she saw that he was right behind her. His face was a picture of concentration as he focused on trying to overtake her.

'Looks like I could be winning this one after all,' he said as he edged slightly ahead.

She grimaced and paddled harder and faster, her muscles burning as her breathing started to become more laboured. They both reached the shallows and jumped out the water to race and touch the shore at the same time.

'I'd say that was a draw,' said Logan. 'Well done.' He raised his hand to high-five her and Kitty forced a smile, reluctant to admit defeat.

'Well done,' she said. 'You know I'll need to challenge you to a rematch some time?'

His eyes widened in surprise. 'Any time you want. You weren't joking when you said you were competitive, were you?'

'Too much?' asked Kitty apologetically.

He shrugged. 'Actually, I quite like it. Come on, how about I buy you lunch?'

'Deal,' she said, pulling the kayak towards the shed and waving at Fergus, who came over to meet them. As she told him about their morning, she couldn't help but notice Logan's defined chest muscles and a smattering of dark hair when he unzipped his wetsuit. Even though she tried not to stare, it was really hard to pull her eyes away.

'I'll give you a call later in the week,' said Fergus. 'Maybe you can come and meet Amelia too?'

'I'd like that very much,' she said. 'And thanks for sorting us out today.'

'Anytime, guys. Logan, are you back for another tour soon?'

Logan nodded. 'Yes, next week, and Kitty has just challenged me to another race, so clearly I'll need to get some training in.'

Kitty chuckled. 'Right, let me just go and get changed, and then you can take me for lunch.'

* * *

They were sitting in the corner of a café that looked out over Lamlash Bay, waiting for their food to arrive.

'Tell me more. What else do you do when you're not at work or being a champion kayaker?'

She mulled his question over. 'I like to bake.'

He eyed her suspiciously.

'What?' she said self-consciously.

'I didn't have you down as a baker either,' he said.

'Just goes to show you have me all wrong. I have lots of hidden talents.' She realised that she sounded as though she was flirting. Then she realised that actually she *was* flirting, and it was quite good fun.

Logan grinned and she fought back a smile.

He leaned towards her. 'Now I'm intrigued. Tell me what sort of things you bake.'

'Well, everything really, as long as it's vegan.'

Just then the waitress arrived with their food, putting a club sandwich in front of Kitty and a plate with quiche and salad down for Logan. He looked at her plate in confusion. 'But there's chicken in that?'

'Oh, I'm not vegan,' she said. 'What happened was that when Cameron was younger, we worked out he had a dairy intolerance, so I started experimenting with cakes and things that didn't have dairy in them. That way he could take his own stuff to parties. And then somehow, without realising it, I had a cottage business of cake making. When I started to cut out eggs too, I could sell them as vegan cakes, which has become a bit of a thing. I was the go-to for making folk's birthday cakes.' She pulled out her phone and opened up her Instagram account, showing him some of the designs.

'These are incredible,' he said as she scrolled through pictures of Disney princess cakes, footballs, a putting green on a golf course, stacks of books and a handbag cake. There was even a kayak. 'You're so creative.'

She smiled sheepishly. 'I never used to bake as a child. But I wanted to make sure Cameron didn't miss out.'

'How do you find the time?'

'I just fit it in around work. Obviously, I'm having a break while I'm here.'

'Is it something you would do full-time?' he asked, putting a forkful of quiche into his mouth.

'I've toyed with it,' she admitted. 'But it might feel like too much pressure and take the fun out of it.'

He nodded. 'Yes, I get that. Then it becomes a bit of a chore rather than something you genuinely enjoy.'

'Exactly.' She took a bite of her sandwich and chewed thoughtfully. Picking up her glass of water, she took a sip and said casually, 'How about you come over for dinner next time you're back? I'll even make my special brownies. All for you.'

Logan looked like he was giving her question serious consideration.

'Or not?' said Kitty lightly, trying to quell the flicker of worry that was forming. Had she read all of this completely wrong?

'Kitty,' he replied, his dark eyes twinkling with amusement. 'I would love to come to dinner next week.'

Kitty let out a quiet breath of relief — she felt a small glimmer of pleasure and anticipation at the thought.

CHAPTER THIRTY-FIVE

Over the next week, Olivia threw herself into organising rehearsal schedules with the kids, spending most of her time down at the community centre practicing routines and helping them perfect their moves. They were so enthusiastic and keen to learn, and it reminded her why she loved teaching so much. Fortunately there weren't too many urgent emails in her inbox, aside from a few invitations to audition for some major tours that her manager had forwarded her. Normally she would have leaped at the chance, but that wasn't where her head was at right now. She had emailed Gina back, apologising profusely for her hiatus, but that she was taking some extended time out. She had previously told Gina that she was taking some compassionate leave but hadn't expanded with any further details. The world of show business could be small at times, and she knew Gina was extremely friendly with Patrick's agent, so she kept the details vague. She didn't want to give any hint of where she was in case the news filtered back to Patrick.

She was so glad Amy had thought to reach out and ask for her help with the competition. A project like this was exactly what she needed. She and Kitty caught up each night for supper, but Kitty was equally busy with sorting out her Instagram account and trying new recipes, and she had started the art class and had a new best friend called Alex, who was Amy and Kirsty's dad.

'I thought you only had eyes for Logan,' teased Olivia.

'Not when Alex is in the room,' confessed Kitty. 'He's great company and so interesting, and did I mention that he's an amazing painter? I've learned so much already just from sitting next to him and watching what he does.'

This particular morning, Olivia woke early to the sound of rain battering against the windows. The house was quiet, which was strange as Kitty was normally an early riser. It was when she liked to bake. But on tiptoeing through to the kitchen, there was no sign that she had been there, and her bedroom door was still closed. She certainly deserved a lie-in, and the weather was extremely gloomy. This is what everyone meant when they said the Scottish weather could change in an instant. Olivia had experienced it that first day when arriving at Prestwick, but the good weather that followed had lulled her into a false sense of security. Especially as she and Kitty had sat up late in the garden last night talking after enjoying another warm and sunny day. Shivering, she grabbed her hoodie that was on the back of one of the kitchen chairs and pulled it on.

Olivia tipped some coffee into the cafetière and filled the kettle. While she waited for the water to boil, she stretched her arms up, certainly feeling the toll all this extra exercise was taking on her body. It was just as well she was so active, as living with Kitty was like having your own in-house baker. She had been whipping up cakes, scones, brownies, traybakes and artfully stacking them or positioning them onto the beautiful stoneware plates in the cottage, before dusting them with icing sugar and then taking some footage and shots for her Instagram reels. She always kept a few aside for Olivia, and then she'd box them up and insist that Olivia take them down to rehearsals and share them with the kids. That was probably what had made her so popular, she thought wryly. Part of the reason they greeted her so excitedly each time was that they couldn't wait to see what was in her Tupperware boxes.

She popped in her earbuds, glad she had packed her old MP3 player. The kids seemed to like her music choices too. They had three minutes to do one dance, and she had suggested they do a medley, or a 'mash-up' as they preferred to say. They weren't shy about correcting her Americanisms and replacing them with some more local words that, thanks to the careful tutelage of Granny Margaret, Isobel and Bella in Italy, she was already familiar with. She had quite the repertoire now with words such as 'bawbag', 'eejit', 'numpty' and 'bampot', which were alternative words for an idiot; 'bolt ya rocket', which meant 'please go away'; and her favourite 'scunnered', which meant 'fed up'. Her attempts to say 'loch' properly were a great source of amusement, as was the way she referred to trousers as 'pants'. That had caused a lot of sniggering.

When it came to sharing the music options for their dance with them, she was fully prepared for their mockery. But they actually surprised her when they'd chosen the medley on her MP3 player that was a favourite of hers, with Justin Timberlake, Janet Jackson, Beyoncé and Missy Elliot. She had shown them a suggested routine — a mix of commercial and street dance — which they'd been excited about and keen to get started on straightaway. Given there was still a few weeks to go until the competition, she was very impressed. The group was a mixture of ages from eight to fifteen, with ten girls and five boys, and they were a brilliant team, all supporting each other, even when Olivia knew they were tired and feeling a bit 'scunnered' if they couldn't quite master the moves immediately.

She looked out the window, staring at the dark sky, and then caught sight of someone behind her, wearing a hood, in the reflection of the window. She yelped and spun round, her heart beating fast until she realised who it was.

'Are you trying to scare me to death, sneaking around like that?' she cried.

'Sorry,' said Kitty sheepishly. 'I didn't mean to scare you. I did call out a few times, but I guess you didn't hear as you had your earbuds in.' She put her shopping bags down and shook her hood off. 'It's horrid out there.'

'I thought you were still in bed. I didn't hear you go out.' Olivia poured the water into the cafetière, stirred it and plunged down the lid. 'And I'm sorry for snapping. I just always feel so on edge. I wonder if that feeling will ever go.'

Kitty went to hang her jacket at the back door and started putting the groceries away. 'Logan is coming for dinner tonight,' she said, in way of explanation for all the food she'd bought.

'Ah, of course. And how many people are you planning to feed?'

'I wasn't sure what to get,' she wailed. 'I've not done any of this stuff for years. I can't remember the last time I made dinner for a man who wasn't a relative or a friend of Cameron's.'

Olivia looked at her. 'So you decided to buy the whole store?'

'I know,' she said. 'You're right. But I didn't know what to make. Lasagne or casserole or steak. I've probably gone overboard, but then I thought you might like to join us?'

Olivia was absent-mindedly tugging at the chord of her hoodie. 'No way am I third-wheeling with you guys. I'll make myself scarce.'

'Don't on my account,' said Kitty pleadingly. 'I could do with the moral support.'

Olivia chuckled. 'I'm sure you'll manage.'

'But what will you do? Where will you go?'

Olivia chewed her lip. 'I'm sure I'll find something to do. Don't you worry about me. Coffee?'

'Please, I'm dying for one.'

She handed a steaming mug to Kitty.

'Ta. I'm so sorry for scaring you like that. How are you doing?'

'Fine,' she said quickly.

'How are you *really*?'

Olivia met Kitty's eyes and sighed. 'I'm terrified that he'll show up. I know it's unlikely, but I don't want to keep looking over my shoulder every two minutes. Every time the doorbell goes, I'm on edge and, well, you saw what happened there when you walked into the kitchen. I feel like I'll end up driving myself mad . . . It's like he's still here in my head.'

Kitty nodded in sympathy. 'I think that's all normal.'

Olivia shuddered. 'It just doesn't feel that way right now.'

'You're doing amazing. You came here knowing nobody, and now you're making a positive impact on the kids here. You didn't need to do that, especially after the time that you've had.'

Olivia considered that, then nodded. 'When you put it like that then yes, I guess I've done more than okay.'

'I hope you don't mind, but can I make a suggestion?'

She put her mug down on the table. 'Sure.'

Kitty's brow was knotted in concern. 'Have you thought about speaking to someone about all of this?'

'What, like a shrink?'

Kitty nodded. 'I think it might help.'

'I can't really just pretend none of this happened, can I?'

Kitty shook her head and smiled gently.

Olivia knew that Kitty was right. Whether she was strong enough to do anything about it was another thing.

* * *

The weather had been appalling all day, and Olivia had sat at the kitchen table talking with Kitty as she prepared dinner for that night. It was late afternoon when Olivia found herself reluctantly agreeing to hang around. 'Just for the dinner bit though, right? It will give me a chance to properly apologise to Logan too, but then I'll make myself scarce,' she said.

'I'm so glad you're going to be here,' said Kitty gratefully. 'It makes it less of a date. More of a night of him coming here to hang out with friends.'

'You tell yourself that if it's easier, Kitty. But I think we both know there's more to it than that.' Olivia smirked. 'Now are you all *prepared*, if you know what I mean?'

'I've got all the food prepped and the brownies are in the oven.' She knew full well it wasn't what Olivia meant.

'Why don't you let me take the brownies out the oven when the buzzer goes, and you go and do that *essential* grooming so that you're date-night ready. If you get my drift.'

Kitty, who was wiping down the kitchen surfaces, froze in horror. 'I'm not about to jump into bed with him,' she exclaimed.

'What about that motto, *always be prepared*. Didn't they teach you that in Girl Scouts or whatever it is you do here?'

'Olivia,' she said admonishingly. 'Please don't make this any worse than it is. I'm not having sex with him *tonight*.'

'Why not?' she argued. 'He's a good-looking guy and you're a beautiful woman.' She paused, then added, 'Maybe you both need a bit of sexual healing . . .'

Kitty burst out laughing and threw the dishcloth across the kitchen at her. 'Would you stop it? Honestly. I'm nervous enough as it is.'

CHAPTER THIRTY-SIX

Kitty answered the door as soon as she heard the first knock. Logan stood on the doorstep, holding a plastic bag that was dripping.

'Come inside,' she said, ushering him in. 'It's awful out there.'

'Not exactly a pleasant summer's evening, is it?' He pulled off his coat.

The weather had got increasingly worse as the day had gone on, and she had wondered if Logan may end up cancelling.

Logan reached down to kiss her on the cheek, which sent a tingle through her. She met his gaze and held it, smiling shyly. Then she gave herself a shake. 'Here,' she said, reaching for his jacket and hanging it on a peg by the front door.

'I did think about wearing a wetsuit here,' he confessed. 'Can you believe I brought my car, and this is just from the dash to your front door.'

As it was, Kitty went to fetch him a towel so he could dry his hair. It also gave herself a moment to calm her breathing and get rid of the mental picture she now had of him unzipping his wetsuit.

'Thanks,' said Logan, after rubbing his hair dry. 'That feels much better.' He glanced out the window at the biblical rain bouncing off the grass. He reached into the plastic bag he was holding and pulled out a bunch of roses and some wine.

'Aw, thank you,' said Kitty. 'That's really kind of you.' They were now standing very close together. She could feel her heart starting to race again. Just then Olivia appeared in the hallway and winked at her, making sure that Logan didn't notice. Kitty narrowed her eyes and glared at her. She was so relieved that she'd managed to talk Olivia into staying but she'd better behave!

'Hi, Olivia,' said Logan. 'How's things?'

'Good, thanks. I'm just on my way out. Better take my canoe,' she joked.

'Are you really going out?' asked Kitty, panicked.

'Maybe . . .' Olivia grinned back.

'Olivia,' said Kitty, as firmly as she could. 'You did say that you wanted to be useful, so how about you put these in a vase for me and fix Logan a drink.' She turned back to Logan. 'Come on through. Welcome to our humble abode.'

'This is such a great place,' he said as he followed them through to the open-plan living space. 'No wonder you two were happy to give house sharing a go.'

'Would you like the full tour?' offered Kitty.

'Sure,' he said.

'Beer or wine, Logan?' asked Olivia.

'A beer would be great, thanks.'

She quickly pulled a bottle from the fridge, pulled the top off and handed it to Logan, who then followed Kitty.

'This is the spare room,' she said, 'which you can see we've managed to keep in show home condition.'

'Impressive,' said Logan. 'I see what you mean. It's pristine. Almost makes you frightened to go through the door in case you knock a carpet fibre out of place.'

Kitty could feel him standing right behind her — she longed to sink back into his chest. 'Olivia's room is through here. Brace yourself,' said Kitty as she opened the door. An array of multi-coloured bras and tops were strewn across the floor.

'Reminds me of a teenage girl's bedroom,' he said.

'I heard that,' yelled Olivia.

'Oops,' said Logan loudly.

'Don't worry. I'll take that as a compliment,' she replied.

'And my room,' she said, opening the door, glad she had thought to leave it in a semi-tidy state. The bed was made, and she had put away any clothes that had been lying around.

'It's such a great find,' said Logan, glancing around her room and then resting his gaze on her face. He put a tentative hand on her shoulder and leaned down to her ear. 'I just wanted to say how good it is to see you. I can't say it in front of Olivia, as I have a feeling she'll take the piss.'

Kitty giggled, a warm glow spreading over her. She was so relieved that there was no tension between them, having been apart, and they were just able to pick things up again from where they left off. 'I'm guessing the rain meant you didn't do your tour today,' she said.

He nodded and took a sip of beer. 'Yes. Normally we don't let a bit of rain affect the walks, but it's been so torrential that those who had signed up were quite happy when I called them to advise it was being cancelled. It wouldn't have been safe to take them out. At least they're experiencing the full variety of the Scottish climate.'

Kitty could hear Olivia bashing about in the kitchen. 'Come on, I hope you're hungry,' she said.

'Extremely.' A smile played on his lips. 'It smells great.'

'Well, it should,' said Olivia. 'I mean, I've been working all day in this kitchen.'

'Ignore her,' said Kitty. 'She's a great actor as well as a great dancer. But she's definitely not a great cook.'

'That's true. And yes, Kitty has been working away, perfecting this recipe.'

'I just made a chilli, nothing fancy,' she said, flushing.

'That sounds great,' said Logan.

Olivia poured her and Kitty a glass of wine, reassuring Kitty and Logan that she would just be having the one and would not be doing a repeat performance of the night in the pub. 'I really am sorry. I'm mortified. I don't usually drink that much.'

Logan nodded his head sympathetically. 'No need to apologise, Olivia. It's okay. We've all been there.'

As the three of them chatted, Kitty realised how at ease she felt with both Logan and Olivia. There was no weird three-wheeler dynamic, and it very much did feel like three friends hanging out. Though the way Logan kept glancing at her, catching her eyes, was a reminder that there was potential for them to be much more than friends.

'Right, guys, I'm off to hit the sack. I need an early night if I'm to be on top form for the kids tomorrow,' Olivia said.

'Don't you want some food though?' asked Kitty.

'I'm all good, thanks. I feel like I've been eating all day. I'll leave you to it. Nice seeing you, Logan.' She ruffled his hair affectionately as she passed him.

'Goodnight, Olivia,' said Kitty fondly, watching her friend disappear into her room.

'That's exactly what my sisters used to do to me,' he said. 'In fact, they still do.'

'Yip. Annoying, isn't it? My brother was the same, and it was usually when I'd just brushed my hair.'

They both sat for a moment in silence, then Kitty jumped up from the table. 'The food! You must be starving. Give me a minute, it's all keeping warm in the oven.'

'Let me help,' said Logan, standing up and walking over.

'Just take these over to the table. The rest is all sorted,' she said, handing him two bowls. Kitty placed a bowl of rice on the table and the casserole dish with chilli and told Logan to help himself. As they ate, she asked Logan about the places he had visited with work.

'Every day is different,' he said. Taking a forkful of chilli, he chewed thoughtfully for a moment. 'This is really delicious,' he said.

Kitty blushed. 'Thank you. It's one of my go-to recipes. Do you cook much?'

Logan shook his head. 'When I'm working away it depends where I'm staying and, even then, it tends to be pretty functional cooking. But when I'm back home for a while then it's something I enjoy.' He smiled at her. 'I'm not sure James's flat really lends itself to a dinner party. But I may surprise you,' he said with a smile.

Kitty placed her cutlery on her bowl and pushed it away. 'Do you ever get tired of living from a bag?' She wanted to reach out and touch him. Telling herself that would be weird, she placed her hands firmly around the stem of her glass.

'Not really . . . though lately it's been bothering me more.' He stared at her intently.

Kitty felt her cheeks flush and she wondered what would happen next. But then Logan stood up and stretched. Surely he wasn't going to go already.

He must have realised she was looking at him quizzically, because he leaned towards her and tucked a curl behind her ear. 'That was delicious,' he said. 'And now I'm just going to do the washing up.'

Kitty helped him clear away the dishes and they chatted as he washed. She dried and put them away. 'This is what I call living life on the edge,' she joked, noticing the amusement dancing in his eyes.

It was then that she noticed just how long and dark his lashes were and she quickly dropped her gaze. She was highly aware that if she lifted her eyes to meet his then they would undoubtedly kiss. The very thought gave her goosebumps. Logan reached his hand out and gently tipped her chin up, his eyes seeking hers. He looked at her for what felt like a very long moment. 'I can't think of anything more exciting than being here with you,' he said, his voice husky.

Kitty continued to stare at him, then took a step forward and tentatively leaned up to kiss him. He pulled her close and kissed her back.

CHAPTER THIRTY-SEVEN

Much to his frustration, Logan spent his days reliving every detail of his time with Kitty. Especially when he was away from the island. In fact, even more so. When he thought about her, he was consumed with a feeling of excited trepidation about seeing her again and kissing her and holding her. Being with her was so easy and exhilarating, and he found himself longing to get back to her. Logan knew Kitty was used to her independence, and he certainly didn't want to suffocate her, even though he was desperate to see her whenever he could. They had both been enjoying the excitement of a new romance, and he kept reminding himself not to think too far ahead or to worry about what would happen when the summer came to an end and she went back to her life in Rosemarkie. Although she had given him a brief summary of what had happened with her late husband, he suspected she was holding something back. But he didn't want to pry, and he hoped she would tell him when she was ready.

Today he was leading a group up Goatfell, and although he had invited Kitty along she had declined, which was not a bad thing. There would have been no way he would have been able to do his job properly or focus on the group if she had been there. She was already dominating his thoughts and she wasn't even in the vicinity.

Everything today felt magnified. The sound of the breeze swishing through the trees, the feel of the scree under his boots and the scent of pine in the air. He rubbed a hand over his jaw. He didn't think he'd ever felt like this. He certainly couldn't remember a time when he felt so alive after spending time with a woman.

This latest group of walkers were enthusiastic about the climb, and he had been pleased for Henry that the numbers had started to look up for the summer, not only in Arran but across Scotland generally. Henry had made a point of thanking him for updating his Instagram account, saying there had definitely been more enquiries as a result of his posts. Logan had shrugged. It wasn't really anything to do with him. Scotland's outdoors could sell itself. There really was no place in the world he would rather be. Where else would you find mountains, hills, glens, lochs and sandy shores, wild swimming pools, waterfalls, forests and glaciers and scattered islands in such a small and concentrated geographical area? He loved the history and the culture and the nuances between all the areas and communities. It was a place he was proud to showcase, so he took no credit at all for his posts gaining extra traction. Yet he felt completely buoyed up today and couldn't wipe the grin off his face. He felt as though he was on top of the world.

* * *

Later, when he waved the guests farewell and made sure everyone was okay, he pulled out his mobile to ring Kitty. They'd made a loose plan to meet up, but she didn't answer her phone. Assuming she hadn't heard the call, he didn't think anything more of it. He went back to James's flat to have a shower and change his clothes, and was about to call her again to suggest a walk, when he heard his phone vibrating. It was Kitty. Snatching it up, he grinned.

'Hi, gorgeous. I've just come out the shower and was thinking about you.' It was the sort of comment that would normally illicit a cheeky response, but it was met with silence. He knew she was there, he could hear her take a shuddery breath.

'Kitty?' he asked, immediately concerned. 'Are you okay?' His heart was pounding now, wondering what on earth was going on.

'No,' she said, her voice subdued.

'What's happened? Where are you?'

'I'm at the cottage . . .' Her voice trailed away.

'You sound different. Kitty? What's wrong?'

He could hear her choke back a sob. 'I don't know what to do,' she said with a wail.

Grabbing his keys, he quickly pulled the door of the flat closed behind him. 'It's okay, I'm on my way to you now. I'll be there as soon as I can.' He had never heard her sound so scared.

'Oh Logan,' she said, her voice shaking. 'What am I going to do?'

'What's happened?' he asked gently. 'Whatever it is, Kitty, I'm here for you. You're not alone.'

'It's Cameron.'

Logan felt a knot at the pit of his stomach. 'What about him?'

Kitty was so overcome with emotion that she was struggling to speak. Logan listened in shock as she garbled out a few words. 'There's been an accident.'

CHAPTER THIRTY-EIGHT

Kitty stared out the living room window wondering what to do. Since she received the call about Cameron, she'd been pacing the house terrified and shaking. Cameron had been on a bus that had crashed on its way back to the camp. Everyone on board had been taken to a nearby hospital and that was all the camp staff member had been able to tell Kitty. She had promised to call as soon as she had any news. They told her to try not to worry. Kitty had immediately called Cameron's phone, which was switched off. Olivia was out and she couldn't bear the silence of being alone. She'd let out a frustrated scream. Then she had called Logan, though she could barely string a sentence together. That's when he said he was on his way.

She knew she was being triggered and tried to push away the memories of what happened when she learned of Ryan's death. Her mind was a swirl of emotions — most of all she couldn't let herself believe that this was happening all over again. Her mind went straight into bargaining mode, and she said a begging prayer, pleading for Cameron to be okay, promising that, if he was, she would be a better mum and a better person. *Please let him be okay.*

She heard the slam of a car door and saw Logan running up the path. Thank goodness she had called him. She couldn't bear to be alone just now. He came straight into the cottage.

'Hey,' he said softly, running towards her. Stretching out his arms, he pulled her close, holding her as the sobs shuddered through her. He waited until her tears subsided, then led her to the sofa to sit down. 'Take a breath. It's okay. I'm here with you, and I'm not going anywhere.'

Kitty wanted to bury her face into his chest and escape this nightmare.

'What's happened?' he asked, placing a gentle hand on hers.

Kitty gazed at him silently, reluctant to talk at first.

'You said there's been an accident with Cameron. Is he okay?'

She took a shuddering breath. 'There's been a bus accident and all the kids have been taken to hospital.' She gulped. 'I don't know if he's alive or . . . or if he's dead.'

'What do you need to do now, Kitty? Is there someone I can call? Do you want to go there to him?'

She stared at him and swallowed. 'I don't know what to do.' She stumbled over her words, feeling lost and over-whelmed by the emotions coursing through her. She wanted to get on the first flight that would get her nearer to her boy, but that would take ages, and what if something happened when she was in the air? She needed the staff to be able to contact her at any time — she wished someone would hurry up and ring her back. She thought about Cameron, lying in pain in hospital. Alone and frightened. Or worse. Desperate not to let her mind even go there, she tried to talk. 'I need to wait for some news . . .' she insisted tearfully. 'They told me to wait by my phone and someone would call . . .'

'That's what we'll do then.' He pulled her close and simply held her. She knew in that moment he was lending her all of his strength. 'It's okay, Kitty,' he said calmly. 'I'm here, and I'm not going anywhere.'

She closed her eyes, focusing on the sound of his heart beating. Anything to distract her thoughts from spiralling out of control. She felt Logan soothingly rub her back and she found herself starting to calm down, her eyelids gently closing.

* * *

Kitty opened her eyes and froze in horror when she realised that she had *actually* fallen asleep. She was next to Logan on the sofa, and he squeezed her hand in his.

'How long have I been sleeping?' she asked, horrified that she might have missed a call. *How could she have gone to sleep when Cameron was in danger?*

'Kitty, it's okay,' said Logan. 'You've only been out for about twenty minutes, and I promise you that if your phone had rung, I would have woken you. You must have needed it.'

Kitty sighed. This was all so surreal. And she couldn't stop thinking about Ryan and what happened that night. Surely the universe wouldn't let this happen to her twice? She couldn't go on if anything happened to Cameron as well. Shaking herself, she sat up and rubbed her eyes, glancing at her phone anyway. There were no missed calls, no messages. *Nothing.*

Logan stood up. 'I'm going to make you some tea.'

Kitty sat for a moment, then followed him into the kitchen, pulling out a chair and watching him fill the kettle.

She sighed heavily. 'This feels like déjà vu.'

He frowned. 'What do you mean?'

Kitty looked at him and thought about how life could change in a tiny heartbeat. 'I told you about my husband dying.' She immediately felt guilty for bringing this up now, but her head felt as though it was going to explode.

'Yes,' he said. 'You told me about the accident.'

'Well . . . I feel as guilty right now as I did back then.'

'What do you mean?' Logan abandoned the tea and sat down next to her, reaching for her hand.

'It was all my fault . . . this is all my fault. If I hadn't agreed that Cameron could go do this camp, then he would be with me at home and fine and safe.'

'Oh, Kitty, you can't blame yourself for this. How were you to know this would happen? It's not your fault.'

She dropped her voice to a whisper. 'Yes, it is.' More tears slid down her face. 'It serves me right.' *Ryan's accident was her fault.*

She told Logan how she had asked Ryan to get home as soon as possible that night. That she'd been so excited, wanting him home so she could tell him of their pregnancy. He'd been going to stay overnight at the conference as it had finished later than expected and he was tired. He was planning on driving back in the morning. But when Kitty said she had some good news for him, he'd agreed to be home as soon as he could. Ryan had died, and it was all her fault. If she hadn't pressurised him, he might still be here and Cameron would have a dad.

'Don't you see?' she said in a whisper. 'I'm the common denominator. I must be bad luck.'

'Oh, Kitty. It was an accident. You mustn't blame yourself.'

She dropped her head onto the table and closed her eyes, feeling as though her heart was being squeezed out like a dishcloth. *Oh Cameron, please be okay. I couldn't survive if anything happened to you.* The pain in her heart was so intense that she wondered if actually she'd been carrying around a broken heart since Ryan died. *It's okay*, she could hear him say to her. *Our Cameron will be okay, Kitty. Just trust.*

Then she felt her phone vibrating next to her on the table, its jaunty *Star Wars* tune sounding so inappropriate at that moment. Snatching it up, she saw the number was withheld.

'Hello,' she said tentatively.

'Is that Ms Galbraith?'

'Yes,' said Kitty, holding her breath and urging the woman to say something.

'It's about your son, Cameron.'

CHAPTER THIRTY-NINE

Kitty's gaze was fixated on a print of Brodick Castle, hanging in a black frame on the opposite wall of the kitchen. She realised she hadn't ever properly noticed it before. Instead she had taken it for granted, failing to notice the detail of the brush strokes and the different shades of brickwork.

'Ms Galbraith, it's Jenny, one of the camp team. I can tell you that your son is okay. Cameron is okay. Can you hold for me a moment, please?'

'Oh, thank God,' was all she could muster. Her gaze turned to Logan, who was watching her, his face etched with concern and his eyes filled with anguish. She gave him a tentative thumbs-up, though she frowned — him being 'okay' wasn't definitive that everything was fine. But he was *alive*. That was all that mattered. Her son was alive.

'There's someone that wants to speak to you,' she said.

'Hey, Mum.'

'Cameron,' she gasped. 'What happened? How are you?'

'I'm fine. Don't worry. Honestly, it's been a drama out of nothing . . .'

'Tell me, tell me,' she said, her words tumbling from her mouth. 'Where are you now?'

'We're at the hospital. Just a precaution. The bus had a bit of an accident and some of the kids got a bang to their heads. And, well, they wanted to make sure we were all okay.'

'And are you?' she asked with bated breath, not daring to contemplate that there could be any casualties.

'Everyone is fine, Mum. We've all been checked over. And the bus driver is fine too.'

'But what happened?'

'He had to swerve to avoid an oncoming car. He's a bit of a hero.'

'Oh Cameron. Are you sure you're in one piece? No cuts and bruises? Do you want me to come over? Do you want to come home?'

Cameron chuckled. 'Mum, I'm not like five years old. I'm fine and I'll look like a right snowflake if you get on the first plane over.'

She smiled and shook her head. 'I'm your *mum*. I'm allowed to worry.'

'I know, and honestly if I needed you, I would tell you. I promise. But we're all okay, and we're heading back for a campfire party tonight. I'd look like a right tool if you turn up tomorrow when I'm supposed to be on kayak duty.'

'Are you sure, sweetheart? I can really easily—'

'Absolutely, Mum. I'm having such a great time, drama aside. I'd be gutted if it ended early.' He coughed to clear his throat. 'Look, I'm actually more worried about you. Are you on your own just now? Is your housemate there?'

'No, she's out but Logan is here,' she said, looking directly at him.

'Good. I'm glad you're making new friends and enjoying your summer. You deserve to have fun as well.'

'When did you get so grown up?'

He laughed.

'And why didn't you answer your phone? It's switched off.'

'Ah, I forgot to charge it. That's why.'

'Okay, I take it back about you being so grown up. You're not. You're such a *teenager*.'

His voice became muffled, and she could hear him talking to someone.

'That's my friend, Donna, just telling me that we're getting ready to head back.'

'Donna?' she asked, her voice teasing.

'Just one of the other camp counsellors,' he said, and Kitty could imagine his eyes rolling. 'Look, I'd better give Jenny her phone back. But I love you and I'll call you tomorrow.'

'Love you too,' she managed to croak. 'Have a great night.'

'Bye, Mum,' he said and ended the call.

'All okay?' asked Logan, smiling cautiously.

Her shoulders sank in relief, and she felt tears of joy pooling in her eyes as she fell into his arms. 'He's fine. Cameron is fine,' she said, her words muffled as she spoke into his chest. 'Thank you, Logan, for being here for me.'

'Hey.' He kissed the top of her head. 'You don't have to thank me. I'm just glad he's okay. I know your son is your world.'

'And I went to pieces. I immediately thought the worst.' She sniffed.

'Anyone would. You know, you're a lot stronger and more resilient than you think. I happen to think you're amazing.'

Looking up at him, she realised how much of a support he had been, and just how special he had become to her over these past few weeks. She had vowed to herself that she didn't want to fall in love again, because if something went wrong it would destroy her. But now, as she smiled at him, she realised that she couldn't imagine this gorgeous and kind man, who had come into her life so unexpectedly, not being around.

CHAPTER FORTY

It was a few days later and Alex was sitting in his usual spot at the watercolour class. Kitty made a beeline for him. 'Good morning, Alex,' she said. 'How are you today?'

He looked up at her, smiled, then placed his paintbrush down. 'I'm fine, thanks. And very much looking forward to this session today. Apparently, we're going to be shown how to paint a Highland cow.'

Kitty nodded enthusiastically and settled herself on the chair next to him. 'This should be interesting,' she said.

These classes had been a real highlight of her summer. She particularly enjoyed the chats she had with Alex, who seemed to thrive in the creative space.

'How's that boy of yours getting on?' asked Alex. 'I'm sorry, I've forgotten his name.'

'Cameron is great, thank you.' She smiled as she thought about his WhatsApp messages and pictures. 'When he finishes working at the camp, he's going to go travelling for a couple of weeks with some of his friends.' He was happy, and that's all she wanted for her son.

'Oh, to be young,' said Alex with a sigh. 'Mind you, I suppose we're all young at heart. I keep thinking that I'm thirty-five.'

Kitty smiled fondly at him. 'Same here.' She nodded, realising that she actually did feel younger and *lighter* than she had for years, which was surely down to her summer on Arran and meeting Logan.

'How's that young man of yours?' he whispered.

Kitty turned and looked at him in surprise. 'How did you know about him?'

He chuckled softly. 'Amy keeps me well informed.'

'He's wonderful.' She beamed, thinking about how much she was looking forward to seeing him again. He was due back on Arran the following day, and her stomach was already fluttering at the thought of seeing him and touching him again. 'I'm a lucky girl.'

'He's the lucky one, dear,' said Alex.

At that point, the tutor cleared his throat and gave them both a look.

'Oopsie,' said Alex. 'We're getting ourselves into trouble again with all our chatting.'

Kitty giggled and turned her attentions towards the process of how to draw a Highland cow.

* * *

When Kitty got back to the cottage after class, she gave the worktops a quick wipe and tidied away anything that didn't need to be on display. Olivia had promised that she would make time to help Kitty with more Instagram cake-making reels. The baking project was supposed to be a bit of fun. She had loved every minute of the actual cake making, probably because it was just a bit of a hobby. Kitty had ended up supplying the distillery and Cèic, the café in Lamlash, with some of her cakes. And she had signed up for a cake stall at the Highland Games, which were fast approaching. She wasn't quite sure she would feel so enthused if she had to rely on it to provide her with a steady flow of cash. She heard the front door open and reached to flick the kettle on.

'Hello,' said Olivia, walking into the kitchen, yawning. 'I'm so sore. Honestly, these kids have boundless energy. I need coffee. Now.' She sighed.

Kitty smiled. 'How was this morning's rehearsal?'

'Great. We had an *immense* session. I can't believe how quickly the routine has come to life.'

Kitty smiled as she made Olivia a cup of coffee. In a lot of ways she was very like her friend from home, Ellen — which reminded her that she'd messaged to say she'd managed to get a few days off work and would love to visit. Kitty was slightly apprehensive about that, though she wasn't quite sure why. Perhaps it was the thought of her two worlds colliding, and her summer retreat merging with her real life, which she would soon return to.

She handed Olivia the mug and watched as she took a sip and stood back against the counter. Even after a sweaty workout, she managed to look effortlessly stylish, with her pale blue shorts and white camisole top that showed off her slim dancer's frame.

Glancing down, she felt embarrassed by her own worn leggings, and she pulled at a thread on her fraying T-shirt that she'd thrown on for the art class. Then she inwardly shrugged. What did it matter? It wasn't like she was trying to impress anyone. Fortunately Logan wasn't around, or perhaps she *would* have made more of an effort.

'Aren't you having one?' asked Olivia, throwing her a quizzical look.

'You know what? I think I will.' She poured the hot liquid into a speckled mug from the cupboard.

'Right, are you going to tell me what's up?'

Kitty frowned. 'Nothing. I'm just thinking about getting the reel done and . . .'

'And? Is everything okay with lover boy?'

Kitty felt her eyes misting. 'Yes, apart from missing him madly . . .'

Olivia rolled her eyes at Kitty. 'Okay, so apart from being lovesick, are you going to tell me what's wrong? You seem a bit distracted.'

Kitty realised that Olivia was right. She had perfected her recipes and figured out what worked and what didn't, and now, this bit they were about to do, it all felt like a hassle. She shrugged and took a nervous gulp. 'I don't want to do this filming stuff. I'd rather go and do something else a bit more fun.'

Olivia's mouth twitched as though she was about to laugh.

'What?' Kitty asked indignantly.

Olivia's voice was gentle. 'You do realise you don't have to do it?'

'What do you mean?'

'The social media stuff?'

Kitty didn't reply.

'Look, do you enjoy the actual making of the cakes?'

'Yes,' answered Kitty immediately. 'I've loved having the time to try new recipes out, and getting the kids to try them.'

'Right, why don't we simplify it? What's the best thing about baking?'

Kitty closed her eyes and thought about the times she and Cameron were in the kitchen, laughing and having fun. Then the times she would be alone and would put on a podcast and potter around, playing with different ingredients. 'The process,' she said, opening her eyes. 'Mixing things together and watching the magic happen. Then seeing how much people enjoy them, especially if they've had to avoid cakes for so long.'

'Okay, and the Instagram page?'

'The Instagram stuff is okay, though it feels a bit indulgent. I've *never* liked being that side of the lens.' Olivia had encouraged her to go in front of the camera and do a couple of small chats.

Olivia clapped her hands. 'And there you go. You've just answered your own question and solved the problem.'

'I have?'

'You should be having *fun*, God knows you deserve it. So just do what feels good and the rest of it will take care of itself. Why don't we forget the reels and do something else instead?'

'Agreed,' said Kitty, smiling warmly at her. 'I do love the way you simplify stuff.'

Olivia laughed. 'Well, I'm only good at doing that for others. When it comes to my life, I'm hopeless. By the way, did I tell you that my aunt Trudy in the States wants a slice of your cake? She wants to know if we can ship some over because they look so good. I know you don't like the social media part but she clearly does. She said she's been following you on Instagram.'

Kitty groaned. 'I don't think I'm ready for shipping across the Clyde, never mind the Atlantic.'

'Don't worry, I told her that it wasn't really sustainable or environmentally friendly, and to source her cakes more locally.' She glanced at the clock. 'Right, what do you say we get out and go and do a yoga class with Amy? She's got one starting soon.'

Kitty paused for a moment and then let herself be swept up by Olivia's infectious enthusiasm. 'Okay, you're on. Just give me a few minutes to get changed.' She washed her mug in the sink and then drank a large glass of water. 'By the way, that reminds me, what do you think of my handiwork from earlier?' She pointed to her watercolour that was lying on the table. 'We did Highland cows today.'

Olivia's eyes twinkled with amusement as she took a closer look. 'Um, it's very, um, *good* . . . A Highland cow, you say?'

'I think it actually looks more like a big orange dog,' Kitty said with a perfectly straight face.

Olivia laughed and shook her head, her blonde curls catching in the sunlight now streaming in through the window. 'Do you want to know something, Kitty?'

Kitty looked at her friend. 'What?'

'I'm so happy.'

'What, my bad painting is making you happy?' she asked with a giggle.

'I'm just so grateful for this summer with you.' She reached to give her a hug. 'It's also made me realise how much

I absolutely love teaching the kids to dance. I feel like it's where I belong. And that's something I've been trying to figure out for a long time.'

'Do you think you'll quit being on the road then and performing?' asked Kitty in surprise. She knew how much Olivia loved that part of her life.

She shrugged. 'I think maybe so. I'm always getting offers in to teach at dance schools across the country and now . . . Well, now it's something I think I may do. It feels like things are starting to fall into place for me, Kitty.'

'And you deserve every happiness as well, Olivia.' Kitty beamed at her friend.

'Isn't it funny how this is all working out?'

Kitty nodded. It did feel like the stars were beginning to align for them both.

CHAPTER FORTY-ONE

In the run up to the Highland Games, Olivia found herself getting more and more excited about the kids' dance event. Everyone had really started to pull together, offering help with whatever they needed. Edie, a family friend of Amy and Kirsty, and a friend of Fergus, had discovered some fabric in her attic and offered to run some costumes up on her sewing machine. Much as Olivia would have loved to have been able to afford to buy in professional costumes, she knew that people were on a budget, and so this had to be made as affordable as possible. It was more satisfying to know that their effort was backed by community spirit, and she found herself hurrying down to the local hall for today's rehearsal. Edie had promised to drop off the costumes and let the kids see them for themselves, and Olivia wanted to make sure she was there early.

'Hi, dear.' Edie walked through the door laden with several huge bags. Although Edie was in her seventies, you would never have thought it. Her bright clothes, high cheekbones and clear unwrinkled skin gave her a youthful look. She wore a purple linen pinafore and had pink flowers in her hair.

'Oh, let me help you with that,' said Olivia, running over to lend a hand.

'Who would have thought that chiffon and glitter and ribbon could be so heavy.' A wide smile lit up her face. 'I've got them in these bags as they're all on hangers. I thought it would be easier for the kids to store them like that and saves them getting mixed up.'

'Ah, you are a genius,' said Olivia, biting her lip, anxious to see the costumes. She watched in eager anticipation as Edie draped one of the carriers over a table. Peeling down the zip, Edie reached inside and took out a hanger. Gently shaking it, she held it up for Olivia to see.

'Well, what do you think?'

Olivia felt Edie watching her as she scanned the costume. 'Oh wow, Edie. I can't believe what you've done. This isn't what we agreed . . .'

'Oh, oh,' said Edie. 'I should have stuck with the plan. I just thought . . .'

'No,' gasped Kitty. 'That's not what I meant. You don't understand. This isn't what I expected.' She threw her hands in the air in exasperation. 'Sorry, Edie. This is coming out all wrong. What I should have said was they are *amazing*. Absolutely, unbelievably brilliant.' And she meant every word. They were incredible, and so much better than she could ever have imagined. 'But how on earth did you add all the extras? Where did you get them from?'

'All the sparkly stuff?' she asked, chuckling.

'Yes, that, exactly.'

'Well, I was running up the chiffon skirts on my machine. That took no time at all. Then I decided that it would be great to add a wee something extra. I mean, red and black are very vivid, but I know sometimes it's good to have a bit of sparkle and glamour. I remembered that I had a bag of Christmas tablecloths in the loft. I'd got them in a sale in Glasgow one year and then completely forgotten about them. Anyway, I thought the golden flowers on them were the perfect appliqués for the costumes.'

Olivia was speechless. The amount of work that had got into the costumes was overwhelming.

'Don't be daft now, don't be thinking that I did it all by myself,' she said, reading her mind. 'I had a team of helpers. Amelia and Thea, my friends in the village, helped me with it all. Once we'd cut out all the shapes, it didn't take long to stitch them into the skirts.' Edie sheepishly reached into one of the other bags and pulled out a T-shirt. 'We didn't want the boys to feel left out either. Fergus had some spare black T-shirts at the outdoor centre, so we turned them inside out and cut the labels off and stitched the appliqué onto them too.'

Olivia chuckled. 'What would I do without you all?'

Edie gave a dismissive wave of her hand. 'That's what community is all about, my dear. We're here to help each other.'

'It's been amazing,' said Olivia. 'Honestly, I can't believe what a summer this has been. It's exactly what I needed. It feels like a fresh new start.'

Edie smiled warmly. 'You know there is something magical about this place, dear.' She reached out to touch Olivia lightly on the arm. It was as though Edie knew exactly what she had been through. Olivia hadn't shared any of the details with her, and she knew that Kitty was discreet. But it was as though Edie just *knew*. 'We owe it to ourselves to make the most of every moment, and to be happy. Life is an incredible gift. You'll be okay, dear.' Edie looked at her so sincerely. 'I just have a feeling that things will work out. Look at how much you've achieved in your short time here.'

That was true. Olivia thought back to Italy and how vulnerable she was then. She had taken a leap of faith and come here, had found a true friend in Kitty, discovered how much she loved teaching dance and managed to prevent Patrick from dominating her thoughts. 'You're right,' she said to Edie. 'It feels like it's all coming together.'

Is it though, Olivia? a voice in her head whispered. *Do you really think Patrick will let you go?*

CHAPTER FORTY-TWO

It was finally the day of the Highland Games. Olivia felt increasingly nervous, checking and rechecking the costumes hanging up in the huge tent that doubled as a dressing room. She had woken early like a child on Christmas Day, so excited about seeing the kids dance on the stage and seeing their little faces light up in front of a crowd. She had stayed late at the community hall last night doing a last practice with the kids, who had done themselves proud. She had grown so fond of the little dance troupe over these past few weeks, and was hugely impressed at what they'd managed to pull together, always keen to push themselves and add in some extra moves.

'We want to win this, Miss Olivia,' they told her every time they met to practice their routine. 'Please show us things that can make us better.'

So she had. She had taken them through their paces again and again, adding extra touches here and there to make sure their routine would stand out.

Now, fuelled by coffee, she was just about managing to hold herself together, knowing that in a couple of hours it would all be over, and she could collapse in an exhausted heap. It would all be worth it. One of the mums had stopped briefly to talk to Olivia, and now Kitty was heading over to the baking stall that she was running with the help of her friend from home, Ellen, who had arrived last night.

'Hi, girls. How's it all going?'

'Brilliant,' said Kitty, emerging from beneath a trestle table with yet more containers of baked goods. 'They're all going like hot cakes.'

'Do you need a hand?'

'Thanks, but I should be okay. Amy's helping, though she stepped away to go to the loo and get some coffees. She should be back any minute.'

'And I'm just going to nip back up the cottage to get the extra cakes. *Just in case*,' said Ellen.

'You are a love. Thanks, Ellen. Bet you're glad you came here for a break.'

Ellen grinned. 'There is no place I would rather be. See you soon. And good luck, Olivia.'

'Aw, thanks,' she said gratefully.

'So, how are you feeling and how are the wee dancers?' asked Kitty.

'They're great, very excited. But my nerves are in shreds,' she admitted. 'The excessive amounts of coffee I've been drinking won't be helping either. I'll be going on a caffeine detox as soon as this is over.'

Kitty laughed. 'I'll hold you to that.'

'One flat white,' said Amy, handing Kitty a coffee. 'Sorry, Olivia, if I'd known you were here, I'd have got you one too.'

Olivia shook her head. 'Thanks, but if I drink any more I'll be spinning on my head, and that's definitely not part of the routine.'

Amy frowned and gestured to the crowd behind them. 'There's a bloke here who's asking about you.'

Olivia felt her legs turn to jelly.

'An American guy who says he knows you from home. What are the chances, eh?'

Olivia felt the colour drain from her face and her body start to tremble. She felt Kitty's hand on her arm.

'It's okay. You're not alone, Olivia. We're all here.'

Amy looked worried. 'Is there something wrong? Have I said something I shouldn't have?'

'I can't believe he would *actually* come here,' said Olivia in disbelief.

'What do you need us to do?' Kitty said gently and calmly.

Olivia glanced at her watch. 'The kids are due on stage in about an hour. I can't let them down. I need to sort this out so I can focus on the kids.'

'Okay. Amy, if you don't mind just keeping an eye on the dancers and making sure they get warmed up and have their costumes on, then that would be fab,' said Kitty, taking charge. 'Olivia, do you want to confront Patrick head-on?'

'Who's Patrick?' asked Amy in confusion.

'My toxic and abusive ex.'

'Oh jeez,' Amy muttered. 'Let me go and brief James and Logan on the situation, then I'll go and sort out things with the kids. Olivia, please don't worry, we're all here to help.'

Olivia threw her a grateful look and saw Kitty mouth her thanks too.

'Don't worry, I'm not leaving your side.' Kitty gripped Olivia's hand in solidarity. 'Just remember to breathe and that you have done *nothing* wrong.'

The pipe band competition had started, and the sound of bagpipes filled the air. Olivia frantically scanned the crowd, looking for Patrick's mop of black hair. She knew he would approach her in a stealth-like way, catching her unawares like he always had. Her breathing started to quicken, and she felt the ground start to swirl.

'You're okay, just breathe. I'm right beside you.' Kitty squeezed her hand. 'Do you want to walk around the field and find him? Or do you want to wait for him to find you?'

'I'm not waiting any longer. He's not controlling me anymore,' she said firmly.

'Okay,' said Kitty, quickly scribbling a *back in five minutes* sign. 'Let's go.'

Olivia gave herself a shake, about to take a step forward, when she felt a hand on her shoulder. She froze.

'There she is! Olivia Kennedy. Where have you been hiding?'

CHAPTER FORTY-THREE

'Surprise!' chorused the women in unison. 'We've been look-ing for you for ages, so we have. Did you not hear us calling your name?'

Kitty watched in astonishment — Olivia's face softened as she became surrounded by a trio of women, spanning the generations, dressed in an assortment of bright floral dresses.

Tears of joy started to roll down her face as she flung her arms around each of them. 'Oh, it's so good to see you all. I'm so glad you're here! Please, meet my friend, Kitty. She's the one I've been sharing the house with.'

'Lovely to meet you. I'm Bella,' said the youngest of the women, who was dressed head to toe in cerise pink and was smiling warmly. 'This is my mum, Isobel.'

'Nice to meet you,' said Isobel, dressed in yellow.

'And this is my gran, Margaret. Also known as Granny Margaret,' she said.

'Bet you didn't think I was the gran, did you, love?' said the oldest of the group, who had a bright orange dress on and a very dirty giggle.

Kitty couldn't help laughing at their infectious and warm manner.

'So, here we are,' said Isobel. 'We thought we'd surprise you.'

'I can't believe you're actually here.' There were tears in Olivia's eyes. 'I can't tell you what this means.'

'Aye, well, what can I say? It's not quite Sorrento, is it?' said Margaret. 'I can't exactly say there's much talent from what I've seen so far, and it's a tad chilly. But anyway, we wouldn't miss it for the world. We can't wait to see your wee dancers in action.'

The women were all so immersed in the moment that they were oblivious to the man that was standing watching them. Kitty shivered when she saw him, realising just who it was. It was like watching something in slow motion as he moved nearer the group, wedging himself between Granny Margaret and Olivia.

'I don't want to interrupt you all, ladies,' he said smoothly. 'But if you don't mind, I would just like a quiet word with my girlfriend.' He smiled and held out his arms. 'Hello, Olivia. It's lovely to see you again. I've missed you.'

Kitty watched as Olivia's face turned puce and she took a step back, folding her arms defensively. As the man took a step towards her, the other women picked up on Olivia's response and flanked her, eyeing him suspiciously.

'Aren't you going to say hello?' he said.

'Now, just you wait a wee minute,' said Margaret, glancing at Olivia in concern. She moved back into the space that Olivia had created and squared up to him. 'Just what is going on here? Who are you?'

'None of your business,' he said, barging past her. 'I have some personal business to take care of and would rather do it without an audience.'

'Now you listen to me, sunshine. There's no need to be rude.' Margaret gave him a steely glare.

'I'm not interested, Patrick. Please go away.' Olivia's tone was icy — she didn't move.

There was a collective gasp. 'So *you're* Patrick then. Well, that explains a *lot*,' said Isobel, narrowing her eyes and staring him down.

Everyone stood rigid as they watched his cheeks flame red. He threw a look of contempt back at Isobel.

'What is this?' he said, a mean smile etched on his face. 'Is this some kind of women's circle?' He looked around, hoping to find someone in the group who might appreciate his joke. But he was met with stony stares.

Kitty glanced around, hoping that Logan and James would arrive soon in case they needed some physical backup. She could see Granny Margaret squeezing her fists together, and she fully expected her to be the one to throw the first punch.

'Olivia,' he said again. 'Can we go somewhere and talk?'

She shook her head. 'No. You can say everything you want in front of these women. They're my friends.'

'Seriously?' he scoffed. 'You've known them for what, about five minutes? You were with me for five years, and this is the welcome I get?'

'What don't you understand, Patrick?' Olivia's voice was steady. 'We're finished, you know that. I *never* want to see you again. I thought I made that perfectly clear.'

'By running away. Like a coward,' he sneered.

'We're done,' said Olivia. 'Finished.'

As Kitty watched him, she wondered what had drawn Olivia to him in the first place. He might have been okay looking with his black hair and dark eyes. But that was it. He had a nasty aura about him, and was quickly demonstrating his mean streak. He had barely even bothered to try to turn on the charm.

'Please just go,' said Olivia.

Kitty sighed with relief when she saw Amy arriving with Logan and James, both wearing their kilts.

'Hey,' Logan said. 'How's things?'

Kitty raised her eyebrows at him and shook her head.

'I'm Logan,' he said, reaching to shake Patrick's hand whether he liked it or not.

'And I'm James.' He followed Logan's lead.

Everyone stood in silence and waited. And waited.

'Well, isn't this quite the gathering?' said Patrick with a hard laugh. 'Which one of you guys in a skirt has charmed my girlfriend then? Because it must be a man she's here for. She can't be staying here for the love of Scotland. It's a shithole.'

'Right *mate*,' said Isobel. 'That's enough. Olivia has politely asked you to leave several times, and now you're just being rude.'

'Piss off,' he said.

Margaret visibly flinched at his tone. 'Oi,' she said, 'you are really starting to try my patience.'

'Uh-oh,' whispered Bella under her breath to Kitty. 'Mum or my gran, or indeed the both of them, are about the lose their rag.'

CHAPTER FORTY-FOUR

'How about you all mind your business?' Patrick snapped.

Olivia glanced at Margaret and could tell she was ready to explode. She knew very well that Margaret wouldn't let anyone be rude to her daughter. She watched as Margaret passed her handbag to Bella and stepped forward.

'Right, sunshine. Do you think we're all buttoned up the back or something?' She stood glaring at him, her hands planted on her waist. 'I know exactly what your game is. I *know* your type. I've seen it all before. You're full of it, but we all know you're talking pish.'

Patrick stared back confused.

'No need to look so glaikit. You know exactly what I'm talking about. There are places for bawbags like you. Away an bile yer heid.'

Patrick shook his head. 'Will you speak English? Or can someone translate? I have no idea what the hell you're saying.'

'Aw, that's my gran for you, she gets totally Glaswegian when she's angry,' explained Bella. She spoke very slowly. 'What Gran is *trying* to say is that you're a bully, we see you and it doesn't take an expert to work out what you did to Olivia.'

Kitty took a step forward. 'You're just lucky that you've not been arrested yet. The law in Scotland comes down hard on domestic abusers. If I were you, I would think about leaving as soon as you can before we call the police and you get thrown in jail. In fact, there are a couple of officers here. I can go and find them if you want?'

Patrick's face turned white. 'And you're happy with this, Olivia, are you? Letting this bunch of old women tell you what to do. I mean, I don't even understand what you're all talking about.'

'Less of the old, you total numpty,' said Margaret crossly.

Olivia looked at Patrick, trying to remember why she had got together with him in the first place. She was suddenly filled with remorse for wasting so much of her life with this man. She didn't think she had *ever* been happy with him. He might have told her he loved her and bought her flowers and chocolates — which he then rationed — but he didn't care about her. Not at all. He just wanted to control her and break her spirit. *And he almost killed her.* Another thought had been niggling her. How on earth did he know she was here, on Arran? 'How did you find me anyway?'

'Your *phone*,' he said cruelly. 'You must have forgotten I was able to track you on it. Then when you switched it off, those dancing brats gave it all away, boasting about you on social media and confirming you were still here. Anyway, Olivia, don't forget that you need me. Without me your career is over,' he said, his tone menacing. 'Are you going to spend the rest of your life teaching brats? When you could be dancing with the stars? I think it's time you stop this nonsense and come home, Olivia.'

She shook her head. 'I'm going nowhere with you.'

'Olivia,' he said, a warning tone in his voice.

'Aw, just bolt ya rocket,' said Margaret.

Olivia could hear Kitty stifle a laugh, especially when she saw Logan and James's eyes widen in a mixture of admiration and fear. Margaret was some woman indeed.

'For your information, that means go away,' said Olivia, now feeling strangely calm. 'I mean it, Patrick. Just leave me alone. I have *nothing* to say to you. I never want to see you again. And if you dare come near me, then I *will r*eport you to the authorities here, and in New York too. And while you're at it, go and get some help. You clearly need it. Now please just go.'

'Gaun yersel, Olivia,' said Isobel proudly.

'The next ferry is due to go quite soon,' said James, his voice steady and firm. 'Why don't Logan and I walk you round there to make sure you get on it, okay?'

Patrick scowled at them as they stepped closer and put a hand on each arm. He shrugged them off, turned to stomp away, but slipped on the damp grass and fell onto his knees. When he stood up, his red jeans were splattered with mud. He turned and kept walking and didn't look back. James and Logan kept their word and followed closely behind, making sure that he was definitely leaving the island.

Margaret guffawed with amusement, and soon Olivia and Kitty were also crying tears of emotional release — but also laughter. Olivia threw her arms around Margaret and Bella and Isobel and they huddled close.

'Thank you,' she said. 'I don't know what I would have done without you.'

'Well,' said Margaret, 'as I said earlier, we're not daft and, well, I've been around long enough to know heartache when I see it. I knew in Italy that you were a wee soul and that something nasty had happened to you, and that a bloke was most probably responsible. Call it my pensioner's intuition.'

'Aye,' said Isobel drily. 'You should see what she did to my ex . . .'

'Well, I can't thank you enough. I love you and will always think of you as my Glasgow girls . . .'

'Aw, I'll totally take that as a compliment. I mean, I'm sure that's a musical or a play or something, is it not? *The Glasgow Girls*? But listen, you would have been fine, love. It looks like you've got some good friends here as well.' Margaret pointed to Kitty.

'Sorry, Kitty, I didn't mean to exclude you ,' said Olivia apologetically.

'I know you didn't, I'm just glad they were here. You're not women to mess with,' said Kitty, chuckling. 'That was a masterclass in how to deal with an eejit. I feel like I've learned a lot.'

'Well, we are experienced in it, isn't that right, Isobel? You've had your fair share of eejits these past few years.'

'Thanks, Mum,' she said, in mock indignation.

'Can you believe we saw that bampot on the ferry on the way over?' said Margaret, who was now on a roll. 'He tried to skip the queue when we were getting our cups of tea, remember? I told him to get to the back and he started gibbering on about how he'd just flown in from New York and was exhausted. I was like, *Did ye, aye? Doesn't mean you're coming between me and my cup of tea.* I think we were supposed to be impressed by him or something.'

Tears of laughter and relief were now streaming down Olivia's face. She would never be able to tell these women, these friends, just what they had done for her. It had been transformational. 'You are my Scottish girls,' she said, pulling them all into a group hug. 'You too, Kitty. Come on, you're part of this.'

'And by the way,' said Margaret, 'I pure take it back what I said about there being no talent over here. Are those two young men single?'

'James and Logan?' asked Olivia.

'Aye, the ones escorting that tosser to the ferry.'

'I'm afraid they're taken,' she said.

'Well, isn't that just typical?'

'Aw, Granny. Honestly, will you behave?' said Bella. 'If it's a new man you're after, you're in the wrong place. You need to get yourself to Corfu.'

'I might just do that, darling. You watch this space,' said Margaret.

'Aw, Mum, you're off your head and still a pure embarrassment.' Isobel shook her head, then grinned. 'But we still love you.'

Olivia was quiet, feeling completely overwhelmed with the surrealness of what had just happened.

'Are you okay?' asked Kitty.

'I think so . . . I mean, I will be, once I've got over the shock,' she said slowly. Then she looked at her watch. 'Oh shoot, I'd better go and see the kids. I should have been there ages ago. I can't let them down. Will I see you all in a bit?' she asked Margaret, Isobel and Bella. 'Sorry, I need to dash off.'

'Don't you worry, love. We managed to get booked into an Airbnb. We're here for the weekend. You're not getting rid of us that fast,' said Isobel. 'And we'll be there cheering the wee ones on.'

Olivia grinned. 'Brilliant. Make sure we can hear you.' She turned to walk away, then ran back to Kitty and gave her a hug. 'Thank you, Kitty, for everything. But most of all for believing in me and reminding me who I am.'

CHAPTER FORTY-FIVE

Logan and James waited until they'd watched Patrick walk onto the ferry. Then they stood until it disembarked before they headed back to the games. James had a quiet word with his friend, one of the ferry staff, to keep an eye on Patrick and make sure he got off at the other end and didn't try and pull any tricks.

'What an utter bellend,' said James as they walked back.

'Part of me thinks that we should have got on the boat with him and quietly pushed him overboard,' Logan muttered. 'There's a special place in hell for blokes like that.'

'At least we were able to make ourselves useful for a change,' said James.

'Speak for yourself.' Logan nudged his friend in the side. 'I've been doing nothing but making myself useful these past few weeks.'

'It's certainly been quite the summer, hasn't it?'

'It has that,' said Logan.

'And now what? What will happen next? Are you going to give it a go with Kitty?'

Logan smiled. 'That's a conversation we're yet to have. But I've a good feeling. She's coming to Perth with me in a few weeks' time to meet Lucie and Bridget.'

'Eek. Well, that's a big step,' said James with a chuckle. 'Have you briefed her?'

Logan held his hands up. 'I've secured a promise from Bridget to reign Lucie in.'

'Good luck with that.' James laughed and shook his head.

'If Kitty can make it through that meeting then she can make it through anything,' Logan said with a sigh. 'I think they'll both be on their best behaviour though, they're so shocked that I'm actually bringing a woman to meet them.'

'Those Glaswegian women were a total hoot,' James laughed. 'I mean, you would not want to mess with them. I couldn't believe it when he started challenging them. I wanted to cover my eyes. It was like watching a car crash happen in slow motion.'

Logan chortled. 'Yes, it's not a scene that I'll forget quickly, and all kudos to them. If Olivia was to want anyone on her side today it would be that trio.'

James sighed. 'Well, I don't know about you, but I could do with a beer. Do we have time before the dance competition starts?'

Logan looked at his watch. 'We have about five minutes and we better not be late. After that, I think Olivia needs all the support she can get.'

CHAPTER FORTY-SIX

Ten teams from across Scotland were competing in the dance competition. What surprised Olivia most was that they all seemed to be rooting for each other. That was not something she had experienced when she was a kid. She had grown used to hostile parents, boos from the crowd and just a smattering of polite clapping from an audience who were supporting the home team. It was heartening today to hear the excited chatter and shouts of encouragement, and for the kids to know it was actually all about the taking part.

Amy had done a brilliant job in helping the kids get stretched and warmed up. Loads of the mums and dads had also stepped in to make sure they were all in their costumes, had their glittery make-up on and their hair pulled back in ponytails if that was what they'd agreed. Edie was also there, making last-minute adjustments and patrolling the room with her needle and thread, just in case.

'I'm so sorry, guys,' Olivia gasped as she sprinted into the large marquee behind the stage. They all cheered when she arrived, and she felt the tears glisten in her eyes.

'Miss Olivia,' said Eilidh, the youngest girl in the group. 'I'm a wee bit worried.'

Olivia sank to her knees, so she was at eye level with the little girl. 'What are you worried about, honey?'

Eilidh's bottom lip wobbled. 'In case I forget my moves.'

'Oh, sweetie,' she said. 'Don't worry about that. Do you remember what I said?'

The little girl nodded. 'Just keep smiling and keep moving and nobody will notice. They'll be too busy watching my beautiful smile.'

'Exactly,' she said, gently high-fiving her. She turned to the rest of the dancers. 'And that applies to you all. This should be about having fun. I know how hard you've worked over the summer. But the most important thing is that you go out there and you have the best time. Keep moving, even if you forget the steps, and keep smiling and the audience will love you. And I will be right beside you every step of the way. I am so proud of you.'

Olivia had to bite back the tears so she didn't upset the kids, but if she could have enveloped them all in a mass hug, she would have. Swallowing back another wave of emotion, she jumped up and down on the spot, and excitedly said, 'Come on, guys. Let's do this!'

They were second last to perform, and she saw the kids becoming more and more nervous as the time grew closer for their slot. She had invited the parents to go off and enjoy the show, knowing full well that if they hung around it could potentially make their children more agitated. Amy had stayed around to help. Fergus's girlfriend, Amelia, had also pitched up with some emergency hairspray and a few cans of glitter spray, and Kitty was now in full nursery-teacher mode, gently brushing hair, adding more glitter make-up to cheeks and generally putting the kids at ease.

Their moment came as they were called to take to the stage. The kids had collectively voted to call themselves Hop and Scotch.

'Come on, guys, let's go. Let's go and dance!'

They quietly followed her out the tent and up the stage steps. She beamed at the kids as she watched them take their place on the dance floor, then she stood at the side, out of sight of the crowd, doing the routine in case anyone needed a prompt. They decided they would start on a dark stage — the music would start and then the lights would turn on. As Olivia closed her eyes, listening to the home crowd scream-ing and yelling encouragement to the kids, she hoped it was something they would remember forever. She was covered in more goosebumps than she could ever remember before. There was a brief hush, and then an ear-splitting whistle. She would bet that it belonged to one of her Glasgow girls.

'C'moan, Hop and Scotch!' someone yelled, almost cer-tainly Granny Margaret. 'Gie it, laldy!'

Olivia chuckled. Thanks to the kids, she knew that meant give it your very best. Then the music started thumping, the lights flooded the stage and her little troupe of talent started to move. There was no need for Olivia to be there at the side doing the dance. She watched in astonishment as they exe-cuted the moves perfectly, along with wide, beaming smiles. The costumes looked fantastic — Edie's appliqué flowers really caught the light and added something extra special to their overall look. Olivia couldn't believe how amazing they were. It was like watching a professional dance troupe.

Every move they had rehearsed was perfect, and the crowd sang along and cheered, which seemed to buoy their mood. Their final move finished with a bang and they stood still, as practised, while the crowd erupted in screaming applause. Olivia had taught them to hold it for that extra moment longer. Despite their excitement and the audience's response, they kept still.

'Go, guys!' she yelled, and watched as they relaxed and smiled, running around the stage excitedly hugging each other. There was just one more act to follow, then the judges would decide. In less than an hour they would know who the winners were.

CHAPTER FORTY-SEVEN

Kitty's eyes snapped open at seven o'clock on the dot. Logan was lying next to her fast asleep, and she leaned gently across to kiss his lips. He stirred briefly but didn't wake. The prospect of everyone coming together today to celebrate was exciting. She was thrilled that she and Olivia were able to host a party to thank everyone for their support. Hop and Scotch had *won* the competition, and Kitty wasn't sure who was more excited — the adults or the kids. Their celebrations had gone on until late and everyone had gone to the ceilidh, which had been great fun, albeit exhausting. Kitty and Logan had sneaked off before it finished. Ellen had insisted she wanted to stay until the end with Olivia, who had managed to master 'The Eightsome Reel' and 'The Dashing White Sergeant' in record time.

Kitty couldn't wait for all their friends to gather with them later for a celebratory barbecue. She wasn't sure why she had worried about Ellen's visit. Her friend had slotted right in, and she and Olivia had hit it off immediately. Kitty contemplated a quick shower, but when Logan opened his eyes and pulled her towards his chest, she decided there was no real rush to get up after all.

'Great night,' he said. 'In fact, what a brilliant day. Well, aside from that pillock turning up.'

'Yip,' said Kitty. 'Mind you, Olivia seemed to be okay. Just as well she had the kids to distract her.'

'That dance was incredible. She's clearly brilliant at what she does.'

'I know. Thank goodness the kids won. They all deserved to after the amount of hard work they'd put in.'

Logan gently wrapped a lock of Kitty's hair around his finger. 'They were so excited.'

'I know. She made such an impact on them. And me . . . I'll miss her,' admitted Kitty. 'I've got a lot to thank her for.' Her voice threatened to crack as she realised the significance of Olivia *and* Logan coming into her life. 'Logan . . .'

'Uh-huh,' he said, his voice sleepy.

'Thank you for helping me realise it's okay to take chances . . . and that I'm more resilient than I think.' She took a moment to gather herself. 'I feel like I can grab life again, and perhaps be a little more like you.'

'In what way?' he asked, hoisting himself up on his elbow to look at her properly.

'More adventurous and free-spirited.'

'Mmm.' He nodded, his eyes twinkling with amusement. 'I'd say you're already both of those.' He dipped his mouth to kiss her. 'Can I make a confession?'

Kitty blinked. 'Okay . . .'

'Don't worry, it's a good confession.' He took a deep breath. 'I want to be more grounded and calm. Like you. I feel so happy when I'm with you, Kitty.'

Kitty smiled and relaxed back into his arms. She could tell how sincere he was. His words came from the heart. Neither spoke as they lay there, content holding each other. Then she hooked her leg over his and pulled him even closer.

* * *

That afternoon everyone was in a joyful mood as they gathered in the garden of Lilybank Cottage. Logan, Ellen, Olivia and Kitty had all worked as a team making a huge salad, prepping meat and taking blankets and chairs out to the garden to make sure the guests had somewhere to sit. Despite the cloudy morning, with rain threatening to fall, there were now only a few fluffs of white in the sky. The fresh breeze from earlier had also disappeared — it was now still and pleasantly warm.

James, Fergus and Kirsty's husband, Steve, insisted they would help Logan with the actual barbecue.

'Because that's not a cliché,' said Amelia, rolling her eyes and kissing Fergus on the cheek.

Kitty loved seeing how smitten her cousin was, and how much Amelia kept him in check. It was refreshing to watch. 'I guess they like to think they're being useful,' she said, smirking.

Pudding was a choice of Kitty's brownies or Ellen's vanilla cheesecake, and Edie also arrived with a huge box of meringues and several punnets of strawberries.

Meanwhile, Granny Margaret, Isobel and Bella had arrived with several bags of clinking bottles, insisting that they had to bring something.

'We wouldn't have dreamed of turning up empty-handed. This is just a few wee bits and pieces to help get the party started,' said Isobel, unpacking what looked like most of the Co-op's alcohol aisle.

They set up a makeshift bar in the kitchen and busied themselves making sure everyone's drinks were topped up. When Kitty had last been inside, Bella was teaching Edie and Amelia how to make cocktails. The latest one was a Long Island iced tea.

Outside, Alex was sitting in a shaded corner of the garden, playing what looked like a very intense game of cards with Ellen. Amy and Kirsty watched in fascination.

'Your dad is *very* good at this,' admitted Ellen, sounding not best pleased. 'It's been a while since I've had such a challenging game.'

'And that's saying something,' said Kitty with a grin. 'Ellen practically does this for a living back home.'

Kirsty gave her a quizzical look.

'She works in a care home, she's renowned for being the queen of cards.'

Kirsty and Amy chuckled.

When everyone had eaten all they could manage of sausages and burgers and salad and buns, Olivia tapped her spoon against her glass, which made a tinkling sound.

'Speech,' said James. 'Everyone gather round.'

The group moved closer to Olivia, who had walked over to stand next to Kitty. 'I just want to say a big thank you for welcoming us both this summer. The past six weeks have felt like six months. But in a good way,' Olivia added hurriedly, to peals of laughter. 'You have all embraced us with your warmth and friendship. I will always be grateful for that, and want to thank each and every one of you for making this summer so special. Not least because of the success of Hop and Scotch last night. That was a real team effort.'

'Hear, hear!' said Edie, raising her glass.

'Cheers,' said Granny Margaret. 'This has been some weekend, eh? Olivia, just wait till you come to Glasgow. You've not seen anything yet.' There was a ripple of laughter.

Olivia gulped. 'That sounds ominous.'

'Och, don't worry, love. You'll have a great time.'

Kitty looked at the smiling faces around her. 'I just want to echo what Olivia said. Thank you all. It has been the best summer, and I can highly recommend a summer house share.'

Just then Kirsty caught her attention. 'Dad's got something for you,' she said.

Alex moved forward with a package for her. When she opened it, she gasped with pleasure. 'Did you do this, Alex?'

'Yes, dear.'

It was a watercolour of the bay in Brodick. 'It's perfect. I will always treasure it and think about the great times we had in class.'

He beamed with pleasure. 'I wanted to give you something to remember Arran.'

She felt her voice crack with emotion. 'I will never forget any of this, or any of you. And don't worry. I'll be back before you know it.'

* * *

It was after nine when everyone finally left, including Logan, who had an early start the next morning. He hugged Olivia tightly. 'Until the next time,' he said.

'You bet. You're not getting rid of me that fast.'

He drew Kitty to him and hugged and kissed her. 'Until we meet again,' he said with a laugh.

'Indeed. I will see you in Perth at the weekend.' They were meeting at his sister's for lunch, then having a night in Dunkeld before she drove back to Rosemarkie.

'That's us offski too, girls. Thanks you for a lovely day and for a brilliant weekend,' said Bella. 'Liv, we'll see you in Glasgow soon. Be ready to paint the town red.'

Kitty glanced at Olivia, who looked fairly petrified.

'Bye for now,' they chorused as they disappeared down the path. 'Logan, are you coming with us or not?'

Logan also looked mildly terrified. He looked at Kitty and shrugged. 'Wish me luck.' He kissed Kitty one last time and then walked after the trio.

Ellen nudged her. 'You have got it bad,' she said, grinning. Her eyes were bright, and it was great seeing her looking so relaxed. A weekend away had clearly done her the world of good.

'I do. I'm not going to lie,' said Kitty, her heart swelling.

'This has to be the best summer I've ever had,' admitted Olivia, who sat down on one of the patio chairs and closed her eyes.

Kitty watched her friend's face relax as she sank back against her seat.

Things were starting to slot into place for them all.

CHAPTER FORTY-EIGHT

Olivia and Kitty had just arrived back at Lilybank Cottage after a morning of kayaking. Kitty had eventually managed to convince her that she'd love it, and she'd been right. Olivia felt exhilarated and happy after a few hours being outside on the water.

They only had a couple of days left together on Arran. Kitty would be going back to Rosemarkie in the next few days, via Perth, and she'd invited Olivia to come up with her and see the Highlands. Olivia had been toying with the idea of returning to New York at the end of August. That would give her some time to gather her things together and get on with the next chapter of her life, though she now knew she didn't want to live in New York anymore.

She was glad she had taken the decision to have counselling. It was definitely helping her process everything that had happened with Patrick, and given her some space to work out what she wanted to do next. She had a few ideas rolling around her head, but if her summer here had taught her anything, it was that her heart was in teaching.

'I'm off to have a quick shower and to warm up,' said Olivia.

'Me too,' said Kitty.

When she came out of the bathroom, Olivia picked up her phone from the bed and saw several missed calls from her aunt. She was about to snatch it up and immediately call her back when she reminded herself to breathe for a moment. Her heart was racing — she practised a few rounds of breathing in for four counts and out for six, and it started to slow down again. She pulled on some sweatpants and a T-shirt, and wrapped a towel around her wet hair. Walking through to the living room, she called her aunt.

It rang once before Trudy answered it. 'Hey, honey,' she said. 'I didn't mean to worry you, but I needed to talk to you.'

'Is everything all right? Are you and Uncle Chuck okay? It must still be early over there.' She looked at the wall clock, frowning.

'You know me. I've always been an early riser. But look, yes, we're absolutely fine,' she said. 'But I did just get a call from one of my lawyer girlfriends in New York.' Trudy paused. 'She said that Patrick's been arrested.'

'Oh,' said Olivia, her legs starting to buckle under her. She sank onto the sofa. 'What happened?'

'Police went to a nine-one-one call outside a restaurant, and a woman there with him told officers that she'd been assaulted. There were several witnesses too. Olivia . . . he's facing charges of misdemeanour assault, aggravated harassment and attempted assault.'

Blood rushed into her cheeks and Olivia couldn't find any words to respond.

'Are you okay, Livvy?' asked Trudy. 'I know it's a shock, but I just thought you would want to know. Talk to me, honey. Let me know you're there.'

Olivia's stomach was doing somersaults and she thought she might stop breathing. 'Oh, Trudy,' she croaked. 'Is the woman okay?'

'She's absolutely fine,' reassured Trudy.

'I feel like it's all my fault,' wailed Olivia. 'If I'd done something or spoken out then he wouldn't have done this to that poor woman.'

'Oh, my darling girl. The woman is fine, and this is *not* your fault. You're not responsible for that dumbass's behaviour. He assaulted that girl all by himself.' She heard Trudy take a steadying breath. 'But there's more . . .'

Olivia clamped a hand over her mouth to stop herself from gasping. What more could there be?

'He's apparently been seeing that woman for a year, and this wasn't the first time it had happened.'

'Okay, wow,' she said evenly. 'I was not expecting you to say that.' She glanced up to see Kitty lingering in the doorway, a look of concern on her face.

'Are you okay?' she mouthed.

All Olivia could do was shrug.

'Is someone there with you just now, Liv? I know it's a lot to process, but I wanted you to know that moron is going to pay for what he did. He's not going to be able to do this ever again. And . . . have a think if you might also want to press charges, dear. My lawyer friend said she'll help you, pro bono.'

'Okay . . .' Her voice trailed away. It was all too much to think about — her brain felt as though it was going to implode. 'Thanks for letting me know, Aunt Trudy. I just need some time to think.' She was so glad that she had a Zoom session booked later with her counsellor. The timing couldn't have been better.

'Will you be okay?'

'Yes, Kitty's here with me.' Her friend sat down next to her on the sofa and gently touched her arm.

'She sounds like a good friend,' said Trudy.

Olivia nodded and looked directly at Kitty. 'The best.'

'Okay, dear, you know where I am if you need me. Call me any time.'

Olivia nodded, feeling the tears sliding down her cheeks and onto her lap. Kitty passed her a pile of tissues. 'Thanks,' she managed to mumble. 'B-bye,' she stuttered, then ended the call.

Olivia sat in silence for a while, dabbing her eyes and waiting for the tears to stop. She was grateful that Kitty was there with her, supporting her by just being there, rather than putting her under any pressure to talk. Eventually she recapped what her aunt had said. When she'd finished, she said what she genuinely felt. 'And you know what, I'm actually fine. Now that I've had a good cry, I'm okay.'

'It's still a shock though,' said Kitty.

'Yeah, not really. I mean, I feel like there's not much that would shock me anymore. And I'm going to speak to that lawyer. Nobody else deserves to go through this. I'm going to do my best to keep other women safe.' She felt Kitty squeeze her hand.

A huge weight lifted from Olivia's shoulders. She knew what to do next. It was like the final piece of the jigsaw slotting into place.

'Let's always stay in touch,' she said to Kitty.

'Obviously,' she replied indignantly. 'I'm fully expecting your presence at my house after your shindig in Glasgow.'

'I wouldn't miss it for the world.'

Kitty hugged her.

'For what it's worth, this summer house share has been the best thing that's ever happened. I'm so glad we decided to try it.'

'I know. Thank you for taking a chance on me,' said Kitty with a chuckle. 'It could all have gone terribly wrong.'

Olivia nodded thoughtfully. 'Instead it all went just the way it should. A perfect summer on Arran.'

EPILOGUE

A trickle of sweat made its way down Olivia's forehead, and she wiped it away with the back of her hand. She just hoped this wasn't a mistake. Kitty's small back garden had been transformed with colourful bunting and paper lanterns. The barbecue was primed and ready to go, there was a large bucket crammed with ice and drinks, and the patio furniture had been wiped in preparation. Olivia had even managed to pick a few wildflowers on her run that morning, which were in a vase on the table. She still had to pinch herself: she was now in the north of Scotland, spending her last few days with Kitty before she flew back to New York.

'How's it going out here?' said Logan, walking towards her. 'Do you think we're all set?'

Olivia nodded. 'I hope so,' she said with a nervous chuckle. 'I just hope Kitty will be okay with all of this.'

Logan screwed up his face. 'Don't say that.'

'Sorry,' said Olivia. 'I'm sure she'll be delighted. You don't think she suspects anything at all?'

He shook his head.

'That poor boy is going to get a shock when he arrives home. He'll think his house has been taken over.' Olivia knew how excited Kitty was that Cameron was coming home after his summer away. When Olivia had suggested that she should cut her visit short to give them some space, Kitty had insisted she stay, telling her how much Cameron was looking forward to meeting her.

Logan brushed his hand over his chin. 'Don't worry, I thought of that. I managed to get his number from Kitty's phone and sent him a message to warn him. He said he can't wait to see his mum's face.' Glancing at his phone, he smiled. 'Kitty's texted to say they're just leaving the airport.' He took a breath. 'I'm starting to feel nervous now.'

Olivia smiled warmly at him. 'It will be fine. How are the girls getting on inside?'

'Ellen has them all under control,' he said, raising an eyebrow.

Just at that moment, Granny Margaret appeared in the garden, closely followed by Isobel, Bella and Ellen.

'In fact, I think I've got that wrong. Margaret looks like she's in charge,' he said drily.

Granny Margaret twirled around and clapped her hands together in delight. 'Oh, I do love a summer party.'

Isobel rolled her eyes. '*Mum*, you just love any kind of party.'

Ellen laughed. 'I agree with that. I just hope the sun keeps shining.'

'Right, do we have a plan?' said Bella.

'A plan?' asked Logan in surprise.

Bella rolled her eyes. 'Uh-huh. How will we know when they're almost here? Are we staying in the garden and letting her come out, or should we be in the kitchen?'

Olivia saw the look of panic on Logan's face. 'Er, I don't know. I hadn't thought of that.'

'Tsk,' said Granny Margaret. 'These finer details are vital.' She shook her head in despair. 'Right. Listen up, team. Logan, you message Cameron and ask him to give you a five-minute warning.'

'Okay,' he said, quickly pulling out his phone and following orders. 'Done.'

'Right,' continued Margaret, 'when we know they're almost here, you, Logan, come with me, Ellen, Isobel and Bella, and we'll wait here in the garden.' She looked around to make sure they were all listening. 'Olivia, you go and meet them out front and bring them round the side to the garden.'

Olivia nodded.

'Then, when Olivia says, "Oh, it's such a beautiful day," that will be our cue to shout out. Capeesh?'

'That sounds like a perfect plan,' agreed Olivia.

'Aye, well, I've organised a few bashes in my time,' she said. 'As soon as she gets here it will be chaos. Isobel, you and Bella sort the drinks. Logan, you turn on the barbecue. And the rest of us can *mingle*.'

'What about the cake?' asked Ellen.

'What about it?' Granny Margaret looked confused. 'I take it you did bring it?'

'Yes,' said Ellen patiently. 'I mean, when will we bring it out?'

'Probably after the food?'

'Okey-dokey,' said Ellen.

'In fact,' said Granny Margaret, 'it might be an idea to show it to me, just to make sure we're all set. Did you bring candles and matches?'

Olivia choked back a giggle when she saw Ellen throwing her a look of exasperation. 'Yes, I did bring candles and matches. Would you like me to show you them?'

Granny Margaret nodded her head. 'I would.' The two women disappeared back into the house and the rest of the party busied themselves, straightening cushions, arranging the pile of presents and cards, and making sure the bunting was hanging properly.

'Right, that's us all sorted in there,' said Granny Margaret, closely followed by Ellen, who had a tight smile on her face.

Just then Logan's phone beeped. He jumped. 'Oh. That's them just a few minutes away.'

Olivia watched as everyone suddenly started to flap and run about.

'Come on. Action stations, everyone,' commanded Granny Margaret with a brisk clap of her hands.

Olivia had learned that she was not a woman to be messed with. Evidently so had everyone else, as they quickly took up their positions to wait.

'*Shh*, stay quiet,' said Granny Margaret in a stage whisper.

'Granny, you're the one making all the noise,' said Bella indignantly.

'Och, wheesht,' she replied crossly.

Olivia heard the sound of a car. She quickly skirted up the side of the house to wait outside for Kitty to arrive. Waving as Kitty pulled up, she couldn't help but notice the huge grin on her friend's face.

'He's home,' Kitty said with a squeal as she jumped from the car and ran round to open up the passenger door.

'Thanks, Mum,' he said, laughing. 'I think the whole street must know I'm back.' Cameron towered over his mum, who was beaming proudly at him.

'Cameron,' said Olivia, 'it's *so* nice to meet you. I'm Olivia.'

Cameron reached out his hand to shake hers. 'I've heard all about you. It sounds like you and Mum have had quite the summer.'

'Indeed we have. And I can't wait to hear about yours,' she said warmly.

Kitty had opened the boot and was about to lift Cameron's rucksack out.

Olivia winked at him.

'Leave it there just now, Mum,' he said, quickly catching on. 'I'm really desperate for some fresh air. That was such a long flight and, er, I've missed the Scottish air. Can we go and sit in the garden?'

'Of course,' said Kitty, looking slightly bemused.

'I've just been out there myself,' said Olivia. 'Come on, let's go and sit in the sun and I'll get you both a cup of tea. You must be tired, Cameron.'

He stretched and pretended to yawn. 'A bit.'

Olivia led the way and, as they reached the gate, she said, 'It's such a beautiful day.' Then she allowed Cameron and Kitty to pass through in front of her.

'Surprise!' everyone shrieked. 'Happy birthday, Kitty!'

'And welcome home, Cameron!' they added.

Olivia watched as Kitty promptly burst into tears. 'Oh my goodness,' she said. 'I can't believe that you're all here.'

Logan stepped forward and extended his hand out to welcome Cameron, then kissed Kitty on the lips. 'Happy birthday,' he said.

'You're meant to be in Loch Lomond just now!'

Logan chuckled. 'That was a wee lie. I'm sorry. I wanted to surprise you.'

Kitty dabbed her eyes with a tissue Olivia had passed her, as she hugged Cameron close on one side. 'This is the best day ever,' she said, looking around. 'I just can't believe you're all here.' She gestured to the Glasgow girls.

'We wouldn't have missed it for the world. And as I've been saying, I do love a wee party.' Granny Margaret looked around. 'Right, team, let's get this party started.'

Isobel took that as her cue to start dispensing drinks. Soon everyone had a cold beverage in their hand while Logan started the barbecue. As everyone moved around the garden, chatting and laughing, Olivia watched them all fondly.

The summer house on Arran had been a gift in so many ways. It had been a shelter for her to hide and lick her wounds and figure out what came next. Even when her worst nightmare came true, with Patrick turning up that day, she realised she didn't need to keep running. She was stronger and more capable and independent than she could ever have believed. Most importantly, she had rediscovered her sense of self. She had made wonderful friends in Margaret, Isobel and Bella. Kitty was like the long-lost sister she never had. In fact, the whole community had gathered round them both, empowering them to take the next steps in their lives. Olivia often thought about Edie's words of advice. *We owe it to ourselves to make the most of every day and be happy. Life is an incredible gift.*

'This has been wonderful,' said Kitty as she walked over with a huge smile across her face. 'Thank you, Olivia.'

'Oh, you don't have to thank me. It was definitely a team effort,' she said.

'I am going to miss you,' said Kitty.

'I know. Me too. But you can come and visit any time, and we'll keep in touch. This is just the beginning.'

Kitty had promised to visit her as soon as she had saved up enough money for the flight. Meanwhile, Isobel had set up a WhatsApp group called *The Glasgow Girls*. Given the comments on that, she knew Margaret, Isobel and Bella would be out to see her too as soon as they could. She'd had to remind them a few times that, no, the men did not all look like Brad Pitt or Channing Tatum.

As she watched Kitty grin at Logan with soppy adoration, she knew this was just the beginning of their story. It was wonderful to see Kitty so happy and in love with Logan, who couldn't take his eyes off her.

The teaching job at the dance school was like a dream come true for Olivia. Her summer on Arran had really helped her find her true vocation in life. She absolutely loved it. She had a few interviews lined up for teaching in dance schools when she went home.

As she admired the vivid blue of the sky, as the sun continued to shine, she had a good feeling that things were just as they should be. She sensed happy times ahead. Most of all, Olivia had learned that the sun would always rise again, and indeed so would she.

THE END

ALSO BY ELLIE HENDERSON

SCOTTISH ROMANCES
Book 1: A SUMMER WEDDING ON ARRAN
Book 2: A CHRISTMAS ESCAPE TO ARRAN
Book 3: A SUMMER HOUSE ON ARRAN

THE CHOC LIT STORY

Established in 2009, Choc Lit is an independent, award-winning publisher dedicated to creating a delicious selection of quality women's fiction.

We have won 18 awards, including Publisher of the Year and the Romantic Novel of the Year, and have been shortlisted for countless others. In 2023, we were shortlisted for Publisher of the Year by the Romantic Novelists' Association.

All our novels are selected by genuine readers. We are proud to publish talented first-time authors, as well as established writers whose books we love introducing to a new generation of readers.

In 2023, we became a Joffe Books company. Best known for publishing a wide range of commercial fiction, Joffe Books has its roots in women's fiction. Today it is one of the largest independent publishers in the UK.

We love to hear from you, so please email us about absolutely anything bookish at choc-lit@joffebooks.com

If you want to hear about all our bargain new releases, join our mailing list: www.choc-lit.com

ACKNOWLEDGEMENTS

I would like to thank the Choc Lit and Joffe Books team for their support and encouragement with particular thanks to Emma Grundy Haigh for being an overall superstar. Thank you to my incredible editor, Sarah Pursey, whose incredible eye for details always helps to make my books so much better. Sarah, you are a dream to work with and I'd like to say a huge thanks for your support when I really needed it! Thanks also to Jasper Joffe, Jasmine Callaghan, Abbie Dodson-Shanks, Alice Latchford and Faith Marsland.

Thank you to the very talented book cover designer — Jarmila Takač — for another gorgeous cover!

Thank you to the Tasting Panel who said 'yes' to the manuscript and made publication possible: Aileen M, Alma H, Brigette H, Fran S, Hilary B, Janet A, Jenny K, Jenny M, Kate A, Laura S, Margaret M, Marie W, Michele R and Sallie D.

Thanks also to Dawn Claire Irvine and Alan Irvine for sharing their dance expertise with me; to Lorna Lyons , Tricia Thompson and Heather Crawford Glass for reminding me of the joy of sisterhood and west coast humour; and to Anouska Woods of Elstons Vegan Bakery for inspiring the vegan cakes!

I must also say a huge thanks to the lovely people of Arran, who always make me so welcome every time I visit.

Although many of the places that feature in this book are the product of my creative imagination, there are many wonderful coffee shops, bars and restaurants worth a visit if you do go to the island.

Thanks also to Dougie, Claudia, Grace and Mum for chumming me on my many Arran trips. I couldn't do any of this without your love and support. Finally, a thank you to my dear Dad, who taught me to have courage, determination, integrity and to always persevere.

THANK YOU

I would like to thank you, the reader, for choosing to read *A Summer House on Arran*. I hope you enjoyed the story of Olivia and Kitty, and that Granny Margaret, Isobel and Bella made you laugh!

The island of Arran has a really special place in my heart, and I hope I have done it justice and inspired you to visit!

If you enjoyed *A Summer House on Arran*, then please do leave a review on the website where you bought the book. Every review really does help a new author like me.

You can find me on Twitter, Facebook and Instagram (details on the 'About the Author' page next).

Please do get in touch for all the latest news. I look forward to chatting with you.

Huge thanks again, Ellie x

ABOUT THE AUTHOR

Ellie Henderson is the author of the Scottish Romance series, which includes her debut romance, *A Summer Wedding on Arran*, and *A Christmas Escape to Arran*, which was in the Amazon Top 100 for several weeks.

She has been a writer in residence with Luminate and Erskine Care Homes and Women's Aid East and Midlothian. This work has twice been nominated in the Write to End Violence Against Women Awards. In 2022 she was appointed as the first storyteller-in-residence at the Fringe by the Sea festival in North Berwick, East Lothian.

She is also part of the Scottish Book Trust's Live Literature Author Directory.

Ellie particularly interested in creative writing for health and well-being and run a small social enterprise in East Lothian, Sharing A Story CIC, where they use creative writing, shared reading and other creative methods to reduce social isolation and build confidence.

You can find Ellie Henderson online:

Twitter: @elliehbooks
Facebook: /EllieHendersonBooks